SLEEPER

SLEEPER

Paul Adam

timewarner
books

A *Time Warner* Book

First published in Great Britain in 2004 by Time Warner Books

A CIP catalogue record for this book is available from the British
Library.

HARDBACK ISBN 0 316 72432 7
C FORMAT ISBN 0 316 72433 5

Typeset by Palimpsest Book Production Ltd, Polmont, Stirlingshire
Printed and bound in Great Britain by Clays Ltd, St Ives plc

Time Warner Book Group UK
Brettenham House
Lancaster Place
London WC2E 7EN

www.twbg.co.uk

Acknowledgements

I would like to thank Giovanni, Marie-Therese and Paola Davico for their help in the research for this book.

1

You expect the momentous events in life to provide some kind of warning. You expect to have some presage of what's about to happen, to be prepared for it when it hits you. But I wasn't prepared. None of us was. Looking back, I was glad that it happened so unexpectedly. Some things hit so hard that you cannot prepare yourself for them. You just have to let them come and hope you survive the blow.

It was a Wednesday evening in June. An ordinary, unexceptional Wednesday evening. We were gathering together – as we have done for close on fifteen years now – for our regular monthly session of string quartets. Rainaldi was the first to arrive. I heard the throaty clatter of his ancient Fiat as it pulled into the drive, then his footsteps as he came around the side of the house. I was on the terrace enjoying the warmth of the waning sun. The garden was streaked with lengthening shadows, the leaves of the olive trees turning silver in the dying light.

'*Ciao*, Gianni,' Rainaldi said. He deposited his violin case on the table and slumped down into a chair beside me, stretching out his thick legs and resting his hands comfortably on his paunch. Even out here in the open air I could smell the distinctive aroma he always brought with him: a mixture of pipe tobacco and pine resin and varnish. I poured him a glass of red wine and he took a long sip.

'Mmm, that's good.'

'Did you come straight from your workshop?' I said. I could see flecks of sawdust on the collar of his shirt, even a few grains in the grizzled hairs of his beard.

Rainaldi shook his head. 'I had a pupil. Rescheduled from Tuesday. Nice kid, pleasure to teach. Keen, listens well, seems to want to improve – God, if only all my pupils were like that. He could be very good, if he did some more practice.'

'Couldn't we all,' I said dryly.

'He has potential. If I keep at him, in a few years' time he might be bad enough to get a job at La Scala.'

Rainaldi gave a low chuckle – always the first to appreciate his own jokes – and drank some more of his wine. Thirty years ago he'd been a rank-and-file violinist in the orchestra at La Scala, but he'd quit because he couldn't bear the drudgery of life in the opera pit, Berlioz's 'black hollow filled with wretches blowing and scraping'. He was a violin-maker like me now, but supplemented his income with a bit of teaching on the side. Being a luthier can be a lonely business and I think he enjoyed the social contact of teaching, the challenge, the rapport with his pupils.

'Where are the others?' he said.

'Antonio rang to say he'd be a little late. Father Arrighi should be on his way. That's probably him now.' I inclined my head, listening to the sound of another car pulling in outside at the front of the house.

I filled a third glass with wine and waited for the priest to come round on to the terrace. Father Ignazio Arrighi was small and slender. His features were delicate, his skin soft and pink and glossy as if it had been swathed in a moist towel for many years. His age was a closely guarded secret, but whatever it was he didn't look it. He was one of those men who never would. At a glance you would think him frail and sickly, like a nineteenth-century consumptive. Until you saw his hands. Father Arrighi had big, strong, square-fingered hands that could shoe a horse or strangle a man. Viola player's hands.

He put down his instrument case and glanced around, his eyes alighting on the glass of wine.

'Gianni, you are a life saver,' he said gratefully, removing the glass from my hand and gulping down a good half of it.

'Communion wine not enough for you, Father?' Rainaldi said provocatively.

'Now, now, Tomaso,' the priest replied good-humouredly. 'I'm not going to rise.' He settled himself down in a chair and placed his glass within easy reach on the table. He'd come directly from church where every Wednesday evening for the past twenty years he'd been celebrating mass with a devout but dwindling group of elderly women. He'd changed out of his cassock and taken off his dog collar because it chafed his neck when he held his viola, but somehow he still looked like a priest.

'Your garden is looking very fine, Gianni,' he said.

'You think so?' I said. 'I've neglected it a little this year. The flowers are thriving, but I fear my fruit crop is going to be down on last year.'

Rainaldi gave me a worried look. 'Not your plums, I hope. I was depending on you for a good supply. You know the shop ones aren't a patch on yours.'

Rainaldi is the main beneficiary of my plum harvest which he uses to produce a potent – and illegal – home-made brandy with the strength and colour of paint stripper, but, alas, none of the taste.

'I'm afraid so,' I said.

3

'That's a disaster,' Rainaldi said.

'We must endeavour to contain our disappointment,' said Father Arrighi, who had tried the brandy, though only once.

It was almost dark now. The blossoms on the trees, the flowers in the borders had lost all colour. They were just shapes, textures in the night. I went in through the French windows and switched on the lamps in my back room. Light flooded out on to the terrace, grazing the clusters of lavender along the edge of the lawn, touching the sage and rosemary and thyme in my herb garden with an ethereal lustre.

Father Arrighi and Rainaldi followed me inside. Rainaldi opened his violin case, took out his bow and began rosining it. He always puts too much on, giving his tone an unnecessary harshness, but he says he likes to feel the bow hair biting into the strings. By the end of the evening the belly of his violin is so covered in rosin dust it looks as if it's been dipped in talcum powder. He gave the bow a couple of swishes through the air and put it down in the lid of his case. Then he lifted out his violin and slung it across his chest like a ukulele, plucking idly at the strings.

'What're we going to play?' he said.

'How about some Haydn?' said Father Arrighi. 'Break us in gently.'

Rainaldi pulled a face. 'Not Haydn. I don't feel like Haydn.'

I lifted down a pile of music from the top of the piano and leafed through it.

'What about Brahms? We haven't played Brahms for ages.'

'No Brahms,' said Rainaldi. 'I'm not in the mood for all that rectitude, that gloomy melancholy.'

I felt obliged to speak up in defence of poor Johannes.

4

I'm rather fond of the old boy. He was German, of course, which is something of a disadvantage in Italian eyes. But he's a dead German which makes it all right.

'It's not at all melancholy,' I said.

'Yes, it is,' Rainaldi insisted. 'It's dark and depressing and dull. No Brahms. That stolid, repressed, boring . . .' he searched for another insult '. . . cat harpooner.'

Father Arrighi turned his head. 'That *what*?'

'Take no notice,' I said.

'Cat harpooner,' Rainaldi repeated. 'Everyone knows that.'

'Rubbish,' I said. 'That's utter rubbish. There's not a shred of evidence to support it.'

This malicious calumny – that Brahms enlivened his mornings of composition by harpooning stray cats from the window of his study – was put about by supporters of Richard Wagner. As any gardener knows – and I am experienced in this matter – it is almost impossible to hit a cat with a stone from ten paces, never mind a harpoon from a second-floor apartment. Besides, where in Vienna would Brahms have got a harpoon?

'Beethoven,' Rainaldi declared. 'One of the Razumovskys. What do you think, Antonio?'

Rainaldi turned to Guastafeste who had just stepped in through the French windows, his cello case in his hand.

'What was that?' Guastafeste said.

He put his cello case down in the corner of the room and looked at the three of us in turn. He was still wearing his work clothes – the worn grey jacket and cheap tie that all the detectives at the *Questura* seemed to favour, as if they were anxious to distinguish themselves as far as possible from the liveried finery of their uniformed colleagues. He looked hot and tired. I handed him a glass of wine. He nodded his thanks, then pulled off his jacket and tie and tossed them casually over the back of a chair.

'We were discussing what to play,' I said.

'I don't care,' Guastafeste replied. He flopped down on to the settee and sipped his wine, in no hurry to start playing.

'Hard day?' I said.

'The usual.'

Guastafeste is in his early forties, twenty years younger than the rest of us. Rainaldi, Father Arrighi and I are old enough to have either realised our ambitions in life, or given up on them, but Guastafeste is in the prime of his career – overworked, underpaid, unappreciated. Sometimes I feared for his health.

'Have you eaten?' I said.

'I didn't have time.'

'I'll get you something.'

'Gianni, that's not necessary.'

'It's no trouble.'

I went into the kitchen and returned with some bread, sliced salami and a bowl of black olives.

'You didn't have to, you know,' Guastafeste said with a weary smile. 'But thank you.' He slid a couple of pieces of salami between two slices of bread and bit into the sandwich.

'Did we decide what we were playing?' Father Arrighi said, tuning up his viola.

'Yes,' Rainaldi replied. 'Beethoven.'

So Beethoven it was, one of the glorious lyrical middle quartets that seem to creep inside you and massage your soul. Midway through – as occasionally happens – the whole thing went to pieces. Rainaldi put down his bow and the rest of us stuttered to a halt.

'That wasn't right,' Rainaldi said. 'Someone was out.'

6

His eyes roved accusingly over us, coming to rest on me. We have a culture of blame in our quartet that would make an interesting psychological study. Rainaldi is a former professional, so of course he is never wrong; Father Arrighi – being a priest – believes in the doctrine of his own infallibility; and Guastafeste is a master at keeping his head down, so I usually end up carrying the can for any mistakes.

'You were a bar out, Gianni,' Rainaldi said.

'Was I?'

'And just after letter F you were all so loud I couldn't hear myself playing.'

'If only we were so lucky,' I said.

Rainaldi snorted and tried to scowl at me, but his heart wasn't in it. 'Let's go back.' He tapped the tip of his bow over his part, counting the bars. 'Twelve before F. And try not to speed up this time.'

I caught Guastafeste's eye and he winked at me. We both knew which of us had been a bar out, but Guastafeste would never come clean and admit it. He'd been a police officer long enough to know that honesty – in music or in life – is most definitely not the best policy.

The Beethoven under our belts, I went into the kitchen to refill the carafe with wine and bring out a plate of biscuits. When I returned, Rainaldi was in the middle of a scurrilous joke about viola players. It seemed somewhat tactless, but he made due allowance for the fact that Father Arrighi played the viola by telling the joke very slowly.

'More wine?' I said.

Rainaldi reached for his glass, but stopped suddenly. 'I almost forgot,' he said. 'What about something stronger?'

He went across to his violin case and bent down, opening a plastic carrier bag he'd brought with him and lifting out a bottle of malt whisky.

7

'I brought this back from England.'

'You've been to England?' I said. 'When?'

'Last week.'

'You never said.'

'It was an impulse decision.'

'A holiday?' Father Arrighi asked.

'Not exactly,' Rainaldi said vaguely. 'More a sort of quest.'

'A quest?' I said. 'What do you mean?'

'Fetch some glasses, Gianni.'

'What sort of quest?' I said when I'd dug out some glasses from a cupboard and Rainaldi had filled them with whisky.

'I can't say,' Rainaldi replied, enjoying the air of mystery he was creating around himself.

'Why not?' Guastafeste asked.

Rainaldi waved a hand in the air. 'It's too soon. I'll tell you another time.' He raised his glass to his lips and sampled the whisky. 'Not bad. Not bad at all. Now, what are we going to play next? I fancy Smetana. What do you think, Gianni?'

'Well, I'm not sure. What about Dvořák?'

Rainaldi turned to Father Arrighi. 'Father?'

'Dvořák for me too.'

'Antonio?'

Guastafeste shrugged. 'Dvořák's fine with me.'

'Okay,' said Rainaldi. 'Smetana it is then.'

Guastafeste stayed on after Rainaldi and Father Arrighi had left. He packed away his cello while I folded up the music stands and sorted through the quartet parts. My own violin I left out on top of the piano, the slackened bow next to it, ready for my practice in the morning. When I'd finished, with the music neatly stacked on the

8

table, I went to the French windows and stepped out on to the terrace. It was cool outside, but not unpleasantly so. The warmth of the day lingers for a long time in summer. I could smell the scent of lavender and jasmine from the garden.

Guastafeste came out behind me and we sat in the chairs at the garden table, drinking more of the bottle of whisky Rainaldi had left behind, and talking intermittently. I'd known Guastafeste since he was a child. We were comfortable with each other, sitting there in the semi-darkness, watching the insects dancing in the light from the French windows.

'I'd better be going,' Guastafeste said eventually, but he made no move to get up.

A heavy lethargy had settled over us, pinning us to our chairs so that we couldn't find the energy even to stand up. Then the piercing ring of the telephone broke through our torpor. I thought about ignoring it, but the bell kept going insistently, demanding to be answered. I dragged myself to my feet and went into the house. It was Clara, Rainaldi's wife.

'Is Tomaso still there?' she said.

'No, he left about . . .' I checked my watch and was astonished to see how late it had got '. . . about an hour ago.'

'He hasn't come home. I'm worried, Gianni.'

'Maybe he stopped off at his workshop,' I said.

'I've rung there. There was no answer. What if he's had an accident, crashed the car?'

'Calm yourself, Clara,' I said reassuringly, though my stomach was feeling suddenly unsettled. Rainaldi *had* had rather a lot to drink. 'Antonio's still here. I'll get him to check and we'll call you back. Okay?'

Guastafeste was at my shoulder. He understood

immediately what had happened. He called the control room at the *Questura*.

'No reports of any accidents,' he said, replacing the receiver.

I rang Clara back and told her.

'Then where is he?' she said. 'He's never been this late.'

'Did he say he was going anywhere on his way home?'

'Where would he go? He always comes straight home. Something's happened to him, I know it.'

'Now, Clara . . .'

'He could be in a ditch somewhere.' Her voice was rising, becoming more agitated. 'Who would notice him? It's just a country road out where you live, Gianni. He could be seriously injured, bleeding to death. Oh God, where *is* he?'

'Clara, stop imagining the worst.'

'What else am I to imagine? He hasn't come home. He always calls if he's going to be late.'

'Listen,' I said. 'We'll go and look for him, if it will put your mind at rest, all right?'

'Would you, Gianni? That's so kind.'

'He might have simply broken down, or got a flat tyre. Stop worrying, Clara. I'll call you later.'

I put down the phone. Guastafeste was slipping on his jacket, folding his tie and stowing it away in a pocket.

'I'll do it, it's on my way home anyway. You don't need to come with me,' he said.

'No, I'll feel better if I do. Two pairs of eyes are better than one. I'd only worry if I stayed here.'

'You think something's really happened?'

'I don't know.'

'Maybe he went to a bar.' Guastafeste paused. 'You don't think he's got another woman, do you?'

'Tomaso? Good God, no. I can't see it, can you? Besides,

even if he did, he wouldn't be stupid enough to call in on her when his wife was expecting him home.'

We drove into Cremona, along the quiet, isolated lanes between my house and the city – Guastafeste at the wheel while I scanned the ditches, the fields for any sign of Rainaldi's car. We reached the outskirts of the city, a scattering of houses along the edges of the road, then the urban sprawl closed in around us oppressively, shutting out the night sky. The buildings were mostly in darkness, their occupants long gone to bed. Occasionally a car came towards us, its headlights and engine noise a jarring intrusion in the deserted streets. There was no one about. No pedestrians, no drunks stumbling home, no stranded motorists waiting for a lift. Guastafeste pulled into the kerb just before a crossroads.

'Where now?' he said.

'Let's try his workshop, just in case.'

Rainaldi's workshop was in a scruffy side-street off the Corso Garibaldi, not one of the more fashionable areas for violin-making in the city, but then Rainaldi was not a fashionable luthier. The road outside was crammed with parked vehicles so we left our car fifty metres further on and walked back along the pavement. The workshop was on the ground floor of a three-storey building. It was set back from the street, accessed through an archway which led into a small paved courtyard. There were no lights on in either the courtyard or Rainaldi's workshop, just an eerie yellowish sheen over the stonework from the lamps out on the street.

'He doesn't appear to be here,' Guastafeste said.

'Then where on earth is he?'

'Probably home by now. We'll call Clara again and find they're tucked up in bed together.'

'You got your mobile?' I said. 'Antonio?'

11

Guastafeste was peering in through the window of the workshop, his hands cupped around his eyes to cut out the reflections from the glass. He'd gone very still.

'Antonio?' I said again. 'Your phone.'

He didn't appear to hear me. He moved away from the window and headed for the archway.

'I'll be right back.'

When he returned, moments later, he was carrying the torch he kept in his car. He shone the beam through the workshop window. Something about his manner alarmed me.

'What is it?' I said. I stepped towards the window, but Guastafeste shifted his position slightly to block me. He clicked off his torch.

'Antonio, what's the matter?' I said.

Guastafeste didn't reply. He went to the workshop door. He took out his handkerchief, wrapped it carefully around the door handle, then depressed the lever. The door was locked. Guastafeste took a pace backwards, lifted his leg and smashed the sole of his shoe into the door. The wood around the lock splintered and the door flew open with a bang. Guastafeste stepped over the threshold. I made a move to follow him but he motioned me back.

'You'd better stay outside, Gianni.'

I stared at him, bewildered. 'Why? What's happened?'

Guastafeste flicked on the light switch just inside the door. I caught a glimpse of a figure slumped over a workbench in the middle of the room before Guastafeste closed the door behind him, shutting out my view. I could have gone to the window and looked in, but I didn't want to see. I didn't want to know. There was a sickness in my stomach, a ghostly touch of premonition on my neck that made me shiver.

12

Guastafeste came back out into the courtyard, his mobile phone in his hand.

'Go and wait in the car, Gianni.' He punched a number into the phone.

'Tomaso . . .' I said.

Guastafeste touched my arm gently. 'Go and wait in the car.'

2

The police were there in less than five minutes. The black and white patrol cars were first, their sirens blaring despite the time of night and lack of traffic, their rooftop lights flashing. They were followed by a couple of unmarked saloons containing plain-clothes detectives. They didn't trouble to find anywhere to park, just stopped in a line in the middle of the street. I saw Guastafeste come out through the archway to meet them, watched him confer for a while with his colleagues before they all turned and disappeared into the courtyard. Uniformed officers were already closing off the street, putting out plastic bollards, running red and white tapes between the buildings.

I felt numb. I knew Rainaldi was dead. Why else had Guastafeste sent me away except to spare me the trauma of seeing my friend's body? Yet, for the police to be there, and in such force, I knew there was more to it than a simple death.

I waited, staring down the street at the garish blue lights on top of the police cars, still illuminated but no longer flashing. One of the officers looked in my direction, saw me

14

sitting in the car. He started to walk towards me, but at that moment Guastafeste came out from the courtyard and overtook him, saying something that made the officer turn back. Guastafeste kept on walking. He pulled open the car door and slid into the driver's seat next to me. He gazed out through the windscreen as if he couldn't bring himself to look at me.

'How did he die?' I asked.

Guastafeste took hold of the steering wheel and gripped it hard, bowing his head and giving a low sigh.

'I have to know,' I said.

Guastafeste lifted his head, still not looking at me. 'He was stabbed in the back of the neck with a chisel.'

'*Dio!*' I felt my chest tighten. I was suddenly short of breath. I wound down the window to let in some air.

'I'll get a squad car to take you home,' Guastafeste said.

'Someone will have to tell Clara.'

'I know. I'll do it. I have to wait for the Scene of Crime team, the forensic people to arrive – it shouldn't be long – then I'll go over and tell her.'

'I'll do it,' I said.

He looked at me now. 'That's not necessary. Not you, Gianni, you were his friend.'

'So were you.'

'I'm a police officer, it's different. I won't put you through an ordeal like that. It's too painful.'

'And Clara? What about her pain? I know her. She'll take it better from me.'

Guastafeste considered the suggestion for a time, then nodded. 'If you don't mind . . . yes, I think it might be better.'

'She'll ask me who, why. What do I tell her?'

'That it's too early to say. But tell her we'll find out. I promise her that.'

Guastafeste looked away again. He was trying hard to remain professional, but I could see the strain in his face.

'Do you want a police officer with you, a woman?' he said. 'We have a special trauma unit. They're trained in things like this.'

'Not with me,' I said. 'But you could send one to Giulia's house. To tell her what's happened and bring her over to her mother's.'

'Of course, I should have thought.' Guastafeste twisted sideways in his seat to face me. 'I'm sorry, Gianni. I'm so very sorry.' He reached over and embraced me, a friend now, not a police officer. Then he broke away and opened his door. 'I'll get someone to run you over.'

The uniformed *poliziotto* said nothing to me on the short journey to Rainaldi's house. I was relieved. I didn't want to talk. Certainly not to him, a stranger I'd never met before. I didn't even want to talk to Clara, but I knew I had to. I owed it to her, to Tomaso. The prospect filled me with dread, but it was the right thing to do.

I could tell from the moment she opened the door that Clara knew her husband was gone. My very presence, my grave expression, the police car behind me on the street must have told her.

'No, no,' she said, so breathless she could barely get the words out. 'It's not . . . no . . . it's not . . .' She backed away down the hall, shaking her head, her gaze fixed on my face, eyes wide open, bleak with shock.

'Come and sit down, Clara,' I said gently. I moved towards her, tried to take her arm, but she shied away from me.

'Tell me, just tell me, Gianni. He's dead, isn't he?'

I nodded. 'I'm sorry, Clara.'

She let out an animal howl of agony, her hand going to her mouth. 'Oh, God. How?'

'Let's sit down,' I said.

'I don't want to sit down. How? He crashed, didn't he? Crashed the car. Had he been drinking? He always drinks too much when he goes to your house.'

'He didn't crash. He was in his workshop.'

'But I rang there. What was it, a heart attack? For God's sake, Gianni, tell me.'

I took hold of her arm. This time she made no move to resist. I led her through into the sitting room and lowered her on to the settee. Her arms were trembling, fragile as twigs. She suddenly seemed very old.

'It wasn't a heart attack,' I said, wondering how I was going to tell her. Accidental death, natural causes were one thing, but murder?

'Someone killed him,' I said. There was no honest way of softening the blow.

'Killed him?' she breathed. 'What do you mean? Deliberately? You mean he was murdered?'

'Yes.'

She stared at me in disbelief. 'Who would do that? Tomaso never harmed anyone in his life. Why? Why would they do it? What happened?'

'I didn't see him. Antonio found him. I think he was stabbed.'

'Stabbed? With a knife?'

'I don't know the details,' I lied, wanting to spare her the image of the chisel that had been haunting me since Guastafeste had first told me.

She continued staring at me, her eyes unblinking, but I don't think she was seeing me. She was seeing through me, beyond me to a place only she could go. I'd expected her to break down. I'd prepared myself for tears, for uncontrollable grief, but she was unnaturally calm now, almost catatonic with shock. I found that more unsettling than the wildest hysteria.

17

'I'll get you a drink,' I said. 'Have you any brandy?'

She didn't answer, didn't seem to register the question. I went out into the kitchen, glad of something to do. I couldn't just sit there and watch her shrivel up, watch a part of her die too. I rummaged through the cupboards, found a bottle of *grappa* and brought it back to the sitting room. Clara hadn't moved. I sat down next to her, poured a glass of brandy and held it to her lips.

'Drink, Clara. It will do you good. Come on, try.'

She opened her mouth and I forced in a little *grappa*. She swallowed, then coughed as the fiery liquor went down. The spasm seemed to jolt her out of her stupor. She blinked and turned to look at me. I saw a terrible sadness in her face, an inconsolable despair. Her features crumpled and she began to weep. I put my arms around her and let her cry, let the pain flood out in great racking sobs.

I was still holding her, quiet now, drained and exhausted, when the front doorbell rang. I eased my arms out from behind her and went into the hall. A woman police officer and Clara's daughter, Giulia, were outside. I showed them into the sitting room.

'Giulia's here,' I said.

Mother and daughter embraced tearfully and I turned away to leave them alone with their grief.

'I'll stay with them now,' the woman police officer said. 'There's a driver outside to take you home.'

I nodded weakly, aware of how tired I was. I looked at Clara and Giulia holding each other on the settee. Giulia glanced up at me over her mother's shoulder, her cheeks streaming with tears.

'I'll call back in the morning,' I said.

My house seemed very quiet and empty when the police driver dropped me off. I went through into the back room and slumped down into an armchair. I was worn out, but somehow couldn't face my bed, couldn't face the effort of trying to get to sleep when my mind was in such turmoil.

I sat there in the darkness, shadows all around me, tears welling up, and thought about Rainaldi, my thoughts running through the half century I had known him in brief, fleeting glimpses, like clips from a dozen films. Seeing him at school with me; sitting beside me in the local youth orchestra; on the day of his marriage, Clara radiant next to him; with our children at a picnic by the river; in his workshop crafting a piece of wood. A palimpsest of memories, each one overlaying the one before, obliterating it so that in the end I was left only with my final image of him – sitting here in my back room, a glass of whisky on the table beside him, his violin tucked under his chin, face alight with joy as he played one of his beloved quartets. That was how I wanted to remember him.

I must have dozed off some time in the small hours. I recall feeling drowsy, seeing the clock on the mantelpiece registering 3:15, but then nothing afterwards. When I next opened my eyes it was light outside. The clock read half past eight. I shifted uncomfortably in my armchair. My eyes felt sore, my head thick. I stretched my limbs to ease the stiffness. For a fraction of a second I wondered what I was doing downstairs, then it all came flooding back with a sickening clarity. I tried to shut out the thoughts, the images, but they were too fresh in my mind, too disturbing, to be erased. I pulled myself slowly to my feet and shuffled through into the kitchen.

I was sitting at the kitchen table, sipping coffee and eating a dried-out bread roll and jam when Guastafeste telephoned.

'I didn't wake you, did I?' he said.

'No, I'm up.'

'Are you free any time today? You knew Tomaso's workshop well. Would you come in and take a look around it for me?'

'Now?'

'Whenever you can make it.'

'Give me half an hour,' I said.

I washed and changed my clothes and drove into Cremona. It was a bright sunny day, too bright for my sombre mood, not to mention the ache behind my eyes which I attributed to either lack of sleep or too much alcohol the night before.

The street outside Rainaldi's workshop was still closed to traffic, the surrounding area still taped off. One or two curious onlookers were clustered on the pavement, but there was nothing much to see. Guastafeste met me by the entrance to the courtyard and escorted me through into the workshop. Rainaldi's body was gone, removed to the morgue for autopsy, Guastafeste explained, but there was a chalk outline on the workbench where it had lain. I tried not to look at it. Two men in white overalls were painstakingly collecting bits of debris from the floor and the top of the bench, and on virtually every surface was a dusting of white powder which I assumed had been used for taking fingerprint evidence. I'd never been present at a crime scene before. It was calm and quiet and unhurried, everyone going about their jobs in a methodical, clinical manner. It was difficult to believe that a few hours earlier a man had died here.

'Try not to touch anything,' Guastafeste said. He was bleary-eyed, unshaven, his clothes crumpled. I knew he'd been up all night.

'What am I looking for?' I asked.

'Anything that strikes you as odd, out of place. Anything missing.'

'You think something might have been stolen?'

'The workshop had been searched, I'm sure of that. Not wrecked, the way you see it in films, but searched nonetheless. The locked cupboard doors had all been forced open, there was stuff spilt on the floor that I don't think Tomaso would have done.'

I let my gaze wander around the room. I'd been here many times before, but always with Rainaldi. Without his loud, gregarious presence it seemed like a different place, one I was seeing for the first time.

'Would he have kept money here?' Guastafeste asked.

'Not large sums,' I replied. 'A bit of petty cash, that's all.'

'What about instruments? Do you know if he was working on any valuable violins?'

'Valuable?' I shook my head. 'Not Tomaso, he wasn't that kind of luthier.' It felt disloyal to say it, but the truth was that Rainaldi had not been a very distinguished violin-maker. He'd come into the business late and had not built up much of a reputation. He'd got by, done a lot of low-grade repair work to pay the bills, but his own violins had not been greatly sought after. I could not see that there would have been any valuable instruments in his work-shop, either his own or anyone else's.

'You think robbery might have been the motive?' I said. I was studying the bench along the side of the room. There was a length of maple in a vice waiting to be sawn, some rough-cut violin backs and bellies, a rib assembly clamped together while the glue dried.

'I don't know,' Guastafeste said. 'It's a puzzle. Why was Tomaso here? Did he call in for something on his way home and was surprised by his killer? The door of the workshop hadn't been forced.'

'Someone with a key?' I said.

21

'Or Tomaso let them in himself. It's possible he was meeting someone here.'

My eyes came to rest on the rack of tools above one of the benches – the saws and planes and gouges, the row of chisels with a gap where one was missing.

'Why would anyone kill him?' I said, voicing my own inner confusion rather than because I expected a reply. 'A man like Tomaso. Everyone liked him. Everyone.'

The two men in white overalls were collecting up their plastic bags and screw-capped containers, recording their finds in a large black logbook. I saw Rainaldi's pipe – the stained wooden briar pipe that he liked to smoke as he worked – in one of the bags. It was such a personal possession, so much a familiar part of the man that I couldn't bear to look at it. I turned away and said to Guastafeste: 'I'm sorry, I can't see anything out of the ordinary.'

He seemed to sense my discomfort for he didn't press me further, just led me out into the courtyard.

'It was worth a try,' he said. 'I'm sorry to have brought you all the way in for nothing.'

'That's all right. I was going to come in to visit Clara in any case.'

'Let's go together. I need to talk to her. She might find it easier if you're there too.'

I looked at him. 'She was in a bad way last night.'

'I won't push her, Gianni. But the sooner I talk to her, the sooner we get a clearer picture of what happened. These first few hours are important in a case like this.'

It was Giulia who answered the door. Her face was pale, taut. She seemed relieved to see us.

'Come in.'

'How is your mother?' I said.

Giulia showed us through into the kitchen at the rear of

the house and only when the door was closed behind us did she answer.

'Not good.'

'Has she slept?' I asked.

'She dozed off for a while near dawn, but she's awake again now. She's exhausted, but too upset to sleep.'

'You should call a doctor,' Guastafeste said. 'He could give her a sedative, something to help her.'

Giulia nodded. 'I think I may have to do that.'

'And you?' I said.

'I'm all right. I don't think it's really sunk in yet. It's Mama that worries me. She doesn't even want to talk. She's withdrawn into herself. Won't go to bed, won't have any breakfast.' She looked at Guastafeste. 'Do you have any idea who did it?'

'Not yet,' Guastafeste replied. 'I was hoping to ask your mother some questions, but perhaps she's not up to it at the moment.'

'No, talking might help her. She's just sitting in an armchair, staring into space. Why don't you go through? I'll bring you all some coffee.'

'We don't want to put you to any trouble,' I said.

'It's no trouble.'

Giulia went to the cupboard, took out a steel espresso pot and busied herself with making coffee. I sensed it was a comfort to her, focusing on the minutiae of life to help erase the magnitude of death.

Guastafeste and I went back down the hall and into the sitting room. Clara was in the armchair in the corner behind the door, the gloomiest part of the room where even the brightest sunshine rarely penetrated. I was shocked by her appearance. It was only a few hours since I had last seen her, yet she seemed to have shrunk. Hunched in her chair, her head tilted to one side as if she lacked the

23

strength to hold it up, she seemed a decade older than when I had been here last night. The skin of her face had tightened, the lines become more pronounced. Her eyes were hollow, the sockets so dark they looked as if they had been rimmed with coal dust.

'Clara,' I said gently. 'Clara, it's me, Gianni.'

She glanced up and her eyes seemed to brighten for an instant, then she looked away, relapsing back into her own dark solitude.

I took her hands. 'Clara, Antonio wants to talk to you. About Tomaso.'

She didn't meet my gaze. 'What does it matter?' she said listlessly. 'He's dead.'

I remembered my own grief when my wife died, the overwhelming feeling of desolation, of utter hopelessness so intense it was hard to motivate myself to do anything. I knew it was important to maintain a semblance of normality, to find something with which to distract Clara – to keep the demons at bay.

'It's important,' I said. 'You may be able to help.'

'Help?' Clara said vaguely.

'We need you, Clara. Antonio's working on the case. You know you can trust him.'

'Do you feel able to answer some questions?' Guastafeste said.

She turned her head, blinking at him as if she had only just become aware of his presence.

'Questions?'

'Just say if it gets too much,' Guastafeste said. 'Do you know why Tomaso went back to his workshop last night, after we'd played quartets?'

Clara gazed at him in silence for such a long time that I wondered whether she had taken in the question. But then she shook her head.

'No, I don't know,' she said.

'He didn't say he was meeting anyone?'

'No.'

'Did he often work late?'

'Not that late,' Clara said. 'And never after he played quartets.'

'Can you think of any reason why he might have done so last night?'

'No.'

'He didn't say anything when he came home for dinner?'

'He didn't come home for dinner. He had a pupil.'

'I can confirm that,' I said to Guastafeste. 'He'd been teaching. He told me that when he arrived.'

'What about his state of mind?' Guastafeste asked Clara. 'Had anything been troubling him? Worries, other people?'

Before Clara could reply, the door opened and Giulia came in carrying a tray of coffee with some cups and saucers. She put the tray down on a table and poured the coffee.

'Mama, you'll have some coffee?'

Clara shook her head.

'It will do you good.'

'No.'

'What about something to eat then? A roll with jam.'

'No.'

'Clara, you should eat something,' I said.

'I don't feel like food.'

I glanced at Giulia and she gave a helpless shrug, as if to say, 'What do I do?' She handed cups of coffee to Guastafeste and me, then sat down on the edge of the settee, gazing anxiously at her mother.

'Yes,' Clara said suddenly. She was looking at Guastafeste, who seemed perplexed by the remark until Clara went on,

'Not worried exactly. More . . . what's the word? Distracted.'

'Distracted about what?' Guastafeste asked.

'He was looking for something,' Clara said. 'It was on his mind all the time. Like an obsession, I suppose.'

I thought back to the previous evening, to Rainaldi saying he'd been to England on a 'quest'.

'Looking for what?' Guastafeste said.

'A violin,' Clara said. 'The Messiah's Sister, he called it.'

I started so violently I spilt some of my coffee on my knee. It was one of those moments you remember for the rest of your life. A turning-point, the beginning of something that changes you for ever – like the moment you first set eyes on the woman who will be your wife, or when your first child is born. Afterwards nothing is ever the same again.

I dabbed at my trousers with my handkerchief. When I looked up, Guastafeste was watching me with his soft, perceptive eyes. He turned to Clara.

'Looking where?' he said.

'All over. He didn't talk about it much. It was his secret. He went to England in search of it.'

'And did he find it?'

'No.'

'What sort of violin?'

'Just a violin. That's all I know. He never found it. And now he's dead.'

Clara was staring across the room, her eyes bleak and empty. Then the tears came, trickling slowly down her wrinkled cheeks.

'And now he's dead,' she repeated. She closed her eyes, but the tears kept coming, forcing their way out under her eyelids.

Giulia went across to her mother and sat down on the arm of the chair. She put her arm around Clara's shoulders. I looked at Guastafeste. He gave a nod and stood up.

'We'll go now.'

I looked at Clara, feeling for her, feeling frustrated by my own impotence. She was my friend. I'd known her even longer than Tomaso. We'd grown up together in the same district of Cremona, we'd started primary school together on the same day. Once, a long time ago, when we were both teenagers, I'd kissed her under the arcade in the Piazza Roma. Yet now, in her hour of greatest need, I could do nothing to help her.

'So tell me, Gianni,' Guastafeste said.

We were at a bar around the corner from Rainaldi's house, sitting out on the pavement under an awning. Guastafeste spooned sugar into his cup of coffee and stirred it for far longer than was necessary to dissolve it.

'You should go home and get some sleep,' I said.

'This violin, this Messiah's Sister, it means something to you, doesn't it? I didn't like to ask you at Clara's.'

Guastafeste has two attributes that make him a particularly good policeman – and friend: he's observant, and he knows when to hold his peace. As a child he was always watching. He used to come to my workshop after school and sit quietly in a corner watching me at my bench; not saying much, just following my hands, absorbing the atmosphere, the smell of glue and pine. I thought at first that he came because he was interested in violin-making. Later I realised it was because he had no one at home.

'There's a violin called the Messiah,' I replied. 'It's usually known by its French name, *Le Messie*.'

'It's a famous violin?' Guastafeste asked.

'The most famous – and the most valuable – on earth.'

Every profession has its myths, its folklore, tales from the past which somehow encapsulate the mystique of the calling, casting an aura of romance over a job which for the most part may be rather dull and monotonous. We all need these myths, to entertain, to embroider the labours we have chosen to fill our working days, for without them life would be intolerable.

The fine arts world is particularly prone, and particularly conducive, to myth-making. A cynic would say it helps keep prices high. Art dealers will talk of a missing Raphael, a Van Gogh that turns up gathering dust in the attic of some eccentric old lady. Musicologists will talk of an undiscovered Schubert symphony, a long-lost Mozart score that is spectacularly unearthed in the library of some obscure collector. And violin-makers tell the story of 'Le Messie', the perfect, unplayed, priceless Stradivari.

'I've never heard of it,' Guastafeste said.

'You should have,' I said. 'It's a work of art to rank alongside the *Mona Lisa*, the *Divine Comedy*, the operas of Verdi. It's a masterpiece as great as anything Michelangelo produced, as profound as a Beethoven symphony, as sublime and universal as a Shakespeare tragedy. To me, it is one of the most beautiful objects ever created by man. Think of jewels, think of a thousand glittering cut diamonds. Think of paintings, a Van Dyck portrait, a Monet landscape. They are nothing. This violin is more beautiful than any of them. Because it is not just for looking at. It is aesthetically beautiful, but it also has a purpose. It creates a sound, a music more heavenly, more inspiring than every jewel, every painting, every poem in history put together.'

Guastafeste stared at me. He is accustomed to my emotional outbursts, but even so my passion seemed to take him by surprise.

'This is some violin,' he said.

'Oh, it is.'

'You've seen it?'

'Yes, I've seen it.'

'Heard it played?'

'No. No man alive has heard it.'

Guastafeste kept his eyes fixed on me. 'I'm waiting,' he said.

I paused a moment, to let the throbbing in my head subside, to bring my emotions back under control.

'You want the story from the beginning?' I said. 'We have to go back to the year 1716. Antonio Stradivari was at the height of his powers, three-quarters of the way through what we now call his "Golden Period". In that year he made a violin which, even by his demanding standards, was superb. It was as close to perfection as he ever got. It was so perfect, in fact, that he could not bring himself to part with it. And he never did. On his death, in 1737, it remained in his workshop. Neither Francesco nor Omobono, the sons by his first wife who continued the violin-making business, parted with it and after their deaths the violin passed to Paolo Stradivari, Antonio's youngest son by his second wife. Paolo wasn't an instrument maker, he was a cloth merchant. He inherited a number of violins, either made entirely by his father or finished by his two half brothers, among them the violin we now know as "Le Messie".'

'It wasn't called that then?' Guastafeste said.

'No, the name came later. Paolo gradually sold off the violins and in 1775 he disposed of the final dozen or so, including Le Messie. The buyer was a nobleman from Casale Monferrato named Count Ignazio Alessandro Cozio di Salabue. Count Cozio, a passionate, almost fanatical, collector of violins, is the first of the three key historical figures in this story. He had a huge collection which he built up over many years and catalogued assiduously – Stradivaris, Guarneris, Amatis, Bergonzis, Ruggeris, Guadagninis, instruments by every leading violin-maker

29

of the time. But towards the end of his life Cozio ran into financial difficulties and was forced to sell off his collection. A large part of it was bought by an itinerant violin dealer named Luigi Tarisio, the second key figure in the story. You are with me so far?'

Guastafeste nodded. He stirred his coffee again, but didn't drink any of it. He was watching me intently.

'Tarisio was a fascinating character,' I continued. 'He was a carpenter by trade but he also played the fiddle – for country dances, weddings, that sort of thing. Like Count Cozio, he had a passion for Cremonese violins. Without Tarisio a good number of the Stradivari, Guarneri and Amati violins we know today would have been lost. This was the 1820s. The old Cremonese makers had fallen out of favour, at least in Italy. Few people wanted their violins.'

'Really?' Guastafeste was astonished.

'It's hard to believe now, but no one regarded them as valuable. Stradivari had been a highly respected, wealthy luthier in his lifetime, but after his death his reputation declined and he faded into relative obscurity. Who knows why? Fashion, taste, the fickle nature of humanity. Today we live in an age of mass-produced shoddy goods. We look back to earlier times and see the craftsmanship, the quality of what was made, and we pay a fortune to own it. But back then people wanted the new, they didn't want some old violin by a dead maker.'

Guastafeste sucked in his cheeks. 'What I wouldn't give to have been around then. To have picked up a few Stradivaris for next to nothing.'

I chuckled. 'That's exactly what Tarisio thought. The Italians may not have wanted old Cremonese violins, but Tarisio knew there was a market for them elsewhere, in France and England. So he scoured northern Italy, travelling around dressed as a pedlar, playing his fiddle and keeping his eyes open for old violins – and it's surprising how many Cremonese instruments were owned by poor farmers or peasants. Or he'd go to the monasteries and churches where there were instruments for the chapel orchestras which were often neglected and in a poor state of repair. He'd offer to buy them for a song, or he'd do carpentry work for the church and ask for the violins in lieu of payment. Then he'd fix up the violins and take them to Paris where he sold them to the great violin dealers Chanot, Aldric and – our third important figure – Jean-Baptiste Vuillaume.'

'Vuillaume?' Guastafeste said. 'I think I may have heard of him.'

'Quite probably. Vuillaume is one of those towering figures of the nineteenth-century musical world. Connoisseur, dealer, a man of the salons and concert halls who somehow also managed to make three thousand rather fine violins himself.'

'Three thousand!' Guastafeste exclaimed.

'You wonder when he found time to sleep. Tarisio did business with Vuillaume for years, selling him innumerable Cremonese violins. Throughout that time Tarisio used to boast about a Stradivari violin he owned that was so magnificent, so perfect he could not bear to sell it. He talked about the instrument so much that Vuillaume's son-in-law, the virtuoso violinist Delphin Alard, said it was like the Messiah: 'One always waits for him, but he never appears.' And that's where the name came from. When Tarisio died, in 1854, Vuillaume went straight to Italy. On the Tarisio family farm and in an attic in Milan he found close on 150 instruments, including *Le Messie*. He bought the lot from Tarisio's relatives and took them back to Paris.'

'And where is it now?' Guastafeste asked.

'In the Ashmolean Museum, in Oxford.'

'Oxford? In England, you mean?'

'Yes. It was acquired by the English dealers, Hills, who donated it to the museum.'

'Has it ever been played?'

'Just twice, and never in public. Delphin Alard played it at a private gathering of friends and family in 1855. Vuillaume said he heard the angels singing. And Joseph Joachim played it briefly in 1891.'

'Never since?'

'No,' I said. 'Hills stipulated that it should never be played.'

Guastafeste leaned back in his chair, his coffee still untouched on the table.

Then with a studied casualness, he said: 'If there were another violin – a sister to this "Messiah", what would it be worth?'

I kept my voice equally off-hand. 'Another perfect, untouched Stradivari coming on the open market. That would be an opportunity that comes once in a lifetime, maybe once in several lifetimes, if ever. A lot of people would be interested.'

'How interested?'

'Well, *Le Messie* has been valued at ten million US dollars.'

Guastafeste's eyes opened wide and I nodded in agreement.

'I know. It's amazing what some people will pay for a few pieces of wood and varnish.'

Guastafeste rubbed his jawline pensively, running his fingertips over the dark stubble. Then he voiced the question I'd been expecting him to ask.

'Would they kill for it?'

I looked away across the pavement, watching the traffic go by, a delivery van pulling in outside a shop, a mother pushing a pram down the street. It seemed odd that life elsewhere was functioning normally when my own felt so disrupted. Guastafeste was waiting for my reply.

'Yes,' I said. 'Human nature being what it is, I think they would.'

3

When I was a boy, I had a violin teacher named Dr Martinelli who was a great believer in the purifying properties of Bach. He said it cleansed the mind, stimulated the production of beneficial hormones, enhancing the body's sense of well-being and lifting the spirits. He was a teacher of the old school, a reserved, very proper man who always taught in frock-coat, waistcoat and dark tie no matter how hot the weather. He could be sharp and critical, but for the most part he was a benevolent tutor who regarded our lessons not simply as instruction in music but as the foundations of a philosophy for life.

To him, music was not something that you tacked on to your life, a secondary consideration or a frivolous distraction. It was an integral part of your very existence, as vital as breathing or eating. To live a day without music was an unthinkable omission, to live a day without Bach a transgression that bordered on blasphemy. 'Giovanni,' he would say to me in his soft, mellifluous voice, 'whatever you are doing, no matter how busy you are, you must always find time in your day for Bach.' And he would exhort me to play an unaccompanied partita every morning before breakfast, much as people today go jogging or to the gym to set themselves up for the day.

I never did, of course. I found it difficult enough getting out of bed in time to go to school, never mind practise my violin. But now I am older, the master of my own timetable, I have finally taken Dr Martinelli's advice. I do not do it before breakfast, nor every day, but as often as I can I go through into the back room after my coffee and roll and I play my violin.

On this particular morning I rose a little after eight, as usual, and had my breakfast in the kitchen. I'd slept badly, my mind preoccupied with Rainaldi's death, with his grieving family and – of less immediate concern but there all the same – the mysterious violin for which my friend had been searching.

After breakfast I went through to my violin and tackled the piece which seemed most in keeping with my melancholy mood – the Chaconne from the D Minor Partita which Bach wrote as an elegy for his beloved wife Maria Barbara whom, on returning home after a long absence, the composer found not only dead but buried as well. His distress must have been excruciating and the Chaconne is shot through with the anguish of his grief.

As I played, I found my conscious thoughts dissolving into the music so that my mind became almost a blank. It calmed me at first, brought a tranquillity which seeped through my body like a drug, then slowly began to energise me, sharpening my senses and filling me with renewed vigour.

When the last chord had died away and I was alone once again in the silence, I thought inevitably of my own wife. She was a fine pianist. We used to make music together almost every day. One of the Brahms sonatas, or perhaps Beethoven or Mozart. Then to end, just for the hell of it, I would take out some bravura piece by one of the great virtuosi composers: Paganini or Wieniawski or Sarasate. I am a violinist whose ambition, alas, has always surpassed his technique. And Caterina would play along with me, her shoulders shaking with laughter as I caterwauled up and down the register, missing harmonics, butchering double stops, searching for notes that never came in tune or never came at all. I thought of her at the piano, her slim fingers dancing over the keyboard, her eyes shining with pleasure, and I wondered again why it is that happy memories are so much more painful than unhappy ones.

My practice complete, I drove to the railway station and caught the train to Milan. There was a time when I would have driven all the way, but not now. Milan is so choked with cars it's difficult to breathe there let alone drive. On the station news-stand there were prominent bills announcing, 'Violin-maker Murdered – Police Hunt Killer'. I could see the stacks of papers with Rainaldi's death on the front page. I was curious to see what had been reported, but I didn't buy one. I knew it would be too distressing to read.

On arrival in Milan, I took a taxi to Serafin's shop, though his premises are really too grand for so common a noun. Serafin would be outraged at the term, deeming it a slur not only on his business but on himself for by extension labelling him a shopkeeper. And no one regards himself as less like a shopkeeper than Vincenzo Serafin.

The salon, Serafin's preferred description for his place of work – if work is really the word for what he does there – was in the heart of Milan's fashionable central district, a rhinestone's throw from the cathedral, the Galleria Umberto II and La Scala. It was sandwiched between an art gallery in which nothing was priced below 5,000 euros and an exclusive *haute couture* clothes shop with one dress in the window and, apparently, nothing else in the entire store. Serafin's establishment was even more minimalist. From its polished mahogany frontage no one would have known that violins were sold inside. Indeed, there was no indication that anything at all was sold there. The front window was completely empty and the room beyond, partially shielded from the street by vertical blinds, contained nothing except a desk and a chair in which a supercilious blonde receptionist had little to do except varnish her immaculate nails. Only a small brass plaque beside the door gave any information about the occupants of the building and that was too discreet to provide anything other than Serafin's name. Clients – never customers – came there by invitation and appointment only. If you didn't already know what went on there, then you were in the wrong place.

I went in. The blonde receptionist, becoming animated for a moment, looked up in what – for her – was a frenzy of excitement. Then she saw who it was and relapsed into her lethargic reverie. What she thought about all day – if she thought about anything at all – was a mystery to me.

'He's upstairs,' she said, raising her plucked eyebrows a couple of millimetres to indicate where 'upstairs' was.

She pressed a button under the desk and the door behind her clicked open. I walked through into a small carpeted hall where a thick-set man in a dark suit sat upright on an antique wooden chair. He didn't make a show of it, but I knew he was armed. Behind the door to the man's left was Serafin's inner sanctum, the sound-proofed music room where his clients tried out instruments. At any one time there were probably several million euros' worth of violins in that room, each one individually displayed in an illuminated glass case. The room had a marble floor, intricately carved oak-panelled walls which looked as if they'd come from the choir of an English church, and was acoustically perfect. Violins were tried one at a time, brought forth from their glass cases by an attendant wearing white gloves like a duke's footman – a wonderful touch which somehow encapsulated Serafin's shrewd nature. Bare hands would have made no difference to the instruments, but it reassured customers that what they were trying, even if it was some rubbishy old fiddle – and Serafin sells a few of those, though never priced accordingly – was delicate and priceless. In the violin-dealing world – far more than outsiders realise – appearances are everything.

I went up the stairs. As I neared the top, I heard voices raised inside Serafin's office. I paused on the landing, listening. I recognised one of the voices as Serafin's, but the other was unfamiliar. It was difficult to make out exactly what was being said, for Serafin's office had a thick, reinforced door, but the tone of both voices was undoubtedly heated, and they were speaking not in Italian but in English. I knocked on the door. There was a sudden silence inside the office, then Serafin called out, 'Yes?'

I went in. Serafin was seated behind his huge mahogany desk. On the other side of the office – as far away from Serafin as it was possible to be – a man was standing. He was tall and gangly with cold blue eyes and sandy hair, receding at the front but long enough at the back to curl over the collar of his white linen jacket. He looked to be somewhere in his thirties. His underlying complexion was pale, spotted with ginger freckles, but right now his skin was flushed with anger. I'd never seen him before, but from his clothes, his appearance, the snatches of conversation I'd overheard, I knew he was English.

'Gianni!' Serafin appeared flustered, not something I was used to seeing.

'We had an appointment,' I said.

'Ah, yes, of course. Our appointment.'

Serafin glanced at the sandy-haired man, who moved towards the door in such a forceful manner that I stepped quickly out of his way for fear he would knock me over.

'I'll be in touch,' he said curtly in English to Serafin, his tone more of a threat than a promise, then he turned and walked out of the room.

I pushed the door to behind him. By the time I looked back at Serafin he'd recovered his composure. He was taking a sip of coffee from the porcelain cup on his desk.

'I'm sorry, did I interrupt?' I said.

'No, no, it's all right. We'd finished.'

Serafin dabbed at his mouth with a napkin and smoothed his neatly trimmed beard with his fingers. There was something very feminine about him – his long, tapering, manicured fingers, his gestures, his soft, fleshy, pampered jowls.

'The violin is over there,' he said, inclining his head.

I went to the side table and opened the case, taking out the instrument inside and holding it up to the light. I knew what it was, of course – I'd carried out work on it in the past – but I still felt a tremor of anticipation as I ran my eyes over the curves, the belly, the waist, as a philanderer might appraise his next conquest. What was it about a violin that, even now, a half century after I'd first begun making them, could still arouse such a powerful sense of – I tried to identify what it was I felt. Was it desire, to possess it, to stamp my ownership on it? Was it admiration? Was it envy because someone greater, more skilful than I had made it? Or was it a nobler sentiment? Did it thrill me because in that beautifully crafted piece of wood there was something more than the sum of its parts? It wasn't just pine and maple and glue, it had been given life by its maker, a soul all of its own.

I couldn't resist looking at the label inside. *Antonius Stradivarius Cremonensis Faciebat Anno 1704.* She was three hundred years old and showing her age a bit, but she was still a magnificent old lady. I tilted her towards the window so the light caught the rich orange-red varnish, making it glow like a liquid sunset. I could see every grain of the pine, imagine Stradivari's hands smoothing over the contours. But on the left side of the belly, just above the f-hole, was a crack which Stradivari certainly would not have recognised.

'What happened?' I asked.

Serafin pushed aside his coffee cup. He dabbed at the corners of his mouth again, then folded the napkin and placed it neatly beside the cup.

'An accident,' he said. He mentioned the name of a distinguished violinist, the leader of one of Italy's foremost string quartets. 'He put it down in his case which was on the floor next to his chair.'

'And?'

'He forgot it was there and trod on it.'

Trod on it! I could barely contain my contempt. This man had a Stradivari violin, worth probably two million euros, a violin that had survived intact for three centuries. And he trod on it.

'Unfortunate,' I murmured, though a more robust exclamation was exploding inside my head.

'Quite,' Serafin said mildly. 'He is greatly distressed and anxious to have it fixed as soon as possible.'

'I'm sure he is.'

I examined the crack more closely through the jeweller's loupe I carry in my pocket. The break looked fairly clean, the wood on either side not too badly shredded.

'How quickly can you do it?' Serafin said. 'He has another instrument – a Bergonzi – but they have an important concert in New York at the end of next month and he'd really like the Stradivari back by then.'

Serafin's clients move in exalted circles. He deals with concert violinists, chamber musicians, orchestral leaders and rich collectors for whom he attends auctions all over the world. If you want a half-size Chinese import for little Luigi to begin on, then Serafin is most definitely not your man. He knows a lot about violins, but not how to play one nor how to make or repair them – I take care of all that for him. I do the labouring, he takes the money, is how I see it. But it's a mutually advantageous arrangement that we have maintained successfully for many, many years. Like all luthiers I deal a bit on the side. I could have a salon like Serafin's, with all the trimmings, but that would bore me. I'd have to wear a suit, acquire a *chaise longue*, some art for the walls, and I can't be bothered with all that. I just want to be left alone in my workshop. I'm an artisan not a businessman.

'I can have it ready for then,' I said.

I put the violin back in its case and sensed a movement out of the corner of my eye. I turned my head. Serafin's mistress, Maddalena, was coming through the door from the small flat behind the office. Serafin has a wife but she seldom comes to Milan. She lives on their country estate near Lake Maggiore, a sad neglected creature destined to share her husband's affections with a steady stream of more sophisticated metropolitan harpies. Maddalena was idle, glamorous, undeniably beautiful yet curiously unsexy. Actually, I don't know why I say 'curiously' for there is nothing curious about it. If there is one thing that I have learnt about women it is that the most stunning of them are rarely the most sexy. Maddalena was so poised and disdainful it was impossible to imagine her ever abandoning herself to the torrid confusion of passion. But then

41

I suspected she was more of an ornament for Serafin's arm than his bed.

'I'm going out now,' she said, barely acknowledging my presence. I'm too old and too poor to interest her. I'm simply a servant hovering in the background.

'All right, darling,' Serafin replied. 'Shall I meet you for lunch?'

'Not today. I'm seeing Teresa. You know, girl talk.'

Maddalena leaned down to allow Serafin to kiss her – her cheek only, to avoid any damage to her make-up.

'I'll see you later, darling,' Serafin said and watched her waggling her bony hips as she left the office.

I sat down and we haggled about my fee for the work. Serafin enjoys haggling. He has cultivated a veneer of culture, a suave, slightly unctuous gloss of refinement that appeals to his wealthy clientele, but underneath it all he's just a market trader, buying low and selling high. In the narrow world of violin dealing he has a reputation as a man who would not just sell his own mother, he would put her out to tender.

'I see you've been having some excitement in Cremona,' he said when we'd sorted out the money.

I gave him a puzzled look.

'The murder,' Serafin explained. 'What was his name again, Tomaso Rainaldi? You know anything about it?'

His tone was casual, almost indifferent. I was instantly on my guard.

'Why would I know anything about it?' I asked warily.

'Oh, I don't know. You're on the spot. He was a luthier. I wasn't familiar with him myself, but you probably knew him.'

'Yes, I knew him.' I didn't expand. I had no intention of sharing my knowledge of the case with Serafin. Ours was strictly a business relationship. 'Why are you interested?'

Serafin shrugged. 'I'm not really. It's just unusual, isn't it? A murder in Cremona.'

He looked away and we chatted about other things for a short while.

'Keep me informed about the Stradivari, Gianni,' he said as we parted. 'If there's a problem, let me know at once.'

'There won't be a problem,' I said.

It was early evening by the time I got back to my house. I had something to eat, then took the Stradivari through into my workshop. My workshop is in the garden at the back of the house, but I also have a varnishing room with skylights in the attic, and this is where I finish my instruments and hang them to dry. Stradivari had the same in his house in the Piazza San Domenico and I attribute some of the lustre of his varnish to the Italian sun which seems to have been absorbed by the wood. They make violins elsewhere, some of them very good, but it is no coincidence that the finest instruments have all come from the warm, but not too warm, pastures of northern Italy.

I laid the violin down on its back on my workbench and composed myself. I've repaired Stradivaris before, and Guarneris, Amatis and most of the other great makers too, but I've never lost the feeling of being privileged to hold them, privileged to be allowed to take the masters' creations and work on them with my own humble hands.

I studied the instrument for a time, examining every part of it carefully to make sure there was no other damage that had been overlooked. Then I concentrated on the crack. The first thing to do was to remove the belly, gently so as not to open the crack even further. I took a syringe and injected a tiny amount of alcohol into the join between the belly and ribs, taking care not to spill any on the varnish which was soluble in alcohol. The alcohol would make the

43

glue dehydrate and lose its grip. Then I inserted a thin knife blade under the belly and put pressure on it with another smaller wedge-shaped blade which I gradually slid in over the ribs. Working my way around the instrument I eased off the front.

I gazed down at the inside of the violin, seeing the two-piece maple back, the ribs, linings and blocks as Stradivari had left them. I could even see the marks of his clamps on the surface of the blocks. I wasn't the first person to open up the instrument. Like all violins of that period the neck, fingerboard and bass bar had been changed – probably at the beginning of the nineteenth century – the neck lengthened and angled backwards to take the additional string tension caused by the increased pitch of the diapason since Stradivari's day. But probably only two other men had seen what I was seeing now, and one of them was Stradivari himself.

I lingered a while, studying the results of the Master's unmatched craftsmanship. Apart from the changes to the neck and bass bar and the switch from gut strings to gut wound with metal, the violin today is exactly the same as it was when Stradivari was alive. Aesthetically, and musically, it cannot be improved, though many people have tried. It is perfect the way it is.

I pulled my eyes away from the body of the instrument and turned my attention to the belly. I took another careful look at the crack with my loupe, this time from the inside of the belly. Not only was the wood fractured, but the plate had been crushed slightly so the two sides of the break were not in alignment. I would have to fix the crack, and also restore the curve of the belly – a time-consuming task that required my making a plaster cast of the plate, then pressing the wood back into shape with a hot sandbag. This was delicate work that needed more concentration than I felt I could summon at this late hour, so I locked the Stradivari away in my fireproof safe and went to bed early. I needed a good night's sleep. My grandchildren were coming to stay the next day.

There are three of them: Paolo, aged eleven, Carla, nine, and the baby of the family, Pietro, six. They live only a couple of hours' drive away, to the east of Mantua, so I see quite a lot of them on day visits. But once a year I have them overnight. My daughter, Francesca, and her husband drop the children off with me on a Saturday morning, then go off somewhere together until Sunday afternoon – maybe to one of the lakes, maybe shopping in Milan followed by an evening at the theatre, a good hotel and some time to themselves.

They arrived early, unloading what appeared to be enough baggage for a month. Francesca, as usual, began fussing over them, torn between her desire to be off and a mother's natural anxiety at leaving her children even for just one night.

'Now be good for Grandpa,' she said. 'Don't make too much noise, eat your food properly and don't wake up too early in the morning.'

The children rolled their eyes and shuffled their feet. 'Yes, yes, Mama. We'll see you tomorrow.'

Francesca's husband was waiting by the car, inscrutable in his expensive sunglasses. He had the driver's door open and was impatient to be on their way. But Francesca had one last duty to perform. She gave me a piece of paper.

'It's the list of dos and don'ts,' she said. 'What they can eat, what time they each have to be in bed. You know.'

I nodded. She gives me a list of instructions every time. After she's gone, the first thing I do is throw it in the bin. Children always forget that you brought them up and

45

know a little about it. Or maybe they don't forget, they just want to do it differently with their own.

Francesca kissed me and the children and we waved them off. Then the kids rushed round into the garden, temporarily free of their shackles, and I didn't see them again for an hour until they came into the house, hot and sweaty, demanding drinks and biscuits.

Towards midday the phone rang. It was Guastafeste.

'What are you doing today?' he asked.

'I've got the grandchildren,' I explained. 'I'm taking them for a swim and a picnic. Why?'

'I wanted to talk to you. About Tomaso.'

'Come with us. Join us for the picnic,' I said.

'I don't have time for picnics.'

'It's Saturday, Antonio. You're allowed a lunch break, aren't you? You've got to look after yourself better, you know. Get more sleep, eat regularly. You won't solve this case more quickly by making yourself ill.'

He gave a dry little laugh. 'Don't fuss, Gianni.'

'I mean it,' I said. 'You know where we'll be. The pool by the woods. Midday onwards. I'll expect you.'

'I'll see,' Guastafeste said.

The pool we were going to was on the river a few kilometres from Cremona. Not the Po, which is hardly one of the world's most attractive rivers – if Johann Strauss had been Italian, I doubt he'd have written 'On the Beautiful Blue Po' – but on one of the smaller tributaries where the stream was still largely water, as opposed to industrial effluent.

We laid out our rug on the bank and the kids stripped off and leaped into the pool. Francesca doesn't like me bringing them here, she thinks it's unsafe and unhygienic, but I take no notice of her. When she was growing up she ignored virtually everything I ever said to her, particularly

46

when she was a stroppy teenager. Now it's my turn to ignore her.

The children were out of the water again and on the bank, drying off in the sun and eating bread and cheese and tomatoes from my garden, when Guastafeste emerged from the trees, his jacket slung casually over one shoulder. He sat down next to me on the rug and loosened his tie.

'You want something to eat?' I said.

'Is there enough for me?'

'Of course there is.'

I passed him a chunk of bread and some cheese on a paper plate. He broke off a piece of the bread and chewed it slowly, looking around at the pool.

'It's years since I was last here,' he said. 'You remember when you used to bring me here? It's hardly changed at all.'

Guastafeste is the same age as my eldest son, Domenico, still friends with him though Domenico has lived and worked in Rome for the past ten years. Antonio was round at our house to play so often when he was a child, came with us on so many outings that he was almost a part of our family. There was a time, indeed, in his late adolescence when he and Francesca seemed sweet on each other, when I thought he might have become a full member of the family, but it was not to be.

'Yes, I remember,' I said.

'Those long summer days. You used to make a wood fire and we cooked sausages on sticks. They always ended up black and charred like lumps of charcoal. I can still remember the taste.'

He smiled at me. He was looking better today, clean shaven, wearing a crisp white shirt and blue tie, but his eyes were still tired.

'Grandpa, can we go swimming again?' Carla asked.

47

'Let your food go down first,' I replied.

'What about the woods? Can we play in the woods?'

'Yes, but don't go too far.'

The children got up from the rug.

'Hey, I brought you something,' Guastafeste said. He felt in his jacket pocket and brought out three packets of sweets. He threw them to the kids.

'Eat them all at once,' he said.

The children thanked him and ran off into the woods. Guastafeste watched them pushing through the under-growth, a soft look on his face. He's always been good with children. He and his ex-wife never had any. He doesn't talk about it, but I wonder sometimes whether that is not some-thing he regrets. Perhaps not though. He likes children, but he also likes his own space, time to himself that children do not allow you. He lay back on the rug, his hands behind his head.

'I should come out here more often,' he said. 'It's so quiet, so peaceful. So different from the *Questura*.'

'Things are bad?' I said.

'The *Questore* wants a result. And he wants it yesterday.'

'And are you going to be able to give him one?'

'Not on what we've got so far.'

A fly buzzed towards Guastafeste's nose. He swotted it away lazily. I helped myself to a left-over tomato and bit into it. There's nothing quite like a home-grown tomato.

'We've almost nothing to go on,' Guastafeste said. 'We've done a door-to-door enquiry, talked to all the neighbours. No one seemed to hear, or see, anything of significance that night. No shouting, no cars arriving or leaving, no strangers hanging around the street.' He sat up and wrapped his arms around his knees, squinting at the sunlight reflected on the surface of the river. 'He was

48

a violin-maker; a gentle, harmless violin-maker. All right, he could be difficult, dogmatic, opinionated, but he wasn't the kind of man who made enemies. He wasn't rich, famous, he wasn't mixed up with any criminal activity – as far as we know. What had he done, what did he know that made someone want to kill him?'

I finished my tomato and licked some juice off my fingers. I waited for him to go on, to clear out his thoughts.

'You know this world better than I do, Gianni. If Tomaso was looking for a violin, this Messiah's Sister, how would he have gone about it?'

'That's difficult to say. He must have had something to go on, some lead. There are always rumours about long-lost Stradivaris. Every luthier hopes – dreams – that one day he'll come across one somewhere. But we never do.'

'Never?'

'It's more than two hundred and fifty years since Stradivari died. The chances of a new, hitherto undiscovered violin of his turning up are almost zero.'

'Tomaso must have thought he had a chance. He went to England, after all, spent money on an air ticket, hotels. He wouldn't do that without a good reason.'

'Do you know where in England he went?'

'We're trying to find out. I spoke to Clara again yesterday. She didn't know where exactly he went. Just that he flew to London, was away for three days.'

'How was she?'

'Depressed, tearful, but better than the day before. She's eating a little, getting some sleep.'

'Did he have any papers?' I said. 'You know, booking slips, hotel confirmation letters, receipts.'

'We're checking. We've got his diary. That might help us. In fact, that's why I wanted to talk to you. There was an entry in the diary, an appointment for last Monday. In Venice.'

'Venice?'

'With a man named Enrico Forlani.'

I reached out for the bottle of mineral water at the foot of the rug and refilled my cup. My mouth seemed suddenly very dry.

'I understand he's a violin collector,' Guastafeste said. 'You ever heard of him?'

I took a sip of water before I replied. 'Yes, I know his name.'

'His phone number was in the diary. I called it. He wasn't very cooperative, refused to talk to me on the phone. Said he'd only speak face to face. Do you know him?'

'Only by reputation. We've never met, but I've done some work on his violins, though only through Serafin, never directly.'

'Is he a big collector?'

'So they say. He's very secretive, keeps his collection out of the public eye. But it's reputed to be big, one of the biggest in the world. He has plenty of money to spend.'

Guastafeste turned his head to look at me. 'I'm out of my depth here, Gianni. So are my colleagues. We know nothing about violins. I'm worried we might miss things, might overlook something, not realise its significance. If I clear it with my superiors, would you be willing to come on board as a sort of expert adviser?'

'Tomaso was my friend,' I said. 'I'll do anything I can to help.'

'Thank you.' Guastafeste looked back at the river, the water still and limpid, dappled with sunbeams and shadows. 'It's tempting, isn't it?' he said. 'I'd just love to strip off and jump in, the way I did when I was a kid.'

'Why don't you?'

'I'm grown up now. I'm not supposed to have fun.'
He stood up and touched me lightly on the shoulder.
'Say bye to the kids for me.'

For dinner, the children helped me prepare kebabs to cook over an open wood fire at the bottom of the garden, something they can never do at home. They live in a town, in a second-floor apartment where the only flowers they see are in a window box. I used to be an urban dweller too. For years my workshop was in the centre of Cremona, tucked away in one of the side-streets with the bustle and noise of the city all around. But seven years ago I grew tired of the cars and pollution and lack of space and moved out into the country. I am only a few kilometres from Cremona – you can see its hazy silhouette on the skyline – but we are surrounded by fields, by swathes of swaying corn, the tranquillity broken only by the distant rattle of a tractor and the intermittent barking of farm dogs.

When we'd finished skewering the kebabs, Paolo and Carla went out into the garden to collect logs from my woodpile, but Pietro lingered behind in the kitchen. He'd been very quiet while we were making the kebabs and I could see that something was troubling him.

'What is it, little chap?' I said.

'Grandpa,' Pietro said in his small, high-pitched voice. 'Why have Mama and Papa gone away?'

'It's only for one night. They'll be back tomorrow.'

'But why couldn't we go with them?'

'They're doing things you wouldn't be interested in, boring grown-up things.'

'Didn't they want us with them?'

'It's not that. Sometimes grown-ups need a bit of time to themselves. They left you with me for a night last year and you didn't seem to mind.'

But he was a year older now, more aware of what was happening, more conscious of rejection yet unable to rationalise it like his brother and sister.

'Are they going to come back?'

He looked up at me and I saw that he was crying.

'Oh, Pietro.'

I put down the knife I was using to chop vegetables and sat him on my lap. With my finger I wiped away the tears on his cheeks.

'Of course they're going to come back,' I said.

'Are you sure?'

'Yes, I'm sure. Shall I tell you something, something your old grandpa has learned over the years? There are very few simple truths in life, but there is one that's universal, that's true for everyone. And that is that your mother and father love you more than anything in the world. You and Carla and Paolo. And they will continue to love you. Even when you're grown up and you've left home and are making your own way in the world they will still love you. Believe me, I know.'

Pietro sniffed and looked up at me. 'So they've not left us?'

'No, you silly old thing. Tomorrow afternoon they will be back for you. You can wait until then, can't you?'

'I'll try.'

'Good boy. Now why don't you come and help me light the fire?'

We made a big blaze at the far end of my vegetable patch and waited until the flames had died down and the logs were glowing red before we put the kebabs on to roast. There were thick chunks of lamb and red peppers and onions on the skewers. We ate them with bread and potatoes and crisp green beans followed by ripe peaches. Then we sat around the embers as night fell and I told them creepy ghost stories, Pietro pressing up close to me, shivering and asking for more.

I regretted it later, though, for when I finally put them to bed they were too terrified to sleep. I sat beside Pietro, stroking his head and murmuring soothingly until at last he dropped off. I stayed there for a while afterwards, remembering when Francesca and her two brothers had been little and I would sit watching over them sometimes while they slept. It seemed such a very short time ago.

I was dozing in my chair under the shade of my cherry tree when Francesca and her husband returned.

'Papa,' Francesca said, shaking me gently.

'Ah, you're back,' I said sleepily, rubbing my eyes and stretching.

Francesca was looking around the garden. 'Where are the children? Are they inside?'

'They're somewhere,' I said vaguely.

'You mean you don't know?'

'They're off exploring in the fields.'

Francesca stared at me. 'You let them go off on their own?'

'I told them not to go far.'

'Papa, how could you be so irresponsible? They could have been abducted.'

'No one would abduct those three, they wouldn't dare.'

'It's not funny. There are all sorts of perverts and weird people out there. Anything could have happened.'

She marched off down the garden, her husband in tow, and disappeared into the fields at the bottom. Twenty minutes later they reappeared herding three sheepish children. The kids were dishevelled, dirt smeared all over their clothes and faces. All three of them were carrying sticks. Even I had to admit they looked pretty scruffy.

'Go inside and clean yourselves up,' Francesca ordered as they drew level with me.

'Aw, do we have to?' Paolo said.

'Now.'

'We saw a rabbit,' Carla said to me proudly. 'Eating grass. It was this big.' She held out her hands to demonstrate.

'Can we go swimming again, Grandpa, before we go home?' Pietro asked.

I looked away, sensing Francesca's steely gaze coming to bear on me. She waited until the children were inside the house before she opened fire.

'Swimming? How did you take them swimming? I didn't leave their costumes.'

'They went skinny dipping,' I said.

'Skinny dipping! Papa, you didn't take them to the river? That filthy, germ-ridden pool?'

'It's not filthy,' I protested. 'It's perfectly all right. I used to take you there when you were little and it never did you any harm.'

'Things are different now. Pollution is worse. That pool's full of bacteria.'

'What's wrong with that? Kids of today don't get enough bacteria. It does them good, builds up their resistance.'

Francesca's mouth tightened, but she didn't pursue the argument. I knew that the moment they got home she'd be scrubbing the children with disinfectant and taking their temperatures.

It was strange when they'd gone. My initial response was one of relief – that the noise, the relentless exhausting activity of young children had ceased. But after I'd caught my breath, I began to miss having them around. My sense of isolation and loneliness seemed more acute than ever, so

54

I did what I always do when melancholy threatens to overwhelm me. I went into my workshop, put one of my old Heifetz LPs on the record player and immersed myself in my work, in the soothing therapy of carving wood.

It was almost dark outside when the telephone rang. I picked up the extension near my workbench and heard Guastafeste's voice.

'It's all fixed,' he said. 'What are you doing for the next couple of days?'

'Just working, as usual.'

'Anything urgent?'

'Not particularly. Why?'

'Pack an overnight bag,' Guastafeste said. 'We're going to Venice in the morning.'

4

We arrived in Venice in the late afternoon. It was several years since I'd last been there, but Venice changes very little and when it does the difference is barely perceptible. When you walk out of the station and see the Grand Canal in front of you the impact is still exhilarating, still sublime, no matter how many times you have been there. And the smell is still the same – a tang of the sea mixed with undertones of fetid water, rank sewage and diesel fumes from the motor boats.

The walk to our hotel – a small *pensione* near the *Teatro La Fenice* which Guastafeste had booked in advance – was the usual Venetian obstacle course of tourists and dog dirt. We left our bags in our rooms, then walked back to the Grand Canal and stood for a moment on the Accademia Bridge. Venice has always been a chiaroscuro city, a place where the light and shadow change suddenly and unexpectedly. One moment it seems dilapidated and tawdry, the next the sunlight alters and you catch a glimpse of a beauty that makes your heart miss a beat. From our vantage point on the bridge, the surface of the Grand Canal, which had looked brown and oily when we arrived, now had the sheen of shot silk. The exposed banks of mud along the edges had the appearance of the expensive youth-giving unguent women apply to their wrinkles rather than the poisonous slime it really was.

Enrico Forlani's home was a *palazzo* on the western side of the Grand Canal. It took us a while to find it in the labyrinth of narrow streets and alleys, and when we finally stopped outside its door it didn't look much like a palace. The stucco had broken away from the walls in large chunks, revealing the brickwork underneath. The paint on the door and windows was chipped, the shutters faded and rotting in the damp air. Guastafeste rang the bell on the entryphone a few times, holding it in for several seconds each time. Eventually a man's head appeared at the window above us.

'What do you want?' he snapped.

'Dottor Forlani?'

'Yes. Who are you?'

'Antonio Guastafeste, Cremona police. We have an appointment, if you remember.'

The head pulled back and a moment later we heard locks and bolts being undone. The front door clicked open on a chain. A dark, suspicious eye looked out through the crack.

'Show me some identification.'

Guastafeste held out his police identity card and a hand like a wizened claw snatched it away for a few seconds, then gave it back. The door snapped shut and we heard the chain being detached on the inside. When Forlani reopened the door it was only a little wider than before. He beckoned us in and we squeezed awkwardly through the gap, Forlani pushing us to one side so he could lock and bolt the door behind us.

The stench was the first thing I noticed. There was the

57

damp odour you get all over Venice, but it was particularly noticeable here and exacerbated by a pungent reek of decaying vegetable matter and a fruitier, more human smell which I realised was emanating from Forlani himself. To my right, a short flight of stone steps led down into the open basement of the building which, like most of the others on the canal, had been constructed as a water entrance and boathouse for the *palazzo*. I could see the Grand Canal through the wrought-iron gates, see and hear the water lapping against the walls of the basement. Even in the gloomy light it was possible to make out the scum on the surface of the water; a thick layer of kitchen scraps and other rubbish which had been dumped there over the years and never been flushed away by the action of the tides. I heard a patter of feet which I knew was rats.

We followed Forlani up the stairs to the first floor. Through an elaborately panelled set of double doors was a large room overlooking the Grand Canal – at least it would have overlooked the canal if the shutters on the windows hadn't been tightly shut. Strips of sunlight percolated in through the slats in the shutters, dimly illuminating the bare floor and walls of the room. The plaster was peeling off like diseased skin, the long curtains next to the windows hung in soiled, shredded tatters. There was no furniture except for a long wooden table and a couple of cheap wooden chairs. The top of the table was cluttered with piles of china plates on which congealed sauce and rancid old meat and rubbery pasta lay decomposing.

I could scarcely believe that this was the Enrico Forlani we were seeking. Guastafeste must have had his doubts too for the first thing he said was, 'You are Enrico Forlani, collector of violins, aren't you?'

'Of course I am,' Forlani replied testily. 'Who else do you think I am? Now what is it you want?'

He was wearing a threadbare old dressing gown and a pair of cheap plastic flip-flops on his bare feet. The smell from his body was so overpowering that I had to step back a few paces from him.

Guastafeste glanced around the room. 'Is there perhaps somewhere more, ah, comfortable, we can talk?'

'What's wrong with here?' Forlani demanded.

'As you wish. First of all, thank you for agreeing to see us. I hope we're not going to take up too much of your time.'

'Get to the point,' Forlani said.

Guastafeste's mouth tightened. 'We're investigating the murder of a man named Tomaso Rainaldi. A violin-maker who was found dead in his workshop in Cremona last Wednesday night.'

Forlani gave an impatient shake of his head. 'You told me all this on the phone. What has it got to do with me? I've never been to Cremona in my life.'

'Rainaldi came to see you two days before he was killed. I'd like to know why.'

Forlani looked at us in turn. He had a pale, unhealthy complexion and hooded eyes like a lugubrious vulture. I put his age at somewhere in his late seventies.

'What if I say that's my business?'

'A man has been murdered, Dottor Forlani,' Guastafeste said mildly. 'I'm sure you would want to give us your full cooperation.' Guastafeste smiled at Forlani, a pleasant enough smile, but one edged with an unmistakable hint of menace.

I sensed Forlani drawing back from us a little, watching us carefully. The Venetians are a green and slippery people, like their city. They have a reputation for hard-headedness, for being calculating and untrustworthy.

Guastafeste fed him a snippet of information, perhaps

trying to head off the evasive reply we could both see coming.

'We know he was looking for a violin, a violin he called the "Messiah's Sister". Was that why he came to see you?'

'You think there's a connection between this violin and his death?' Forlani said.

'We're exploring every possibility. You're a wealthy collector. Was he searching for the violin for you?'

Forlani didn't answer. He turned away so we couldn't see the expression on his face. It was stiflingly hot and airless in the room. I was beginning to feel sick.

'Was he?' Guastafeste asked again.

'What if he was?' Forlani said, swinging back to face us. 'That was between him and me.'

'Not any more,' Guastafeste said. 'Not now he's dead.'

Forlani walked across to the shuttered windows and fingered one of the catches. I hoped he was going to open it, to let some air and light into the oppressive room, but he didn't. He shrugged.

'I don't suppose you know the story of *Le Messie*, do you? A provincial policeman like you.'

Guastafeste ignored the slur. 'I know it. My friend here told me.'

'Did he?' Forlani turned his gaze on me. 'Did he tell you what it was worth?'

'Yes. He's quite an expert on violins.'

'Oh yes?' Forlani's lip curled. 'I didn't think the police were experts on anything, except corruption, of course.'

'I'm not a policeman,' I said. 'I'm a luthier.'

'A luthier? Your name?'

'Giovanni Battista Castiglione.'

Forlani screwed up his nose. 'I believe I may have heard of you,' he conceded. Then his eyes became wary. 'Why are you here?'

'He's assisting us in our enquiries,' Guastafeste said. 'Perhaps you would be good enough to answer my question, *dottore*. Why did Tomaso Rainaldi come to see you?' His tone was sharp. He was starting to lose patience.

Forlani gazed at him for a long moment. Then he said indifferently, as if his reply were of no consequence: 'He had a proposition for me. He told me he was sure there was another Messiah out there and he could find it for me.'

'And you believed him?' Guastafeste said.

'Yes.'

'Were you paying him?'

'I gave him some money for expenses, yes.'

'How much?'

'Five thousand euros.'

'That's a lot of money.'

'It may be a lot to you. It's not to me.'

'Did you know Rainaldi? Had you met him before?'

'No. I'd never set eyes on him until he showed up on my doorstep.'

Guastafeste regarded the old man sceptically. 'So this stranger you've never seen before comes to your door and tells you some tale about a violin and you give him money? I find that a little unlikely, Dottor Forlani.'

'Do you?' Forlani's voice took on an edge of aggression. 'Do you have any idea what is at stake here? I don't think you do. Come with me, I'll show you.'

Forlani went out of the room, his flip-flops slapping on the marble floor. We followed him up another flight of stairs and down a gloomy corridor. Through open doors I caught glimpses of more derelict rooms, of collapsed ceilings and piles of rubble. The smell of decay was everywhere. Forlani moved slowly, pausing regularly to catch his breath. At the end of the corridor he opened a door and we entered a small, unfurnished antechamber which

61

contained nothing but a metal cabinet on the wall. In front of us was a large steel door, like the entrance to a bank vault.

Forlani unlocked the cabinet and, shielding his fingers with his body, punched in a combination on a keypad. The steel door clicked open and swung out towards us, its electric motor purring softly.

Beyond the door was another room, a vast chamber that must have taken up half the total area of the second floor. It had no windows – the light was all artificial, beaming down from recessed lamps in the ceiling – and from the breath of cool air that gusted out I could tell it was air-conditioned and humidity-controlled. I knew Forlani's reputation, had seen fine collections many times before, but nothing could have prepared me for what I saw when I entered that room. Around all the walls and in the centre of the chamber, immaculately presented in individually lit glass cases, were violins.

I paused on the threshold, suddenly breathless. It wasn't the quantity of instruments that struck me – though there must have been a hundred or more – it was the quality. I could tell at a glance that this was a truly exceptional collection, maybe the finest ever put together since Cozio di Salabue had amassed – and then lost – his own.

Forlani was watching me, gauging my reaction.

'What do you think?' he asked.

'It's incredible.'

I stared around at the glass cases, at the violins bathed in light, their varnish glowing orange and red and russet like a sunlit autumn forest.

'You see now?' Forlani said. 'For forty years I have been building this collection. Forty years, that's a long time. I have instruments by all the giants of violin-making: by Stradivari, the Guarneris, by every one of the great luthiers. I have spent a fortune on it.'

He wandered deeper into the chamber, holding out his arms as if to embrace his precious possessions.

'This is why I gave Rainaldi money. Maybe he was wrong about the violin, maybe he was even lying to me, trying to cheat me. But think of the prize: a perfect, undiscovered Stradivari, as fresh and untouched as the day the Master finished it. If there was just a one per cent – no, a fraction of one per cent – possibility that Rainaldi was right and could find it, then that was good enough for me. He was offering me a chance to have it. What collector could turn down an opportunity like that?'

Forlani's eyes had the glint of the fanatic in them, a hard coruscating light which was just this side of insanity. I believed him. I'd met collectors before. I'd seen how the desire, the greed to own a violin could consume and corrupt a man.

Forlani was rich and shrewd, the scion of a shipowning family which dated back to the Middle Ages when the Venetians had made a killing transporting the Crusaders to the Holy Land, their support for their passengers' Christian cause always tempered by good sense and the clear-headed philosophy that has almost become the unofficial Venetian motto: 'On what terms?' Forlani was tough and ruthless, but he also had that other dominant Venetian characteristic: a willingness to gamble.

I walked in a daze around that perfect room, that shrine in a cathedral of squalor, my head swimming with an intoxicating cocktail of emotions: awe, astonishment, envy, admiration. But also anger. A deep, powerful resentment directed against Forlani. I despised him for hiding away treasures that the whole world should have been able to share. I have no quarrel with people who collect art. Its only purpose is to be looked at; whether in a public gallery or on a collector's wall is irrelevant except for the number of people who can enjoy it. But a violin is different. A violin is meant to be played and heard, not put in a vault or a glass case. Forlani could have lent out his instruments to gifted but impoverished players, to young musicians who would use them as their makers intended, but he had chosen instead to hoard them away where only he could look at them.

I could see that there were at least ten Stradivaris in the room. Why did he want another? What was it that drove his desire to own yet more violins that would never be played? I knew he wasn't a violinist himself. No true musician would ever have put instruments like these in glass cases.

Forlani was watching me. 'Let's see how much you know, shall we? Our police "expert". Are you up to the challenge?'

'What do you want me to do?'

'Identify my violins. Without looking at the labels inside them.'

I stifled a snort of contempt. No one but an amateur would have made such a remark. No violin expert worth his salt bothers much with labels. Too many of them are false or have been changed. He assesses the instrument from the outside first, examining the shape, the feel, the colour and sheen of the varnish, the cut of the f-holes and scroll, searching for the fingerprints of the maker which are there as surely as the fingerprints of a careless thief at the scene of a burglary and are just as clear to the expert eye. Only then does he bother to look at the label, if there is one. It may confirm his assessment. If it does not, then I would always trust my own judgement first – the label is probably false.

'Where would you like me to begin?' I said.

'Try this one,' Forlani said, pointing at one of the glass cases near the side wall.

64

I stepped over to the case and studied the violin inside it. I knew instantly what it was.

'Maggini,' I said.

'Your reasoning?'

Who could resist such an invitation to show off?

'Several things,' I said. 'The varnish, for a start. That rich golden orange. Then the arching is very full towards the edges, the waist a little more discreet than, say, the Amatis' instruments which were being made at about the same time. The sound holes have the small lobes and wings characteristic of Maggini and, of course, it has his trademark double purfling which – as every violin-maker knows – is dedication beyond the call of duty.'

I walked round to the back of the case. The violin had a one-piece maple back, cut on the slab, with a pattern in the grain that resembled the head of a snake. I peered closer. 'It's hard to tell without holding the violin, but from this distance it looks to me as if the white part of the purfling is fig tree bark. Maggini, and his teacher Gasparo da Salò, are the only great makers to use fig tree bark in their purfling. The Cremonese and Venetians always used poplar wood for the white part, except Ruggeri who favoured beech like the Neapolitan and Tuscan luthiers.'

Forlani pursed his lips. 'Not bad. A date?'

I gave him a look. 'Please, *dottore*, you will have to do better than that. Everyone knows that Maggini never dated his instruments.'

Forlani sniffed. Round one to me.

'All right, what about this one?'

'Amati,' I said.

'Which one?'

'Nicolò.'

I gazed at the violin. Amati instruments have fallen out of favour with modern soloists because they lack the power

of a Stradivari or a Guarneri, but they are beautifully crafted and have an unmatched sweetness of sound. Nicolò was
the third generation and greatest maker of the family. His
influence on the art of violin-making was immense, not just
because of his own instruments but because of the pupils
he taught – Andrea Guarneri, Giovanni Battista Rogeri,
Bartolomeo Cristofori, who would go on to invent the
pianoforte, and of course Antonio Stradivari.

'And this?' Forlani said.

'Guadagnini. Giovanni Battista.'

'Care to hazard a guess at the date?'

'Somewhere between 1759 and 1771,' I said. 'When he
lived and worked in Parma.'

'What makes you think that?'

'The sound holes. He cut them higher and higher up the
table during that period and so had to cut the notches to
mark the position of the bridge correspondingly lower.'

'Pretty good. I'm impressed,' Forlani said. 'But how
about this one?'

And so we worked our way around most of the room.
He had several more Amatis, violins by every member of
the Guarneri family, Bergonzis, Stainers, Gaglianos, the ten
Stradivaris, including one extremely rare *pochette*, a dance
master's fiddle which was made narrower than usual to fit
in the player's coat pocket. Each one – to Forlani's increas-
ing irritation – I identified correctly.

Finally, we came to a glass cabinet set apart from the others in the centre of the room. A chair was drawn up in front
of the case as if Forlani liked to sit there admiring this one
violin in particular.

It was certainly a magnificent specimen, its back two
pieces of striking flamed maple, its varnish a dazzling mixture of colours which seemed to encompass and meld
together every red, orange and gold in the spectrum.

'Guarneri "del Gesù",' I said without a moment's hesitation.

Giuseppe Guarneri 'del Gesù', like Nicolò Amati, was the most gifted member of a distinguished violin-making family, one of the two greatest luthiers of all time, Stradivari being the other. When people speak in awe of a Guarneri violin this is the maker they mean, the suffix 'del Gesù' coming from the cross and the letters IHS – the Greek for Jesus – he inscribed on his labels. His craftsmanship falls short of Stradivari's sheer perfection, but for tonal beauty his instruments are unsurpassed. Paganini played a 'del Gesù'. So too did Heifetz, Stern, Grumiaux and Kogan. If I were a concert violinist, given the pick of any instrument on earth, I would choose a Guarneri 'del Gesù'.

'But do you know what's special about this Guarneri?' Forlani asked me. It was time for him to show off, to bask a little in his superior knowledge.

'It belonged to Louis Spohr,' he said in the tone of veneration priests use when speaking of the Holy Father. And just in case I'd missed the significance, he repeated the name of that illustrious nineteenth-century virtuoso and composer. 'Louis Spohr. This is Spohr's missing Guarneri.'

Guastafeste, who'd remained silent all this time, peered more closely at the glass case.

'Missing?' he said.

'He lost it back in the early 1800s,' I explained.

'1804, to be precise,' Forlani added and I knew he was going to give us the full history. Spohr's stolen Guarneri, like the tale of *Le Messie*, is familiar to every student of the violin. But I let Forlani tell us anyway. This was the moment he'd been waiting for ever since we'd entered the room.

'Spohr was on tour in Germany with the cellist Beneke,' he said. 'His violin was packed inside his trunk and fastened with ropes to the back of the carriage in which they were travelling. The carriage had no rear window so Spohr was continually leaning out to check that the trunk was still there. When they reached Göttingen and were stopped at the town gate, Spohr asked the sergeant of the guard if the trunk was secure, to which the sergeant replied, "What trunk?" Spohr leaped out and saw that the ropes had been cut. He drew a hunting knife and raced off back down the track to look for the thieves. But they had melted into the night. The next day the trunk and empty violin case were found in a field near the town, but there was no sign of the Guarneri. It was never recovered in Spohr's lifetime.'

'But you found it?' Guastafeste said.

'Not personally. I acquired it seven years ago from a dealer. It came with letters and other papers which gave conclusive proof of its provenance. It cost me two million dollars.'

I started. 'Two million?'

'You seem surprised,' Forlani said. 'I know, it was a lot of money. But I'm prepared to pay whatever it takes to get what I want. How much would you say this collection is worth today?'

His eyes were gleaming with avarice, the tip of his tongue touching his lips, wetting them in anticipation of my reply. This was the point of his collection. They weren't living instruments to him, nor even simply objects of beauty, they were investments. Their value was all that mattered to him. I could see him in here, sitting for hour after hour in his chair, gazing around at his violins, as sad and futile an occupation as Midas counting his gold.

I gave him the answer I give everyone who asks me what a violin is worth.

'Whatever someone is prepared to pay.'

Forlani's disappointment, and his displeasure, were manifest.

'Is that the best you can do?' he said in disgust. 'What kind of reply is that?'

'An honest one. A violin, like any other object, is only worth what a buyer is willing to pay. And that price will vary according to the market conditions, what else is on offer, what other buyers are competing to acquire it.'

'But millions, you would say?' Forlani pressed his point.

'Of course. Many millions, but I wouldn't like to be more specific than that.'

'Dottor Forlani,' Guastafeste said gently. 'If we could return to Tomaso Rainaldi.'

'What? Oh, yes. Rainaldi. The dead man.' Forlani's gaze drifted away from us. 'What a waste.'

For a moment I thought he was talking about the waste of a life. Then the real train of his thoughts became apparent.

'Five thousand euros, I gave him. All for nothing. Where's my violin now?'

'You said he told you he believed there was another Messiah somewhere,' Guastafeste said. 'You surely didn't just take his word for that. He must have given you some evidence to support his claim.'

Forlani squinted at us with his pale, moist eyes. He was scruffy and unwashed but that didn't make him a fool. I suddenly caught a glimpse of the wily, calculating nature that lay at the core of his character.

'Why should I tell you that?' he said. 'So someone else can go and find it? *My* violin.'

'Withholding evidence in a murder inquiry is a serious offence, *dottore*,' Guastafeste said. 'I have powers to compel you to cooperate, but I'm sure neither of us wants to go down that route. Look at it like this, you're an elderly man, you're obviously not in the best of health. You're not going to find the violin by yourself, are you? But if it's discovered in the course of our investigations, it may well come on the open market and you'll have an opportunity to acquire it.'

It was an astute approach, appealing to Forlani's avarice, his self-interest. The old man moved away from us and stood looking at the Spohr Guarneri for a time.

'He showed me some documents,' he said eventually. 'Some papers – photocopies of some papers – he'd found in England.'

'You have the photocopies?' Guastafeste asked.

'No, he took them away with him.'

'What did they say?'

'I can't remember in any detail. They were old letters, very old letters. Correspondence between a firm of cloth merchants in Italy and one of their suppliers in England.'

'Cloth merchants?' Guastafeste said, frowning. 'What has that got to do with violins?'

'The firm was in Casale Monferrato.'

Guastafeste stared at him blankly. 'So?'

Forlani had his eyes on me. 'Your colleague understands.'

'Anselmi di Briata?' I asked.

Forlani nodded, appraising me quietly. 'Indeed.'

'Who?' Guastafeste said.

'Your colleague will explain later,' Forlani replied impatiently.

'And these letters were enough to make you believe Rainaldi?' Guastafeste said.

'Enough to make me take a chance, yes. For five thousand euros what did I have to lose?'

'That's all, just some papers?'

'Yes. That's all I can tell you.'

Forlani walked to the heavy steel door of the room and

waited for us to leave. It was an incongruous sight, this dirty old man in flip-flops surrounded by his priceless collection of violins. He activated the electric motor that swung the massive door shut behind us. It clicked smoothly into place and the locks engaged. We followed him back downstairs to the front door.

'You've been privileged,' Forlani said smugly, unfastening the chains and bolts to pull open the door, 'to see a collection like mine. There isn't a finer one anywhere in the world.'

I stepped over the threshold into the narrow alley outside the door. Guastafeste made a move to follow me, but Forlani clutched at his sleeve, holding him back.

'If the violin is found, it is to be mine. No one else's. You understand?' the old man said in a hoarse whisper. 'Mine.'

'I promise you nothing,' Guastafeste said, breaking free of Forlani's possessive grasp.

'I am a rich man. I will make it worth your while.'

Guastafeste gave him a look of withering contempt.

'Policemen are not violins, *dottore*. Not all of them have a price.'

We went to St Mark's Square for a drink before dinner. It's what all the tourists do, but somehow in Venice it's the only place to go for an aperitif. The city is so cramped, its open spaces so small and few in number that the Piazza alone gives any relief from the suffocating claustrophobia. Only in St Mark's can you really see the sky, only there can you savour the exquisite atmosphere of the Venetian dusk, the sunlight touching the pinnacles of the basilica, the shadows stretching out across the footworn stones, the water by the Piazzetta iridescent as a sheet of polished mother-of-pearl.

That is the romantic view, of course, a guidebook

description of St Mark's. In fact, when you get to the square you find it brimming over with braying foreigners, unscrupulous street sellers and overfed pigeons which spatter droppings on your head as you fight your way through the throng.

In days gone by, the Venetians had a reputation for savage cruelty. The two men who made the fantastic zodiacal clock in the Piazza were supposedly officially blinded to prevent them making another for somebody else. Traitors were sometimes found buried alive head first, their legs sticking up through the slabs of the Piazzetta, and the Bridge of Sighs and the terrible tortures of the state dungeons sent shivers throughout the civilised world. The citizens have mellowed over the centuries, but the tradition of inhuman punishment still continues in a modified form in St Mark's: not the garrotte or the rack of yore, but something infinitely more subtle and pitiless – the cafe orchestra.

There are three of these excrescences in the square and two more in the Piazzetta, all competing to be the most nauseatingly sugary and trite. It's impossible to escape them. Their noise blends together in a sickly *mélange* and reverberates around the surrounding buildings, assaulting your ears from every direction. Short of throwing yourself off the top of the campanile, the only sensible course of action is to take a table at one of the cafes and thereby ration your senses to just a single orchestra. The drinks are outrageously expensive and the proprietors have the gall to charge you a supplement for the 'music', but it is possible to survive a half hour or so of the torture without serious long-term consequences for your health.

We ordered a couple of drinks and settled back in our chairs, watching the people milling about the square. The Venetians have always been renowned for their style and fondness for clothes. Back in the days when the city was a republic, the women used to vie so much with one another in the richness and splendour of their dress that the authorities introduced a sumptuary law to restrict ostentation, but it never worked. Well, it wouldn't, would it?

There wasn't much ostentation on show this evening. Most of the people huddled together around the square were scruffy backpackers and foreign tour groups. I watched a young man pause to take a photograph of the campanile. It's an impressive bell tower in its way, but not a patch on the one in Cremona which – as everyone should know – is the tallest brick structure in Europe. The basilica too seems to me to be inferior to the duomo in Cremona. St Mark's is an architectural wonder, but with all those Byzantine domes and pinnacles it looks gaudy and vulgar, like a Mafia *capo*'s wedding cake.

There was a flurry among the cooing carpet of pigeons in the centre of the Piazza. Someone was tossing out birdseed. A woman posed for a photograph, the mangy, bedraggled creatures perched all over her head and outstretched arms. I wondered if she realised what ghastly avian disease she risked catching for the sake of a holiday snap.

'So what did you make of Forlani?' Guastafeste said, sipping his beer. 'Do you think he's quite right in the head? Living in a dump like that, the place falling apart around his ears. He stank to high heaven, did you notice?'

'It was impossible not to,' I said. 'He's a rich man. They live by different rules to the rest of us.'

'So what was he on about? All that stuff he said you'd explain to me. You know, about the letters, the cloth merchants.'

'Casale Monferrato. I mentioned it to you the other night.'

'You did? All I know about Casale Monferrato is that it's a town in Piedmont. What's it got to do with violins?'

'Casale Monferrato was the home of Cozio di Salabue.'

'Salabue?' It came back to him. 'Ah, you mean the guy who bought the Messiah from Stradivari's son? The violin collector.'

I nodded. 'Count Cozio bought the Messiah from Paolo Stradivari. But he didn't buy it directly. He used an intermediary called Giovanni Michele Anselmi di Briata who – like Paolo Stradivari – was a cloth merchant. Anselmi acted as agent for the count in several transactions, including a later deal whereby Cozio bought all of Stradivari's remaining tools from Paolo.'

'His tools?'

'Yes. Cozio wasn't just interested in Stradivari's violins. He wanted anything the Master had used to make them – tools, patterns, moulds.'

'Why?'

I shrugged. 'He was a fanatical collector. He was like Forlani. He hoarded violins, though unlike Forlani he wanted to do more than merely gloat over them. He studied how they were put together, measured them in painstaking detail. He was planning to write a book on violins and violin-making but he never got round to it.'

'So this agent, this cloth merchant, what was he called again?'

'Giovanni Michele Anselmi di Briata.'

'He was mentioned in the papers Tomaso showed to Forlani?'

'So it would seem.'

'And that's all we've got to go on. We don't know what these letters said, what they were about.'

'Just that they were sufficient to persuade Enrico Forlani to risk a gamble on them.'

'They must have been pretty convincing. Forlani didn't strike me as a man who throws his money around much.'

'Except on violins. He lives in squalor, but I think he would blow his whole fortune to own another Messiah.'

I watched the leader of the five-piece orchestra, who bore an uncanny resemblance to Chico Marx – though without the hat. He wasn't a bad player. Too much vibrato, too many showy glissandi, but his technique was solid. They were finishing a medley of Neapolitan tunes – *Torna a Surriento* and the cod dialect *Funiculì, Funiculà* which the English always think is a song about a mountain railway.

An elderly woman came out on to the steps next to the bandstand as the music ended. She clapped her hands and blew kisses to the musicians who bowed to her graciously in acknowledgement. I recognised her as a well-known Italian actress, more famous for her longevity and flamboyant clothes than her talent. She was caked in orange make-up and around her shoulders – despite the warm evening – she was wearing what appeared to be the last surviving North American buffalo.

'Why did Tomaso go to Forlani?' Guastafeste said. 'Why not find the violin first, then put it in an auction and sell it to the highest bidder?'

'Money,' I replied. 'You know how Tomaso lived. Always on the edge, always exceeding his income. He'd already been to England. That must have cost. He needed someone to pay the bills. Particularly as his search might well have proved unsuccessful. Forlani could afford the risk, Tomaso couldn't.'

'We need to find those letters – if the killer hasn't found them already.'

'You think that was why Tomaso's workshop was searched?'

'It's a good bet. The violin's the key, I know that.'

75

Guastafeste finished his beer. 'We pick up the scent of the violin and we'll pick up the scent of Tomaso's killer.'

We left our table and strolled across the Piazzetta to the Molo. The gondolas were bobbing up and down at their mooring posts, the water slapping against their hulls, making a sound like wellington boots squelching through mud. The church of Santa Maria Della Salute, at the end of the Grand Canal, looked as timeless and ravishing in the sunset as she had when Canaletto captured her in oils.

We walked along the Riva degli Schiavoni, stopping for a while to look at the Bridge of Sighs. Below, in the small canal that runs behind the Doge's Palace, a long line of gondolas was gliding towards us. In the first boat, an accordion player and a balding tenor with a shrill voice were serenading their passengers. The gondolier had one hand on his oar, the other pressing a mobile phone to his ear. In the gondola at the rear of the line sat a single Japanese tourist with only his camcorder for company. I felt a twinge of pity for him. Venice is not a place in which to be alone.

Beyond the Hotel Danieli we turned left down an alley and found a *trattoria* near Campo San Zaccaria, an inferior, overpriced tourist establishment like most of the restaurants in Venice. We had spaghetti with clams, veal cutlets and a carafe of the house red wine, then wandered back to St Mark's. It was late, but there were still plenty of people about, drifting aimlessly around the piazza, seated at the tables outside the cafes where the orchestras were still churning out their saccharine medleys.

I paused, soaking up the atmosphere, in no particular hurry to get back to our *pensione*.

'I need to catch up on some sleep,' Guastafeste said. 'You stay here, if you like. I'll see you in the morning.'

I sauntered slowly across the square. The lights were on in the open galleries around the edge. The shop frontages shone as brightly as the glass and silverware in their windows. It was cooling down. I could feel a breeze gusting in from the lagoon, stirring the debris, the litter that was scattered over the paving stones. The people were starting to move, getting up from their cafe tables, slipping on jackets or pullovers, heading back to their hotels. Even the pigeons were thinning out, returning to their roosts for the night.

In the gallery at the western end of the piazza I turned to look back at the floodlit basilica and my attention was caught by a figure crossing the square. He was fifty metres away, walking purposefully towards the exit from the square. Tall, gaunt, wearing a white linen jacket, I recognised him as the Englishman I'd encountered in Serafin's office in Milan. He was staring straight ahead, taking no notice of his surroundings, as if his mind were focused on more important matters. I watched him pass by, then made an impulse decision, curious to know who he was, what he was doing in Venice.

I set off after him, following him through the Campo San Moise and along the well-trodden path to the Accademia Bridge. The streets were quieter here, the pavements washed with a sickly greenish light from the wall lamps. Not once did the Englishman look back. We were across the bridge and into the dark alleys on the western side of the Grand Canal when I felt a strange, disconcerting tingle in the nape of my neck. I had a curious feeling that I too was being followed. I paused and looked round, listening. But I heard no footsteps, saw no figures, no shadows behind me. I turned to look ahead again. The Englishman had vanished. I hurried on along the street, unnerved now – by the night, by the sinister atmosphere, by the continuing suspicion that I was not alone.

77

There was no sign of the Englishman. I turned down an alley and emerged into a tiny unlit courtyard. I paused again. This time I heard footsteps – in front of me, not behind. I walked quickly under an arch and out into another alley. Ahead of me I saw a flash of the Englishman's white jacket and went after him. Moments later he turned off into a narrow passageway. I crept to the mouth of the passage and watched him stop outside a door and ring the bell. The door opened a fraction. I caught a glimpse of a pale face before the Englishman stepped inside and disappeared from sight. I was close enough to hear a lock snap shut as the door closed.

I retraced my steps and stood on the Accademia Bridge looking out over the Grand Canal. A barge loaded with crates of beer passed by beneath me, then a water taxi cruising for hire. I shivered as a gust of cool air swirled up from the canal. There is something fundamentally untrustworthy about Venice. She is like a moody, enigmatic mistress whose loyalties cannot be relied on, a mistress whom you continually fear will leave you for someone richer, more powerful. No man can hold on to her indefinitely, though many have tried. I thought of the great historical figures who had been here before me: Goethe, Stendhal, Mendelssohn, Dickens, Hemingway, the list was endless. Robert Browning died in the Ca' Rezzonico, I could see it clearly a few hundred metres away up the Grand Canal. Richard Wagner died surrounded by silk in the Palazzo Vendramin further north beyond the Rialto Bridge. Byron swam in the waters just below my feet and miraculously survived.

I thought about all these things in passing. But mostly I was wondering why the Englishman should have been visiting Enrico Forlani at half past eleven at night.

5

'You know something?' Guastafeste said over breakfast the next morning. 'I think Forlani is holding out on us.'

I spread some apricot jam on a bread roll and looked up. 'How do you mean?'

'He must know more than he's letting on. The letters Tomaso showed him – Forlani said he couldn't remember what they contained. I don't believe that. A man like Forlani; he's peculiar, but he's not senile. I want to talk to him again before we leave Venice.'

'Go back to his house? With that stench?' I said.

'It won't take long,' Guastafeste replied.

We paid our bill and left our bags at the *pensione* while we walked back over the Grand Canal to Forlani's *palazzo*. The front door of his house was ajar when we got there. Guastafeste looked at it, frowning, then he pushed the door open with his foot.

'Dottor Forlani?' he called.

There was no reply. Guastafeste examined the door without touching it. The locks were still intact. There was no sign of a forced entry.

'Maybe he's gone out to the shops,' I said. 'He has to buy food some time.'

'And leave his door unlocked? I don't think so, not Forlani. Did you see his alarm system yesterday? He'd close up the place like a fortress.'

We stepped inside and went upstairs. On the first-floor landing we paused to look into the room with the long table. There was no one there. We continued on up the stairs. The smell was just as bad as before, the air just as stale and hot.

Guastafeste came to an abrupt halt. At the far end of the second-floor corridor the door was open. Beyond it the heavy steel door guarding the violin room was also open. We walked quickly down the corridor and stopped on the threshold. The lights were on inside the chamber, all the glass cases illuminated as they had been yesterday. But one thing was different. On the floor of the room, lying in a puddle of congealed blood, was Enrico Forlani.

He was sprawled on his front, his head twisted side-ways, his eyes wide open, unseeing. He was still wearing his dressing gown and plastic flip-flops. On the floor all around him, mixed in with the blood, were fragments of glass from the shattered display case which the old man appeared to have fallen against and broken.

Guastafeste went in. I hung back near the door, averting my gaze. The air-conditioning was on in the room, but even so I could detect a faint putrid odour which I guessed was the smell of flesh starting to decompose. I put my handkerchief over my mouth, wondering if I was going to be sick.

I glanced at Forlani. Guastafeste was bending over his body, examining it more closely. He had a policeman's stomach, the ability to tolerate sights and smells that would make most people nauseous.

80

Guastafeste straightened up and walked across to me, his hand delving into the pocket of his jacket, pulling out his mobile phone. Another image came to me: Guastafeste outside Rainaldi's workshop, doing the same thing. He'd spared me then, shielded me from the shocking realities of violent death, but this time I'd had no such protection. I'd seen Forlani's body. The sight was etched immutably in my mind: horrific, bloody, a vision of nightmares to come.

Guastafeste took me by the arm. 'Let's wait outside.'

He punched in a number on his phone as we went back along the corridor and down the stairs. I was in a daze, aware only distantly of him talking to the emergency operator, asking for the Venice police, then we were outside in the alley by the front door and I was leaning back on the brick wall, taking deep gulps of fresh air.

'You okay, Gianni?' Guastafeste asked.

'I think so. It's just the shock. Two dead bodies in less than a week.' I tried to shut out the images, but they wouldn't go. No matter how hard I tried to direct my mind elsewhere it stayed resolutely on Forlani. 'What happened?' I said. 'Was he murdered?'

'That's hard to tell.'

'What else could it be? All that blood everywhere.'

'It looks to me as if he fell – or was pushed – against the display case. Severed an artery on the broken glass. Maybe it was an accident. He was an old man. He could have had a heart attack and fallen into the case. Only an autopsy will give us a clearer picture of what really happened.'

We walked along the alley. It was an unprepossessing passageway, little more than a metre wide, hemmed in by Forlani's *palazzo* on one side and another high wall on the other. Yet when we got to the end, the Grand Canal was suddenly there before us in all its shabby splendour, the buildings along the banks bathed in sunlight, some pink, some orange, some sugar white. A *vaporetto* cruised past, sending a wash of cloudy green water to lap against the steps by our feet.

'There's something you should know,' I said.

I told him what had happened after we'd split up the previous evening.

'He went to Forlani's house?' Guastafeste said, a note of urgency in his voice. 'You're sure it was the same man you saw at Serafin's?'

'Yes.'

'You know his name?'

'No.'

Guastafeste handed me his mobile phone. 'Call Serafin. Find out who he is. It could be very important.'

I rang Serafin's office in Milan. His secretary said he hadn't come in yet, she didn't know where he was. I tried his mobile number, but there was no reply so I left a message on his voice-mail asking him to call Guastafeste's number as soon as possible.

I was handing the phone back to Guastafeste when I saw the police launch surging towards us. The helmsman brought the vessel in fast then, at the last moment when it seemed a collision with the bank was inevitable, thrust the throttle into reverse to allow the side of the boat to brush gently up against the steps. An officer leaped ashore with a rope and secured the launch to one of the red and white mooring posts along the edge of the canal, then five or six more officers – two in plain clothes – clambered out and headed down the alley with Guastafeste.

I stayed where I was, watching the boats on the canal, trying not to think of the body in the building behind me, until Guastafeste returned.

'Can you face coming back upstairs?' he asked. 'The police want to talk to you about last night. And there's something else you can help with. Something I overlooked. The broken glass case. The violin that was inside it is missing. We need to know which one it was.'

I followed him back into the *palazzo* and upstairs to the second floor. The Venetian police officers were grouped around Forlani's body, two of them crouching down by the corpse so that – to my relief – I could barely see it. One of the plain-clothes detectives came across to meet us, introducing himself as Gian Luigi Spadina. I repeated everything I'd told Guastafeste earlier.

'We're waiting for a call giving us the name,' Guastafeste added when I'd finished.

'And the missing violin?' Spadina said.

I looked around at the illuminated glass cases, recalling the order in which I'd examined them the previous day. I knew immediately which violin had been in the broken case.

'The Maggini,' I said.

'You're sure?' Guastafeste said.

'Positive. It was quite a well-known instrument. The Snake's Head Maggini, it was called.'

'Valuable?' Spadina asked.

'Fairly. Though nothing like as valuable as some of the other violins here.'

Spadina gazed around the room. 'Why just that one?' he said contemplatively. 'Why didn't the killer take more?'

'Killer?' I said, glancing at Guastafeste.

'I'm afraid it's looking more and more like a homicide,' Guastafeste replied.

'Thank you for your help, Signor Castiglione,' Spadina said. 'We'll need a full statement from you later. Now, if you'll excuse me.' He went back across to Forlani's body.

Guastafeste looked at the display case in the centre of the room. 'Why didn't he take that one, the Guarneri that belonged to Louis Spohr? It must surely be the most valuable in the collection.'

'That's a fake,' I said, not really thinking about what I was saying.

Guastafeste turned and squinted at me. 'Pardon?'

I hesitated. 'It's a fake.'

'How can you tell?'

I took my time replying, wondering why I'd told him, whether it was too late to withdraw the remark. But I *wanted* him to know. I kept my voice low, so the other police officers wouldn't hear.

'Because *I* made it.'

When you look back at your life from my age it's difficult to be sure at exactly what point key events happened. Our memories are unreliable, the ebb and flow of our existence so blended together that it's impossible to distinguish the tide which led on to greater – or lesser – things. For most of us the greater things rarely come. Our lives are a continual process of coming to terms with failure. We all want to make our mark somewhere, to leave some trace of our passing. But how do we make that mark?

I was seven years old when I started to learn the violin. By the age of twelve I could play Bach and Haydn concerti. At fourteen I could play the Mendelssohn. I used to dream of being the next Paganini, of making a career as a concert virtuoso. At what point did I realise that dream would never be fulfilled? There was no single, identifiable point. We cling on to our ambitions until they are wrenched away from us. I am sixty-three years old with greying hair and creaking joints, but I still daydream about scoring the winning goal for Italy in the

World Cup final the way I did when I was ten. I still dream about playing the Brahms concerto at Carnegie Hall. Why shouldn't I? Our lives would be unbearable without illusions.

But in reality? I knew in my teens that I would never be a concert soloist. I might have made a rank-and-file orchestral player, but that is a life of frustration and dissatisfaction, as my friend Rainaldi discovered. It comes as a shock, the realisation of your own limitations. But if you're sensible, you put the disappointment behind you and turn to other things, something you *can* excel at. That's when I turned to violin-making.

At fifteen I was apprenticed to a local Cremona luthier named Bartolomeo Ruffino. I made his coffee, sharpened his tools, swept the wood shavings from the floor for several months, then he let me have a go at making an instrument myself. At sixteen I finished my first violin. It was not very good, but I persevered. The next one was better. I discovered I had a gift.

It was at that moment too that I understood there was more to Ruffino than met the eye. He was a well respected luthier whose instruments were highly regarded in both violin-making circles and in the marketplace. But working alongside him each day, it gradually dawned on me that my apprentice master was not simply a maker of new violins: he was also a faker of old violins. He made no attempt to conceal from me what he was up to. Indeed, he made it clear that he expected me to help him in his nefarious activities, thus becoming complicit in his dishonesty. Because if I was involved, I too was tainted and therefore less likely to betray him.

'What choice did I have?' I said to Guastafeste. 'I was just a boy, an apprentice. Ruffino paid my wages. I wanted desperately to learn how to make violins – not fakes, but instruments of my own. In retrospect, I know I should have left, refused to have anything to do with his schemes, but I was young, pliable. Apprenticeships were not easy to come by and I didn't want to jeopardise my career.'

Guastafeste studied me intently. He was finding it hard to absorb what I was telling him. We were in a cafe in one of the squares near Forlani's house, sitting out on the terrace with a couple of glasses of mineral water on the table between us.

'I was with Ruffino for nine years,' I said. 'When I was twenty-four I left and set up on my own. I didn't make another fake after that. Except for the Spohr "del Gesù".'

'You really made that Guarneri?' Guastafeste said incredulously. 'And you got away with it? Didn't Forlani have it examined, checked over by an expert?'

'Oh, yes. It was examined by an expert all right. One of Italy's leading authorities on Cremonese violins.'

'Who?'

'Me.'

'*What!*'

'You are a policeman, Antonio,' I said. 'But you are an innocent when it comes to the world of violin dealing. The criminals you encounter, the thugs, the thieves, the dregs of society, are paragons of virtue compared to your average violin dealer.'

'You authenticated your own fake?'

'Wonderful, isn't it? Yes, I forged the violin and then I was called in as an expert to verify its provenance.'

'Called in by whom?'

'By the dealer who was selling it, Vincenzo Serafin.'

'Couldn't Serafin tell it was a fake?'

'Serafin knew it was a fake. It was Serafin who asked me to make it in the first place.'

86

Guastafeste gaped at me. This was more than he could handle.

'Serafin asked you to make it? You mean he's a crook?'

'Of course he's a crook, he's a dealer,' I said.

'Vincenzo Serafin, the respected Milanese businessman who mixes with politicians and opera stars and goodness knows who, who hosts a glittering annual fundraising event for children's charities and all that kind of bullshit . . . is no more than a common criminal?'

'Not common,' I said. 'He'd be appalled at the suggestion. Serafin is a very sophisticated criminal.'

'Who sells fake violins.'

'Only a few fakes. Most of them are genuine. You have to be careful.'

'And how long has he been doing this?'

'Oh, years. His father did it before him. Selling fakes is in his blood.'

'And he's got away with it all this time? How come no one has found out?'

'You have to remember that in this business there is no such thing as an independent expert. The people who sell violins authenticate them. That's how it works. If Vincenzo Serafin tells you a violin is a Guarneri "del Gesù", then it is. You could take the instrument somewhere else, to a dealer in London or New York and get a second opinion, but they're unlikely to want to contradict Serafin's opinion. They're all at the same game and it's a very small pitch. If they undermine Serafin's reputation, they know it won't be long before he starts undermining theirs and that's not good for any of them.'

'So none of them can be trusted?' Guastafeste said.

'You can never trust someone who wants to sell you something.'

Guastafeste took a sip of his mineral water. He had few

illusions about human nature. He knew that no one is completely honest, that hypocrisy is the oil that lubricates our relations with other people. But nevertheless I could tell he was shocked; that he was seeing me suddenly in a new light.

'Why, Gianni? Why did you do it?'

'Serafin pressured me. After Ruffino died, Serafin lost his master forger. He wanted someone to take his place. He knew I could do it. He kept on at me for years, trying to persuade me to cooperate, but I always resisted. Until seven years ago. When Caterina became ill.'

I thought back to that time. Those long months of watching my wife slowly fade away. Watching her suffer so much that I prayed every night for the end to come so that she might find peace.

'We needed the money,' I said. 'For nursing care, for treatment. I thought moving out of the city might also help her. Caterina had always wanted to live in the country. So I faked a violin for Serafin and used my share of the proceeds to buy our house.'

'What did Forlani say he paid? Two million dollars, wasn't it?'

My face clouded for a moment. 'Yes, that was a revelation to me. Serafin said he only made eight hundred thousand.'

'So he cheated you too?'

'Like I said, you can trust no one in this business.'

I wondered why I'd told Guastafeste. To clear my conscience, to purge a secret that had been festering inside me perhaps. Certainly I felt cleaner for getting it off my chest.

'Don't think ill of me, Antonio. I know it was wrong. I'm ashamed of what I did. You're a policeman. You must do what you think best.'

Guastafeste stared at me. 'You think I'd turn you in? What do you think I am? You're my friend. What do I care that that miserable old man paid two million dollars for a fake violin? But now he's dead, someone else will examine that Guarneri. I don't want you to get caught, Gianni.'

'I won't get caught.'

'I thought there were ways of detecting fakes now, scientific ways that can give a true, independent assessment of when a violin was made.'

'There's dendrochronology,' I said. 'A technique for analysing and dating the tree rings in a piece of wood. But that only gives the age of the wood, not the age of the violin.'

'You used old wood?'

'Of course. Ruffino bequeathed me a store of old wood when he died. I don't know where he got it from. Forlani's Guarneri "del Gesù" was made from wood cut in the early eighteenth century. A dendrochronological investigation of the instrument would confirm unequivocally that the wood was of the right period for Guarneri to have used it. Every tool I used, every technique was exactly the same as the ones Guarneri used. I doubt there's an expert on earth who wouldn't be fooled by it.'

'And the sound? Does it sound like a Guarneri?'

'Ah, now that's the question. No, it doesn't sound like a Guarneri. I can copy the appearance of a "del Gesù" but, alas, I cannot give it the touch of genius that produces that special, wonderful tone. If I could, I would be another Giuseppe Guarneri instead of a Giovanni Battista Castiglione. But Forlani was a collector. He didn't play the violin. He didn't buy the "del Gesù" to listen to, he bought it to look at, to gloat over.'

Guastafeste looked away across the square, watching

the tourists passing through with their cameras and guidebooks. An elderly lady dressed all in black shuffled past clutching a string bag of vegetables. We could hear the low wheeze of her breathing from where we were sitting.

'It's ironical, isn't it?' Guastafeste said. 'Forlani had all those violins, yet the one he prized most was a fake.'

'Believe me,' I said, 'he would much rather have had a fake he believed to be genuine than the other way round.'

'You think so?'

'I know it. I've seen it many times. People come to my workshop with a violin. They tell me it's a Gagliano or a Pressenda or something. The label inside seems to confirm that. I examine the instrument and tell them it's a fake. It's not a Gagliano, it's a nineteenth-century German copy. They go away despondent. Why? The violin hasn't changed. It looks the same as before, it sounds the same. But to them it's different. It now looks and sounds like an inferior instrument.'

'But it's worth much less.'

'That's true. On the open market its value has suddenly plummeted. But as a violin to play, why should its worth have changed? Because when people buy a good violin they aren't just buying an instrument, they're buying a name. They're buying a dream, an association with greatness. I think of it as the Holy Grail Syndrome. Wanting to possess, to touch something that some great figure of the past has touched. Like all those gullible souls in the Middle Ages who bought the bones of saints or strips from the shroud that covered Christ in the belief that they were genuine. Or like those people today who pay ridiculous sums for celebrity memorabilia. You know, the cup that Elvis Presley once drank a Coke from,

Marilyn Monroe's childhood teddy bear, John Lennon's toenail clippings, that sort of thing. What on earth do they do it for? Is it because they hope some of the magic that made those people famous will rub off on them?'

'Is that why you chose Louis Spohr?' Guastafeste said.

'Yes. Collectors want something special. They have plenty of money so any old Guarneri won't do. They want one with a name, with a history attached to it. And in the violin world the most celebrated Guarneri – after Paganini's *Cannone*, which is in the town hall in Genoa – is Spohr's stolen "del Gesù".'

'Wasn't it a bit risky?'

I shrugged. 'It was a private sale, not through auction, so there was no public scrutiny. The documentation – also fake, of course – was so thorough and convincing that even I half believed it. Serafin forged letters, bills of sale, certificates, a whole pile of papers to explain what happened to the violin after Spohr lost it, to account for its sudden reappearance in a junk shop in Warsaw.'

'In Warsaw?'

'Eastern Europe, former Communist bloc, in turmoil for centuries. It's an ideal place for lost violins to surface. With a con you have to think big. Look at Konrad Kujau who forged the Hitler diaries. If he'd forged a couple, or even a dozen, people would have been instantly suspicious. But he forged fifty-eight volumes. No one could believe anyone would go to that kind of trouble for a scam so they thought they were genuine. Or back in the 1920s a Czech nobleman successfully sold the Eiffel Tower for scrap. Twice. We are an astonishingly easy species to dupe.'

'But Forlani? A rich, shrewd businessman like him.'

'Can be the easiest to fool, if you pitch the con right. If you go to a financier with some small plan to open a shop that will bring only a modest return, he'll go over your business plan with a magnifying glass, ask you hundreds of searching questions. But go in asking for fifty million for some unproven crackpot scheme that looks as if it may pay out big in a year and he'll fall over himself to give you the money. Look at the dot.com bubbles. People are greedy, they want their money to come easily. So make your con special, that's what hooks them. Appeal to that greed.'

'And Forlani was taken in, just like that?'

'You have to understand his mentality, the collector's mentality,' I said. 'He wanted something no one else had, something unique. He wanted desperately to believe it was Spohr's "del Gesù". His greed blinded him, overrode his natural suspicion.'

Guastafeste looked at me. 'I'm still finding this incredible, you know. You, a forger.'

'Please, it's not something I'm proud of.'

'I don't condemn you, Gianni. I understand why you did it. I'd have done the same in your position.' He pushed back his chair. 'I'd better get back to Forlani's.'

'You want me to come too?'

Guastafeste shook his head. 'We're not going to get away today. Spadina wants us to stick around. Why don't you go back to the hotel, tell them we want to hang on to our rooms for another night? And try Serafin again from the hotel.'

I walked slowly back to our *pensione*, not really aware of where I was going. I was preoccupied, agitated, my brain in a state of turmoil. I was approaching the *Teatro La Fenice* when a strange thing happened. I don't know whether I was falling prey to my own fevered imagination, but as I negotiated the congested streets I glanced down a side alley and caught a fleeting glimpse of a woman passing by at the other end. I saw her for only a moment, so I may have been mistaken, but she looked very like Vincenzo Serafin's mistress, Maddalena.

6

I lay on the bed in my room at the *pensione* for a long time. It was only the middle of the morning, but I felt utterly drained. Venice is a tiring city. Too much walking, pavements hot and hard on the feet, constant crowds to endure, but it wasn't just physical weariness that afflicted me. I was emotionally exhausted. I closed my eyes and tried to doze off, but my mind would not let me rest. Forlani's body was there at the forefront of my thoughts, illuminated like a neon sign, searing my retinas with his sprawled form, his lifeless face, the pool of blood all around him. The image still turned my stomach, filled me with revulsion, yet I could not switch it off.

I forced myself to get up, knowing that the longer I allowed those disturbing memories to seep inside my consciousness the more unsettling, the more damaging they would become. If I could not erase them with sleep, then I could attempt to do so with activity. I dialled an outside line on the telephone beside the bed and rang Serafin's office again. He still hadn't come in. I tried his mobile phone. No success there either. I put on my jacket and went out, hoping that the noise and activity of the city would distract me.

St Mark's was already packed with tourists. There was a queue a hundred metres long outside the basilica, the line snaking away into the Piazzetta next to the raised wooden boardwalks that – with the area flooding so frequently – have become a permanent, and unsightly, feature of the piazza. I walked round on to the Molo where a string of artists and caricature-sketchers had set up stall next to the Doge's Palace, almost blocking the thoroughfare. I pushed my way past them and up the steps on to the Ponte della Paglia from which everyone views the Bridge of Sighs. The crowds here were so dense – people posing, cameras clicking – that it took me half a minute or more to get through them. Then almost immediately I saw a vast tour group swelling towards me like a tsunami, the guide at the front – a diminutive oriental woman – holding aloft an umbrella to avoid being swallowed up by her charges. Fearing for my safety, I stepped smartly sideways, seeking sanctuary in the serene portals of the Hotel Danieli, the grandest, most famous hostelry in Venice. The transformation was absolute: from the raging, boiling maelstrom outside to the cool, calm haven inside, the soothing green marble of the hotel foyer like a windless lagoon on which I found myself suddenly becalmed.

I looked around. The architecture had a gloomy, Gothic style that could only be described as early Dr Frankenstein. Stairs and pillars and balconies rose up above me like an Escher *trompe l'oeil*, the old-fashioned crystal chandeliers and liveried staff adding to the sensation that I had stepped back into an earlier century.

I went through into the lounge and ordered coffee. It came in an elegant white, gold and maroon china cup with the Danieli crest on the side and – beneath a small silver jug of milk – a bill for nine euros. In Venice you pay for your tranquillity. I drank the coffee slowly, eking out every sip to pass the time, and delay the dreaded moment at which I would have to step back into the clamorous theme park outside.

Almost a full hour had passed before I felt obliged to leave my comfortable seat. Returning to the foyer, I made a detour to the payphone at the back near the stairs and tried Serafin's mobile phone again. This time he answered.

'Gianni, my friend. What can I do for you?' he said.

'Did you get my message?' I asked.

'Yes, I got it. I called the number you left, but it was engaged. What's the matter? You sounded upset.'

'I was upset. It was something of a shock finding Enrico Forlani dead in his house.'

There was a silence on the line. Then Serafin said: 'Forlani? You're in Venice?'

'Yes.'

'Forlani is *dead*? How?'

'I don't know. The police are handling everything.'

'The police? What're you saying, Gianni? The *police*? What's happened?'

'Never mind that, I need some information,' I said. 'The man who was in your office last Friday, the Englishman, who was he?'

Serafin didn't reply.

'Vincenzo, I need to know who he was.'

'Why? Why're you interested in him?' Serafin said, evasion second nature to him.

'It's not for me to say.'

'Is he implicated in the death?'

'The Englishman, Vincenzo, what's his name?'

There was another pause on the line while Serafin weighed up his response. I waited impatiently, watching a middle-aged couple come in through the hotel entrance and collect their key from the reception desk.

'Vincenzo . . .' I prompted. 'Do you want the police turning up on your doorstep and charging you with obstructing the course of justice?'

'Scott,' Serafin said. 'His name is Christopher Scott.'

'Who is he?'

'A violin dealer from London.'

'You have an address for him?'

'In Italy?'

'Anywhere.'

'Not in Italy. I don't know where he is. I have his address in England, but it's at the office.'

'Where are you now?'

'Oh, out and about,' he said vaguely.

'The police will want that address.'

'I'll take care of it, don't worry. Has Scott got something to do with Forlani's death?'

'I can't say any more.'

'When did Forlani die? What were you doing there, Gianni? You can tell me that, can't you? Come on, an old friend like me.'

'Sorry, I didn't catch that,' I said. 'You're breaking up. *Ciao*.'

I depressed the button on the top of the phone, inserted some more money and punched in Guastafeste's mobile number.

'I got through to Serafin,' I said when Guastafeste answered. I gave him the information I'd acquired.

'Thanks, Gianni. I'll pass it on to Spadina.'

'Where are you?' I asked.

'Still at Forlani's. Keeping an eye on things.'

'You don't trust the locals?'

'No, it's not that. They know what they're doing. I just want to be in on everything from the start. It's quite

97

possible that whoever killed Forlani also killed Tomaso. What are you doing? Where are you?'

'The Hotel Danieli.'

'Why there?'

'It's quiet. I'm just filling in time really, giving myself something to do.'

'I'm sorry about this, Gianni. Do you mind fending for yourself?'

'No, you do what you need to do. I'm fine.'

'I'll see you later, okay?'

I couldn't face the heat and the noise of the streets just yet so I remained in the Danieli, going upstairs to the rooftop restaurant and having a glass of wine and something to eat, though I didn't feel much like food. When I finally left to go back to our *pensione* it was the early afternoon – the hottest part of the day, but the temperature seemed no deterrent to the swarms of visitors thronging the streets. The paving stones seemed white hot, burning the soles of my shoes, reflecting the glare of the sun so that they were painful to look at. The air was close, as if all the people had sucked the oxygen out of it.

In my room at the *pensione* I bathed my face in cool water, then lay down on the bed and dozed off. The harsh ring of the telephone woke me at four o'clock. I'd slept for almost two hours.

It was Guastafeste. 'Gianni, can you come over to Forlani's house?'

'Now?'

'Please. The police want to talk to you. They want a full description of Christopher Scott.'

'They haven't found him?'

'He checked out of his hotel first thing this morning. They don't know where he went after that.'

* * *

98

It was the detective named Spadina who interviewed me, Guastafeste sitting in, not interfering, just watching. We sat at one end of the table in Forlani's first-floor dining room. The shutters had been swung back, a couple of windows opened, but it was still unpleasantly warm. Spadina was in shirt sleeves, his tie loose, collar undone to reveal a clump of dark curly chest hair. He apologised for taking up my time, then noted down a detailed description of Christopher Scott. He gave his notes to a uniformed officer to take back to the *Questura* for circulation to every police force in the country, then took down a statement from me about exactly what I'd observed when I'd followed Scott to Forlani's house the previous evening.

'You're absolutely sure it was this house?' Spadina asked.

'Yes.'

'And the time? You're sure about that?'

'Not to the exact minute, but it was somewhere around half past eleven.'

'Did you see Scott leave the house?'

'No, I didn't wait around after he'd gone inside. I went back to our *pensione*.'

I read through the statement and signed it, then Spadina went out of the room.

'Will I be able to go back to Cremona tomorrow?' I asked Guastafeste.

He nodded. 'You've done your bit. You don't need to stay around any longer.'

'What happens now?'

'They try to find Scott.'

'You think he's the killer?'

'He's a suspect.'

'Who else could have done it?'

'There's no one else in the frame at the moment. But the times aren't conclusive.'

99

'What do you mean?' I said.

'Scott came here at half past eleven yesterday evening. The police doctor puts Forlani's time of death as somewhere between six and eight o'clock this morning.'

'Maybe Scott stayed the night.'

'It's possible. Or maybe he went away, then came back. Or maybe someone else came here early this morning. We simply don't know.' He looked at me sympathetically. 'It's not your concern, Gianni. Go back to the *pensione*, try to forget what you saw this morning. I'll be back for dinner.'

I stayed where I was for a time after Guastafeste had left the room. There were two or three hours to kill before dinner. I wondered how I was going to pass them. Then I heard footsteps out on the landing and a woman appeared in the doorway. She was breathing heavily and looked very hot. In her right hand she was carrying a suitcase which she dropped to the floor with a low gasp of relief. She put a hand out, steadying herself on the door frame, and looked at me.

'*Dio*, those are steep steps,' she said with feeling.

I stood up and pulled out a chair for her. 'Signora, please . . .'

She nodded gratefully and sat down, leaving her suitcase by the door.

'I knew it was a mistake, bringing that case. But I never could travel light.' She sighed. 'It's a longer walk from the station than I thought.'

'From the station?' I said. 'You've carried that case all the way from the station? You should have taken the *vaporetto*, signora, there's a stop just by the Accademia Bridge.'

'There's a half-day strike by the drivers – is that what you call them, the boat crew?' she replied. 'I thought about taking a water taxi, but the queue was so long I'd have been standing there until midnight.'

She took a handkerchief out of her shoulder-bag and dabbed at the perspiration on her face. She was a good-looking woman. A few years younger than me, I would have guessed, maybe in her late fifties. She had shortish dark hair – just a hint of grey showing through at the temples – which right now was slightly dishevelled, strands curling untidily around her ears, her fringe straggling over her forehead. I could detect the faint scent of her perfume, a sweet, subtle odour that seemed out of place in Forlani's rank *palazzo*.

She glanced around the room and noticed the peeling plaster, the tatty curtains, the piles of dirty crockery on the table, the leftover food that was turning blue with mould.

'My goodness, is this how Uncle Enrico was living?' she said, aghast.

'Dottor Forlani was your uncle?' I said.

'I'm sorry, I should have introduced myself. Margherita Severini. I'm his niece.' She held out her hand. Her grip was warm and firm. 'You must be with the police.'

I took that as a compliment. I must have looked younger than I thought. 'No, I'm not a policeman,' I said. I introduced myself and told her briefly why I was there. Her hand went to her mouth, suppressing an exclamation of horror.

'You found his body? That must have been awful.'

'Less so than your own shock on hearing of his death, I'm sure,' I said. 'I didn't know him. I met him only for the first time yesterday. You have my sincere condolences, signora.'

'Thank you. Yes, I suppose it was a shock. Not so much his death – he must have been nearly eighty – as the

101

manner of it. The police were very reticent on the phone. How exactly did he die?'

'I don't know,' I said. 'I'm not sure the police really know yet.'

'Perhaps it would be better if I didn't find out. But it *was* murder?'

'It would appear so.'

She grimaced. 'They want me to identify the body. I'm not sure how I'll cope with that.' She looked around the room again. 'I can't believe this place. Is the rest of the house like this?'

'I'm afraid it is somewhat rundown,' I replied.

'It must be – what? – fifteen years since I was last here. But it was nothing like this. What on earth happened?'

It wasn't a question I could answer. Nor did I have to make an attempt for at that moment Spadina came back into the room. He shook hands with Margherita.

'Signora, they told me you were here. Thank you for coming, and so swiftly.'

'It was the least I could do,' Margherita replied.

Spadina noticed her suitcase. 'You came straight here? Where are you staying?'

Margherita shrugged. 'I haven't booked anywhere. I didn't think about hotels. I just threw some things in a bag and jumped on the first train I could get. I'll find somewhere, I suppose.'

'The *pensione* where I'm staying has rooms vacant, I believe,' I said. 'It's not very luxurious, but it's clean. Would you like me to take you there? It's not far.'

She smiled at me. 'Thank you. That's very kind.' She turned to Spadina, a look of anxiety on her face. 'My uncle's body, is it . . . still here?'

Spadina shook his head. 'It's been taken to the morgue.'

'When do you want me to identify it?'

'There's no immediate hurry. Go to your *pensione* and settle in. Someone will come and pick you up in – shall we say an hour?'

I carried Margherita's suitcase to the *pensione* for her. She tried to refuse my offer, but I had to insist; a gallant gesture for which I paid the price with a sore hand and aching shoulder. But I didn't regret it for an instant. I'm old-fashioned enough to believe that carrying luggage is a man's work. The proprietor of the *pensione* found her a room on the floor above mine and I saw no more of her until half past seven when – showered and changed and waiting for Guastafeste to return – I answered a knock on my door. Margherita was outside, quite obviously in a state of some distress.

'I'm sorry to bother you,' she said.

'Come in, please.' I stepped back to let her enter. 'It must have been an ordeal for you.'

She gave me a momentary blank look, then shook her head, understanding my meaning.

'No, it's not that. Not the morgue. That was over very quickly. No, it's something else.'

'Take a seat,' I said, directing her to the chair by the window.

'No, I won't stay. This is a terrible imposition. I'm sorry, I know this sounds very silly, but I don't know what to do. A man's been calling me. Three times since I got back. He's downstairs in the foyer now. He says he wants to see me.'

'About what?'

'About my uncle's violin collection. He wants to – "discuss terms" was how he put it.'

I was outraged. 'Discuss terms? My God, who is he?'

'He said he was a dealer.'

'A dealer?' I knew who it was before she said his name.

'Serafin, I think he said. Something Serafin.'

'I'll take care of him,' I said.

'I don't know how he found out I was here. I mean, it's absurd. I know nothing about my uncle's collection. I'm his next of kin – his only kin, in fact – but that doesn't mean I inherit his estate. What should I do? I daren't go out in case he accosts me.'

'Don't worry,' I said. 'You go back to your room. I'll handle him.'

She looked at me doubtfully. 'I don't want you to get into any kind of trouble. He was quite aggressive on the phone.'

'I'm not going to ask him to step outside or anything. I'm a little old – and far too sensible – for that.'

I went downstairs to the foyer, reining in my anger. Serafin was sitting in a wicker armchair near the reception desk, plump and immaculate in a dark grey suit and pink silk tie. He started in surprise when he saw me.

'Gianni! What are you doing here?'

'I might ask you the same thing.'

He waved a hand dismissively in the air. 'Oh, you know. Business.'

I sat down in the chair next to him. 'How did you know Forlani's niece was here?'

'His niece?' Serafin said evasively.

I knew him well enough to hazard a guess. 'You've been to his house, haven't you? Did the police tell you? How much did it cost you?'

Serafin smirked, unable to resist telling me how clever he'd been. 'I slipped the *poliziotto* on the door fifty euros. I really wanted to get inside to check out the collection, but he was wise to that, wouldn't let me past. He mentioned the niece arriving though, gave me the name of this *pensione*.'

'She doesn't want to see you, Vincenzo.'

'How do you . . .' He stopped. 'You've spoken to her? You know her?' His eyes narrowed, staring at me suspiciously. 'You're not trying to steal a march on me, are you?'

If I'd been younger, and more inclined to violence, I would have punched him on the nose. Instead, I said icily: 'Don't impute your own base motives to others.'

He was taken aback. 'That's rather harsh. I'm doing her a favour. She could make a lot of money out of this.'

'Have you no sensitivity?' I said, though I knew it was a silly question. Serafin had had a sensitivity by-pass operation at birth. 'She's just lost her uncle. Couldn't you have waited before coming touting for trade?'

'What, and let someone else sneak in before me? Believe me, as soon as word of Forlani's death gets around, every dealer in the world will be beating a path to her door. All I want to do is have a chat with her, get my offer in first.'

Serafin stroked his beard, smoothing the hairs over his jawline as if they were the finest sable. He was particular about his beard, the only man I knew who called in at his barber's on the way to work each morning to have his whiskers groomed – the edges clipped, any traces of grey touched up with dye. He looked away across the foyer, then back at me. I recognised the devious gleam of cunning in his eyes.

'Gianni, my friend,' he said slyly. 'If you have this woman's confidence, perhaps you could have a word with her on my behalf? Persuade her to see me.'

I stared at him incredulously. 'You just don't get it,

do you? I have no intention of doing your dirty work for you.'

'Dirty work?' Serafin's expression hardened. Then the real Serafin broke through, the man behind the avuncular façade. 'Don't be so self-righteous, Gianni. Never forget what I know about you.' He leaned closer. 'Did you see Forlani's collection?'

I didn't reply.

'Did you recognise any of his violins?' Serafin continued. 'A certain Guarneri "del Gesù", for example? We don't want that falling into the wrong hands, now do we? That might be dangerous for you.'

'Don't threaten me, Vincenzo. You were the one who sold it to him.'

'And I want it back. I want the others too, the rest of Forlani's collection. Remember that, Gianni.'

Serafin pulled himself to his feet and felt in his jacket pocket, producing one of his business cards.

'Give her my card, there's a good fellow,' he said, reverting to his benign persona. 'I'm staying overnight at the Gritti Palace Hotel.'

I held the business card distastefully between my fingers while Serafin left the hotel. When he'd gone, I tore the card to shreds and dropped it in the bin by the reception desk.

I had dinner with Margherita that evening, at a small, family-run *trattoria* round the corner from our *pensione* that had been recommended by the guesthouse proprietor's wife. It was only a short distance off one of the busiest thoroughfares between St Mark's and the Accademia Bridge, but in Venice you can pass from bustling streets to deserted squares in the space of just a few metres. The *trattoria* was refreshingly quiet, its five or six tables occupied by diners who looked, and sounded, more like locals than tourists.

It was just the two of us. Guastafeste had phoned shortly before eight o'clock to say that he was going to sit in on the Forlani autopsy with Spadina and would not be back until late. Reluctant to dine alone, and suspecting that Margherita might have had similar sentiments, I'd called her room and invited her to join me.

'It was very kind of you to accept, signora,' I said when we were seated at our table in the restaurant. 'I hate eating out by myself.'

'Please, call me Margherita.'

'I'm Giovanni, but everyone calls me Gianni.'

'I'm the one who should be thanking you,' she said. 'You saved me from a lonely, hungry evening in my room. There's nothing worse for a woman than sitting alone in a restaurant. Everyone staring at you, wondering who's stood you up.'

'I'm sure no one would ever stand you up,' I said.

She gave me a dry look. 'You'd be surprised.'

She took out a pair of reading glasses from her shoulder-bag and studied the menu. She looked cooler, more composed than earlier. She'd changed into a pale blue blouse and dark trousers, no jewellery except a couple of gold stud earrings. Her hair was brushed, gleaming in the light from the candle on our table.

'I'm very bad at this,' she said, looking at me over her spectacles. 'What shall we have?'

'How hungry are you?'

'Very. I haven't eaten since breakfast, except for a couple of biscuits on the train. What do you think might be good?'

'You want a starter?'

'Why not?'

107

'The seafood is supposed to be good here. Or would you prefer pasta?'

'I don't mind. The ham looks tempting. Or maybe the artichokes. Or perhaps I should have a salad?' She ran her hand through her hair, scraping it backwards with her fingers. 'Oh, God, I hate having to make decisions.' She glanced at me apologetically. 'You know the joke about economists? You could lay every one in the world end to end and they still wouldn't come to a conclusion.'

I laughed. 'You're an economist?'

'I teach economics. At the university in Milan. I'm a classroom economist. In theory I could run the Bank of Italy. In practice – like most of my students – I can't even handle my own overdraft.'

She tossed the menu down on to the table and folded away her glasses.

'You decide, I'm too hungry to think.'

I ordered for both of us – *antipasto misto*, seafood risotto and a bottle of chilled Soave. Margherita waited for the wine to arrive, then raised her glass to me.

'Thank you.'

'For what?' I said.

'A whole list of things. For finding me a chair at my uncle's house, for finding me somewhere to stay, for carrying my bag to the *pensione*, for inviting me out for dinner, for ordering the food . . . oh, yes, and for getting rid of that dreadful dealer for me.'

'I fear your reprieve may only be temporary,' I said. 'Serafin is nothing if not persistent.'

'You know him?'

'I'm afraid so.' I saw her expression change, a hint of mistrust creep into her eyes, and added hurriedly: 'This isn't some plot, I assure you. I'm not a dealer. This dinner isn't a pretext for bludgeoning you with offers. I have absolutely no interest in your uncle's violin collection. No financial interest anyway. You believe me, don't you?'

Her face relaxed. 'Yes, I believe you.'

'I know Serafin through my work, that's all.' I told her what I did for a living. Then I told her more fully what I was doing in Venice, about Rainaldi, about Guastafeste. She stared at me.

'My God, someone else was murdered? Your friend. You must be reeling.'

'I've had less turbulent times,' I said phlegmatically.

'I'm sorry, Gianni. I'm stunned. What can I say? You must be in shock. Was he a close friend?'

'We grew up together. Played the violin together for more than fifty years. Yes, we were close. He was a very old, very dear friend.'

I heard my voice start to crack a little and took a sip of my wine. Margherita reached across the table and touched the back of my hand lightly with her fingers. A brief, fleeting touch of sympathy, perhaps of empathy, for she too had lost someone.

I looked away. The waiter – a young boy I assumed was the proprietor's son – was approaching our table. I let him serve our starters and withdraw before I said: 'Were you close to your uncle?'

'Not really,' Margherita replied. 'I hadn't seen or spoken to him in years. Or rather, he hadn't seen or spoken to me. He fell out with my father – his younger brother – a long time ago. He cut us all off, refused to speak to my father. He had no quarrel with me, but you know how it is, I was my father's daughter and therefore tainted.'

'What was the quarrel about?'

'Oh, I don't know for sure. It seems strange, doesn't it?

Something so serious and yet I don't really know what it was.'

'Perhaps not so strange,' I said. 'People fall out over all manner of ridiculous things. Often very trivial.'

'Uncle Enrico wasn't the easiest man to get on with. He was stubborn, obsessive, suspicious. He never married, lived all alone in that vast house after my grandfather died. He nursed all kinds of grievances, some maybe real, most, I suspect, imagined. And he got worse as he got older.' She spiked a piece of tomato on her fork and slipped it into her mouth.

'He certainly seemed a little eccentric when I met him yesterday,' I said.

'I think it was the violins that did it in the end. Money, I suppose. Uncle Enrico – being the eldest – inherited the bulk of my grandfather's estate. My father always resented that. It infuriated him that Enrico spent so much money on violins. Squandered so much money was how he saw it. My father thought it was wasteful and self-indulgent. Families are messy, aren't they? Blood's thicker than water, but it turns bad more easily.'

'You had no contact with your uncle at all?'

'I used to send him Christmas cards, but he never replied. Perhaps I should have made more of an effort. Come and seen him, even though I know he'd probably have closed the door in my face. When I saw his house this afternoon – the state of it, the dirt, the smell – I felt guilty. Guilty for neglecting him.'

'The way he lived wasn't your fault. It was his violins that made him happy. Everything else was an irrelevance.'

'Perhaps so. If that dealer – Serafin, was it? – only knew our family history, he'd realise how unlikely it is that I'll inherit my uncle's collection. He's probably left it to a museum somewhere.'

I ate my *antipasto*, thinking about my visit to Forlani's

vault, that room full of glass cases. At the time it had felt like a mausoleum for dead violins. Now Forlani was gone it seemed even more like a tomb. I hoped that perhaps the instruments might be resurrected from their air-conditioned grave, given a new life in the outside world where their music might be heard again. Yet I couldn't help having misgivings. The Spohr Guarneri 'del Gesù' would inevitably come out into the open. It would be examined by experts, by dealers, auctioneers, subjected to the kind of intense scrutiny it had so far avoided. Did I really want that?

'But let's not dwell on my uncle,' Margherita said, forcing a weak smile. 'Tell me about *your* violins. My grandson's interested in learning the violin, you know.'

'You have grandchildren?'

'Three. Stefano is six. Is that too young to start?'

'Not at all.'

'He'll need a small instrument, of course. He's not a very big boy. Are they hard to find?'

'He'll probably need a quarter size,' I said. 'No, they aren't difficult to obtain. Is he in Milan too?'

'Yes. All my grandchildren are nearby.'

'You're lucky. Mine are further away than I would like. And your husband? He couldn't come with you?'

'My *ex*-husband,' Margherita said. 'We divorced four years ago.'

'Ah.' I refrained from saying more. With divorce it's always difficult to know whether to offer your congratulations or your condolences.

'And your wife?' she asked.

'She died six years ago.'

A shadow passed across her face.

'Oh, I'm sorry.'

I picked up the bottle of Soave to cover the uncomfortable silence that followed.

'Have some more wine. How is your *antipasto*?' I said.

I didn't want to talk about Caterina. At that particular moment, having dinner with another woman, it didn't seem right.

I'd been back in my room for only ten minutes when there was a knock on the door and I heard Guastafeste's voice outside.

'Gianni, are you awake?'

I pulled open the door to let him in.

'You weren't in bed?' he said.

'No, I haven't been back long. How was the autopsy?'

Guastafeste sat down in the chair near the window, his legs splayed, his arms dangling down limply. He rubbed his eyes. He looked very tired.

'Inconclusive,' he said, yawning. 'We've established the cause of death. It was what I thought. Forlani severed the artery in his left wrist when he crashed through the glass display case. He basically bled to death.'

'That sounds pretty conclusive,' I said.

'But we still don't know how it happened. Whether it was an accident, whether it was murder. The pathologist found no evidence that Forlani had had a heart attack or a sudden stroke or anything that might have made him black out and fall into the case.'

'What about the missing Maggini? The open front door. Doesn't that indicate that someone else was there at the time?'

'Not necessarily. The Maggini might have been taken earlier. That's one of the things we're going to ask Christopher Scott when we talk to him.'

Something in his tone, his phrasing, made me look at him sharply.

'*When?* He's been located?'

'Picked up two hours ago as he tried to board a flight from Linate to London. Spadina's laid on a car. We're driving to Milan now, the two of us.'

7

I had breakfast alone on the small, enclosed terrace at the rear of the *pensione*. I'd hoped that Margherita might have been there to keep me company, but she didn't appear until I'd finished my coffee and roll and was preparing to return to my room.

She came out into the courtyard and smiled when she saw me. 'Would you mind if I joined you?' she asked.

'Of course I wouldn't. Here.' I moved my plate and cup to clear a space for her on the opposite side of the table.

'Just a coffee, please,' she said to the proprietor, who had emerged from the door to the kitchen. She sat down and glanced around. We were the only guests on the terrace. Our table was in the shade, but above us the sunlight was creeping slowly down the whitewashed walls. The sky was a cloudless cobalt. I studied her. Her face was showing signs of her age – lines around her eyes and mouth – but she still had the bone structure that in her youth would have made her a strikingly attractive woman. Perhaps not beautiful in the conventional sense, but I've never been much of a one for convention.

'It's going to be hot again,' she said. 'Venice is insufferable in the heat. And smelly. Are you staying on?'

I shook my head. 'I'm catching the train back to Cremona this morning.'

'What a shame. I enjoyed our dinner last night.'

'When do you go back to Milan?'

Margherita shrugged. 'Who knows? The police want me to go over to the *Questura* this morning. Apparently there are forms I have to sign. Then I have to see my uncle's lawyer, start dealing with his affairs.' She gave a shudder. 'The whole business fills me with dread. I hate lawyers and legal matters. I never understand what any of it's about. I'll probably be here for days.'

She looked up as her coffee arrived, nodding her thanks at the proprietor. Then she saw me glance at my watch.

'Please, don't let me keep you.'

I smiled apologetically. 'My train leaves at half past nine. I'm afraid I'll have to go.' I pushed back my chair and stood up. 'It was nice meeting you. I hope you manage to get everything sorted.'

'Sorted?' she said dryly. 'This is Italy. Since when has anything here ever been sorted?'

I held out my hand. Her fingers touched mine.

'Goodbye.'

'Safe journey, Gianni.'

I thought about her in the *vaporetto* on the way to the station, heading up the Grand Canal in the morning sunshine. Thought about her perhaps more than I should have done. I wondered why. I considered whether I should have given her my phone number, or asked for hers. But what would have been the point? I was no longer a young man. I'd reached an age when such things weren't really acceptable, perhaps weren't even respectable. We'd met,

115

had dinner, then parted. That was all it amounted to. There was nothing else to be said.

I made myself a cup of coffee and a sandwich when I arrived home, then went out to my workshop. It was hot and stuffy after being closed up for the previous two days. I threw open the windows to let in some air before unlocking my safe and taking out the damaged Stradivari that Serafin had entrusted to me.

What was it that made Stradivari so great? What was his secret? Hardly a year goes by without some scientist or so-called 'expert' coming up with a new theory: about the wood Stradivari used, how it was seasoned, how it was treated, above all how it was varnished. There have been countless treatises on the magical ingredients of his varnish. Experts have tested the vibrations of his plates, the movements of air inside the body of his violins. They have examined his tools, his drawings, scoured the Alps for the source of the timber he used. To what end?

We are a strange species. We have an immense ability to hope. We want Stradivari to have had a secret because we want to hope that, if only we could discover that secret, we could equal him as a luthier. But there is no secret. Violin-making is not alchemy, the transmutation of base metals into gold. It is woodwork.

When I was a schoolboy I was a reasonably bright pupil – not the best in the class but a good all-rounder. I could no doubt have stayed on at school, perhaps gone to university, but academic study didn't interest me. I always had a preference, a particular aptitude, for art and craft so I was put with all the numbskulls and delinquents in the class who because they couldn't add up or read were assumed to be 'good with their hands'. Well, they were. They were good at thieving and fighting. But woodwork? They could no more craft an object in wood than they could explain

116

Einstein's Theory of Relativity. The ability to work with your hands is not some leftover that is given to those who are not intellectual. It is a gift, just as surely and just as precious as an aptitude for maths or languages. You are given the gift, but then you have to work at it to realise your true potential. That is something we do not want to acknowledge today. We do not want anything to be hard work.

Stradivari did not emerge from nowhere, a genius arriving fully formed from a vacuum. He was born in a city of luthiers where violin-making had been a widespread and profitable calling for a century and a half before him. There was a rich established tradition, a wealth of experience and knowledge on which he could call. He was fourteen when he was apprenticed to Nicolò Amati and he continued making violins until he was ninety-three. That is almost eighty years of practice. Who today can boast that in any calling? He learned his trade and he worked at it day in and day out. He didn't have four or five weeks' holiday to go off skiing in the Dolomites or to sun himself on a Tuscan beach. He worked six days a week, ate a piece of bread and cheese at his bench for his lunch and worked on into the evening. Violin-making wasn't just his life's work, it was his life.

By contrast, young luthiers today do a course at some college lasting three or four years at the most. They come out with a diploma, a piece of paper with a seal on it, and think they know how to make violins. What's more, they think people will buy them. They are living in a dream-world. After fifty years in the business I don't need any experts to tell me Stradivari's secret. I know what it was. He was simply a better craftsman than any violin-maker – Guarneri 'del Gesù' excepted – before or since.

I gazed at the instrument on the workbench in front of me, then I found my eyes lifting and being drawn towards another violin that hung on the wall in a corner of my workshop – a violin that I had not made and would never sell. I stood up, walked across to the violin and brought it back to my bench. I placed it next to the Stradivari and compared the two instruments. The similarities were marked. The varnish, the arching of the tables, the cut of the f-holes, the carving of the scroll, they all bore the distinctive marks of the same maker, so much so that I would have sworn they were both the work of the Master. Yet I knew that the instrument on my left was a genuine Stradivari whilst the one on my right was a fake manufactured by my old apprentice master Bartolomeo Ruffino – an unsold fake that he had bequeathed to me on his death, along with his tools and stock of wood.

I had to admire his skill. He'd been an exceptionally gifted forger, practising in a long, if dishonourable, tradition. Violins have been forged since the days of Andrea Amati and Gasparo da Salò, the fathers of the instrument. It is human nature. When an object is in demand and highly prized, there will always be someone looking to cash in on the market and meet that demand from more dubious sources. So many violins were forged in the nineteenth century that it was a veritable industry, employing hundreds of luthiers. I'd guess that probably half the total number of instruments made at that time are falsely labelled. Add in the copies made by honest luthiers making instruments in the style of the masters but not labelling them as such and it's no wonder that it is difficult to be sure a particular violin is genuine. With this kind of history, dealers and buyers are naturally going to be suspicious of any instrument that purports to be either old, or Italian, and particularly both. A forger must be very careful which makers' violins he chooses to fake.

Ruffino had been cautious. He hadn't produced many

fakes a year and had concentrated mainly on the lesser-known luthiers of the late nineteenth and early twentieth centuries. Their violins are much easier to slip out into circulation without arousing suspicion and their prices can be remarkably rewarding. The great makers' instruments are riskier. They are subject to closer scrutiny and because they were ostensibly produced so long ago it is harder to explain plausibly where they have been in the intervening two or three hundred years. But Ruffino had faked them nevertheless. The temptation, the money, the challenge had been too much to resist. In my time with him as an apprentice he'd faked instruments by Giovanni Grancino, Nicolò Gagliano, Giovanni Battista Guadagnini and Carlo Bergonzi – actually three Bergonzis: he took a genuine Bergonzi, dismantled it piece by piece and then built three new instruments using some of the original parts and adding others. This is a wily way of fooling an expert – confronted with an undoubtedly genuine Bergonzi belly, say, he is much more likely to believe the whole instrument to be genuine.

This fake Stradivari before me had come much later, long after Ruffino and I had parted company, but I remembered him making it all the same. It had taken him years to finish. Occasionally it would be out on his bench when I paid a social call on him in his workshop and he would show me with glee exactly how he was faking it – finishing the back and belly with scrapers which, like Stradivari's, were made from the blades of sabres, completing the final smoothing of the wood with dried dogfish skin and horsetail, a coarse, abrasive grass which still grows along the banks of the Po as it did in the Master's day. He was disarmingly honest with me, much as he had been when I had been apprenticed to him. He knew I would never turn him in to the police. I had too much affection for him as a person and, besides, I had spent my apprentice years helping him. To expose Ruffino would have been to destroy my own hard-won reputation as a luthier and Ruffino knew I would never do that.

His painstaking work on the Stradivari had paid off. Even my expert eye could not detect any flaws in its construction. Ruffino had imitated every facet of Stradivari's style with consummate mastery, and in addition he had 'aged' the violin convincingly. He had darkened and dirtied the varnish, simulated wear and tear on the upper treble bout where a player's hand would have rested in third position, and rubbed away some of the varnish on the middle of the back and the chamfers of the scroll. Even the label inside had been discoloured to make it appear three hundred years old. It was the most perfect fake I'd ever seen, yet Ruffino had never tried to dispose of it. I wondered sometimes if he'd hung on to it because he knew it was the apotheosis of his forger's craft, something never again to be equalled. There again, Stradivari was a dangerous subject for a deception. He produced a large number of instruments – probably close on 1,100, of which only around 650 survive – so there would appear superficially to be scope for finding a few hitherto undiscovered examples. In fact, those 650 are so well documented, and so many people over the years have tried unsuccessfully to track down the remaining 450, that the arrival in the marketplace of an unknown Strad would arouse the most profound suspicion and a *prima facie* assumption that it was a fake. Maybe Ruffino had kept his 'Stradivari' because he feared he might be caught if he tried to sell it.

I picked up the instrument and hung it back on its hook. It had been there for almost a quarter of a century. Sometimes I had thought about destroying it – in case on my own death it was brought out into the light and believed to be genuine – but I'd always resisted the impulse. I liked having it there on the wall. It was a memento of my old teacher, a reminder of the skills he had taught me, and perhaps also a warning to me about how those skills should be used.

For the next two hours I worked on the genuine Stradivari, making the plaster of Paris mould I needed to repair the damaged belly of the violin. I was so engrossed in my task that I didn't notice Guastafeste coming into my workshop until he closed the door behind him with a loud click. I looked up sharply.

'Sorry,' Guastafeste said. 'I didn't mean to startle you.'

'Come in,' I said. 'What time is it?'

'Seven-thirty. Am I interrupting?'

'It's time I stopped. I'm tired.' I stretched my shoulders and slid down off my stool. 'How about a drink?'

We sat out at the table on the terrace with a glass of Valpolicella each and a large bowl of olives between us. Guastafeste looked unkempt, a dark stubble on his face. He was wearing the same shirt and tie he'd had on in Venice almost twenty-four hours earlier.

'What happened with Christopher Scott?' I said. 'Or is that confidential?'

'You're inside the loop, Gianni,' Guastafeste replied. 'What I know, you can know.'

'Did he kill Forlani?'

Guastafeste chewed on an olive, spitting the stone out into the palm of his hand.

'He has an alibi. Corroborated by several witnesses. He would seem to be in the clear.'

'What kind of an alibi?'

'He was staying at the Cipriani in Venice. You know it?'

'No. I'm not very familiar with Venice.'

'It's an exclusive, very expensive hotel on the Giudecca. The kind of place film stars like to hide out. It's private, secure, yet only a five-minute boat ride from St Mark's. The hotel has its own taxi service across the lagoon – a fleet of swish luxury motorboats to ferry guests to and from the city. The drivers keep a log of who they transport – stops the *hoi polloi* and *paparazzi* from sneaking into the hotel compound. Christopher Scott, according to both the taxi driver and the hotel night receptionist, came back to his room at half past twelve on Monday night. He had an early-morning alarm call at seven, then took a water taxi from the hotel to the airport at Jesolo at eight. He caught a nine-thirty Alitalia flight to Milan.'

'And Forlani died some time between six and eight a.m. on Tuesday morning?' I said. Guastafeste nodded. 'What if Scott somehow slipped out of the hotel during the night, went back to Forlani's house and then returned to the Cipriani in time for his seven a.m. alarm call?'

'Can't be done. The only way off the Giudecca is by boat. The Venice police have spent the day checking out Scott's alibi, talking to every water taxi operator in the city. They're pretty sure he never left the island until he went to the airport. Not unless he swam across the lagoon which, frankly, is not a credible option.'

'Did he admit he went to Forlani's that evening?'

'Oh, yes, he was very forthcoming.'

'He say why?'

'To discuss violins.'

'Any violin in particular?'

'A Guarneri that's coming up for auction in London next week. Scott had the catalogue with him. He showed it to us. He said he was going to be bidding on Forlani's behalf and they'd met to discuss how high he should go.'

'At half past eleven at night?'

122

'That was the time specified by Forlani, apparently. I can believe it, having met him.'

'Did you ask Scott about the Messiah's Sister?'

'He said he'd never heard of it.'

'Or Tomaso?'

'The same.'

'Do you believe him?'

Guastafeste helped himself to another olive and toyed with it between his fingers.

'I'm not sure. We had to conduct the interview through an interpreter. Scott speaks very little Italian and my English – as you know – is atrocious. Spadina's is even worse. That makes it hard to pick up the nuances. But from his demeanour, his facial expressions, his body language, he didn't strike me as a particularly trustworthy individual. When you've been a policeman as long as I have, you get a feeling for these things.'

'He's a dealer,' I said sardonically.

Guastafeste smiled. 'That's not yet a criminal offence in Italy.'

'Are you holding him?'

'We had no grounds to. He's gone back to England.'

'So what now?'

'As far as Forlani is concerned, that's Spadina's problem.'

'And Tomaso?'

Guastafeste slid his hand into the inside pocket of his jacket and took out a thin sheaf of papers.

'I've been back to his workshop, checked his house. I can't find any trace of the photocopied letters he showed Forlani. Clara knows nothing about them either. They seem to have disappeared.'

'Do you know any more about his trip to England?'

'We've obtained his credit card records. He was there for

three nights. The first night he stayed in a hotel in London, the third night he stayed in a hotel in Oxford. The second night is unaccounted for. We don't know where he was, but he didn't use his credit card.'

Guastafeste unfolded the sheaf of papers in his hand and spread them out on the table.

'We've also got his telephone records – this is a photocopy of them. His two land lines, that is – home and workshop. He didn't have a mobile phone.'

'Nor do I,' I said. 'It's a generation thing. Mobile phones are toys for the young.'

'We've identified most of the numbers he called. There were three in England. Two were the hotels in London and Oxford I mentioned – calls to book his rooms, I would guess. The third we're not sure about. We've tried it a few times and got no answer. It's registered to a Mrs V. Colquhoun. You ever heard the name?'

'No.'

'Tomaso never mentioned it?'

'Not that I can recall.'

'I'll leave you the list. Will you have a look through it? See if you recognise any of the numbers?'

'Of course.'

'I'm going home to bed. I was up all night. Thanks for the wine.'

I went into the house after Guastafeste had left and made myself a light supper. Then I poured another glass of Valpolicella and retired to the armchair in my back room to study the list of phone numbers. Several entries I recognised as my own – Tomaso and I had spoken on the phone almost every week – and there were others I knew: mutual friends, other luthiers in Cremona, for we are a close-knit community of craftsmen. Most of the calls were local. Only three – the three to England Guastafeste had mentioned –

were international. Next to most of the numbers was the name of the subscriber. There were lengthy calls to Tomaso's daughter, Giulia, and his granddaughter, Sofia, who was studying music at the Conservatorio in Milan. There were calls to members of Clara's extended family, who were spread all over northern Italy.

I took a sip of my wine and turned to the final page of the list of calls from Tomaso's workshop. One number stood out immediately – a number in Milan that I could identify even without the subscriber's name written next to it. It was Vincenzo Serafin's office line. I felt my pulse rate increase and sat back in my armchair until the throbbing had subsided. Serafin? Tomaso had called Serafin just five days before he died; a call that had lasted nearly six minutes. And yet when I'd visited Serafin in Milan last week he'd told me he didn't know Tomaso.

Our passage through life is marked by births and weddings and funerals, though when you get to my age the last seem to predominate. I am not an unduly old man – sixty-three is not a great age these days – but I am aware that the years are ticking away. In my more morbid moments I feel the darkness drawing nearer. Perhaps He does not have me in His sights just yet, but I am acutely conscious that I am within range.

For my generation, our births and marriages are long behind us. When we gather together now it is more likely to be grief than joy that unites us. In the last few years I must have attended half a dozen funerals; some for family members or close friends, others for little more than acquaintances. And now Tomaso was gone. He had been so much a presence in my life that it was almost impossible to believe that he would no longer be around – that I would never again hear his voice, share a bottle of wine with him or play quartets beside him. Irrationally, I was angry with him for leaving me, for pulling such a monstrous disappearing trick on us all, and as I watched his coffin being carried into the church I half expected him to leap out suddenly and laugh at us for our gullibility.

We were in San Sigismondo – after the cathedral, the most magnificent church in Cremona. Built by Francesco Sforza, the Duke of Milan, and his wife Bianca Maria Visconti in the fifteenth century, almost every centimetre of the interior – from the walls to the vaulted ceiling – is decorated with elaborate paintings of Biblical scenes. The ostentation is quite overwhelming. It was in this church that the young Luigi Tarisio – the itinerant dealer who bought *Le Messie* from Cozio di Salabue – is said to have acquired his remarkable gift for discovering precious violins. At harvest time San Sigismondo was famous for its Festival of the Dove. A high tower was erected outside the church with a wire stretching from the top of the tower through the main doors to the altar. A 'dove' made of straw and gunpowder, said to be a manifestation of the Lord, was attached to the wire and set alight. The gunpowder ignited, sending the blazing dove whizzing along the wire. It was considered a blessing to touch the flames. Tarisio, the story goes, stretched up his arm as the dove sped by and his hand passed directly through the fire.

I thought briefly of that tale as Tomaso's coffin was placed on the catafalque before the high altar and I saw the flickering light of candles reflected in its polished sides. The church was crowded with mourners, almost every seat occupied. Tomaso had been a sociable man. He had had many friends. Then Father Arrighi turned to face the congregation, his sombre, powerful voice reaching out to us, joining with us in a celebration of Tomaso's life.

I listened to Father Arrighi's words, but I didn't really

hear them. I knew the kind of man Tomaso had been. I didn't need a priest's oration, however heartfelt and eloquent, to tell me his qualities. His personality, his being had infected my life for more than half a century. In the days since his death I had thought at length about him, reconciled myself to his passing and tried to make some kind of peace with my emotions. The funeral was simply a formal valediction, a ceremony to bring us all together and send Tomaso on his way. But I had already said my farewell to him.

I looked around the walls of the church, at the frescoes of saints and apostles and angels, and I thought of a different place, a different funeral. It was six years since my wife had died, but I still thought about her every day. At strange moments – at my workbench, in the garden, even doing mundane things like the washing up – I felt she was beside me. Sometimes I woke in the middle of the night with the feeling that she had been watching over me while I slept. And I found my pillow damp from my tears as I wondered who was watching over her while she slept.

Father Arrighi was asking us to join him in prayer now and I slipped to my knees automatically though I was no longer sure I was a believer. Once I had had faith in the goodness and the mercy of the Lord, but the day Caterina was taken from me I knew it was all a lie. I knew then that He did not exist, yet even so I raged against Him like a madman chasing a shadow, for who else could I blame for my grief? He had taken her from me. Taken her in suffering and pain and for that I could never forgive Him.

But listening to the voices around me, the voices of Tomaso's friends and family murmuring in prayer for him, I wondered whether I had been unjust. I looked up at the figure of Christ above the altar and thought of Tomaso, and of my wife, two souls lost to me for eternity, and I hoped with every particle of my being that I had been wrong about God.

You could feel the sense of relief sweeping through the room. A collective sigh as the people seemed to exhale as one, letting go of their emotions, shrugging off the solemn traces of the funeral, their damp eyes and heavy hearts, and returning to a state of welcome – if slightly subdued – normality. They could talk of other things than Tomaso, catch up with old acquaintances, drink wine, even laugh. I felt my own shoulders lighten, my spirits lift. It was over.

'How are you doing, Gianni?' Guastafeste put a solicitous hand on my shoulder.

'I'm all right.'

'You want a drink?'

He squeezed his way across the crowded room and returned with two glasses of red wine.

'It was a fitting send-off,' he said. 'Father Arrighi excelled himself. And so many people. If I have a quarter that number at my own funeral, I'll be amazed.'

'You won't be around to be amazed,' I said and Guastafeste smiled.

'It's nice for the family,' he said. 'To see how well loved Tomaso was. Who are they all, violin-makers?'

'A lot of them, yes,' I replied. 'He'll be missed. Tomaso had that knack of getting on with almost everyone. That's a rare virtue.'

I saw Tomaso's daughter, Giulia, coming towards us through the throng, pausing to exchange greetings, to receive words of condolence as she passed.

'Good, you've both got a drink,' she said, coming to a halt before us. 'There's some food in the kitchen. Please have some. Mama has overcatered, as usual.'

'How is she?' I said.

'Coping. She's lifted herself for the occasion. All the preparations have kept her busy, taken her mind off things a little. But it's what happens now that worries me. When all the fuss is over and she's left on her own.'

I nodded. The funeral had brought to an end that first, intense period of grief, but I knew it would be years – if ever – before Clara fully recovered from her loss. People talk of closure, but most of us who have lost a partner never truly achieve closure. Reconciliation, resignation perhaps, but rarely closure.

'Is she staying here in the house?' I said.

'She wants to. I'm trying to persuade her to come and stay with us for a few weeks, but she's reluctant to leave. I don't want her here on her own, getting depressed.'

'It will take her a long time to adjust.'

'I know.'

I took Giulia's hand. I knew money would be tight for Clara. Tomaso had been a man who had lived for the moment. Pension plans, savings had not been a priority for him.

'If there's anything I can do to help, just let me know. You only have to ask, you know that.'

'Thank you, Gianni. There was something . . .' Giulia paused. 'I don't know if this is the right moment. Not about Mama, but about Sofia.'

'Sofia?'

Giulia turned to scan the room. She caught the eye of her daughter and beckoned her over. I'd noticed Tomaso's granddaughter in the church, but hadn't spoken to her. She was tall and willowy, dark hair falling around her shoulders. I'd met her only infrequently over the past few years. My last vivid memory of her was of a shy, awkward fifteen-year-old girl winning first prize at the Cremona Music Festival. Seeing this confident, self-possessed young woman before me now was a salutary reminder of how quickly children grow up.

'You remember Sofia, don't you?' Giulia said.

'Of course I do,' I said, smiling at Sofia. 'Your grandfather used to talk about you. How are your studies at the Conservatorio?'

'Fine. They're fine,' Sofia replied. 'That's what I wanted to talk to you about. To ask you a favour.' She glanced at Guastafeste. 'To ask *both* of you a favour.'

'Please, ask away.'

'It's about my recital. My début recital,' Sofia began.

'Ah yes, I remember,' I said. 'Your grandfather mentioned a recital. It's soon, isn't it?'

'The day after tomorrow. I wasn't sure whether to go ahead with it. It doesn't seem, well, appropriate with Grandpa dying.'

'My goodness, you mustn't think about cancelling,' I said hurriedly. 'That's not at all what Tomaso would have wanted.'

'That's what I said,' Giulia interjected, then turned to her daughter. 'It's an important day for you. Very important.'

'Well, I know it is, but . . .' Sofia hesitated, looking at Guastafeste, then me. 'But there's a problem. Grandpa was going to do some work on my violin for me – fit a new bridge, check the soundpost. I only left it with him last week. I don't think he will have had time to do the work. I have another instrument – one Grandpa made – but I'd rather have my other one back for my recital, if possible.'

'Leave it to me,' I said. 'I'll have a look at it.'

Sofia's eyes went to Guastafeste. 'Unfortunately, the violin is in Grandpa's workshop. And the police have sealed it off. I went over there yesterday and was told that no one is allowed into the workshop and nothing can be taken out of it.'

'What sort of violin is it?' Guastafeste asked.

'A Romeo Antoniazzi. It's in a black case with my name on the outside. There was a policeman guarding the workshop door. He said I'd need a court order to get the violin back.'

'Put your mind at rest,' Guastafeste said reassuringly. 'I'll take care of it.'

The photocopies of Tomaso's phone records were on the table in my back room where I'd left them the previous evening. I picked up the sheets of paper and leafed through them pensively. The international calls to England had been heavily underlined in black ink: the Marlborough Hotel, London; the Randolph Hotel, Oxford; and a Mrs V. Colquhoun, whom the police – as far as I was aware – had still not managed to contact. I stared at her number for a while, then picked up the phone. I suppose, technically, I was interfering in police business, but Guastafeste had said I was 'inside the loop', hadn't he? I was trying to help. What harm would it do? I dialled the number and waited. It rang for a long time. I was contemplating abandoning the call when I heard a click and a voice came on the line, speaking English.

'Hello.'

It was a woman. She sounded elderly, perhaps a little frail.

'Is that Mrs Colquhoun?' I said in English.

'Yes, I'm Mrs Colquhoun.'

'My name is Castiglione.'

'Speak up, I can hardly hear you.'

'I'm sorry, the line is bad. I'm ringing from Italy.'

'Did you say Italy?'

'Yes.'

'How wonderful. Whereabouts in Italy?'

131

'Cremona.'

'Ah, I've never been there. How is the weather?'

What? 'Well, it's hot,' I said.

'It's overcast here. A bit muggy.'

Muggy? What did that mean?

'I'm sorry to trouble you . . .'

'Cremona, did you say? I don't know Cremona, but Florence, ah, now there's a city. Firenze, you call it, don't you? It must be . . . let me see, twenty, no, thirty years since I was there, but one never forgets Florence, does one? Or is that Sorrento? I'm not sure . . .' She broke off. 'Timmy, get down from there. You know you're not allowed on the table. Such a mischievous little thing. Now where were we?'

'Mrs Colquhoun, I wanted to ask you about a friend of mine, Tomaso Rainaldi. I believe he telephoned you recently.'

'Signor Rainaldi? Oh, yes, I remember . . .' She broke off again, her voice getting fainter. 'Timmy, I won't tell you again, you naughty boy. Get down at once.' Her voice became stronger again. 'Do you have cats, Mr . . . I'm sorry, I've forgotten your name.'

'Castiglione. No, I don't have cats.'

'I'm very fond of cats. You Italians love cats, don't you? I remember in the Forum in Rome once, there were hundreds of them. All over the place they were.'

'Could you tell me why he telephoned you?' I said, steering the conversation back on track.

'Who?' said Mrs Colquhoun.

'Signor Rainaldi.'

'Such a nice man. He brought me a box of chocolates, you know. Most kind of him. Thornton's Continentals, they were. I'm very fond of Thornton's Continentals. Do you have them in Italy?'

132

'I don't think so.'

'How odd. They call them Continentals, but they aren't available on the Continent.'

'He came to your house?' I said.

'Oh, yes. We had such a nice chat. His English was a little, well, strange, but I have some Italian. Your English is very good, Signor . . . I'm sorry, it keeps going.'

'Castiglione.'

'Where did you learn it?'

'I've picked it up over the years. Could you tell me why Signor Rainaldi came to see you?'

'To look at some papers. Old family letters.'

My heart gave a sudden jolt.

'Old letters?' I said.

'Yes, they've been in a trunk for years, centuries actually.'

'What was in the letters?'

'Oh, I don't know that. I've never really looked at them properly.'

'Do you still have the letters?'

'Of course, they're upstairs.'

'Would it be possible for me to look at them?'

'But you're in Italy.'

'To come over and look at them.'

'If you wish. I don't believe they're very interesting though. Just old family correspondence.'

'Whereabouts in England are you?'

'Highfield Hall.'

'And where exactly is that?'

'In Derbyshire, the Peak District. Near Manchester.'

'May I call you back to arrange an appointment?'

'Of course. Come whenever you like.'

'You've been very kind. I look forward to meeting you.'

'Bring some of that Italian sun with you. Goodbye.'

133

I replaced the receiver, then called Guastafeste at the *Questura*.

'Now I know I shouldn't have done this,' I said. 'But I think I have something.'

8

I have lived in the Lombardy countryside for seven years and would not want to be anywhere else. I enjoy the space, the scents of my garden, the blue sky filling the horizon wherever I look. But increasingly, when I venture into Cremona, I feel a strange, almost maudlin nostalgia for my time in the city.

My youth and middle age were spent there. My most enduring memories are inextricably bound up with the friends and experiences of that time. I miss the companionship of my urban days, the comforting feeling that one is not entirely alone, and I take great pleasure in wandering around my old haunts. I call in at my old workshop which has been taken over by a younger luthier, share a drink or a meal with some of my former neighbours and for a time I bask in the warmth of friendship and shared recollection that, more than anything these days, bring a genuine happiness into my life.

The Piazza Roma was cool and quiet. Cremona is something of a backwater. The adjective most frequently applied to the city – when anyone bothers to describe it at all – is 'sleepy'. Comatose would be a better word. Everything passes us by. If Milan is the beating heart of northern Italy, the motorways radiating out from it like arteries, then Cremona is a bit like the appendix: people have heard of it, know vaguely where it is, but they can't quite recall what it's for. The local tourist board and the city fathers make earnest but essentially doomed attempts to attract visitors to the area – tourists, businessmen, students. But despite these valiant efforts the place remains noticeably uncontaminated by outsiders.

I sat on a bench under the trees in the piazza and watched the water dancing in the fountain in the centre of the square. Three hundred years ago this was the Piazza San Domenico. It had a church in the centre and a row of houses across the far side where Stradivari lived and worked. The houses and the church have long since been demolished, but there is a pinkish marble copy of Stradivari's tombstone set amidst the flower beds. The original headstone is in the civic museum, but Stradivari's bones have been lost. In one of the more shameful episodes in the city's history, the great man's remains were dug up and dumped in an unknown mass grave when the church of San Domenico was razed.

The piazza is now surrounded by unprepossessing office buildings, many occupied by banks which can be guaranteed to suck the soul out of any area they inhabit. At one corner there is even a branch of McDonald's, for the infamous golden arches have colonised our humble community too, though I notice – in an irony suitable for our times – that a McDonald's paper cup is now the vessel of choice for every beggar on the street to hold forth for alms.

There is an air of neglect about the place. The band-stand, which these days is more often used to shelter from the rain than for musical performances, is looking distinctly rundown. The statue of Ponchielli, a son of Cremona who wrote some ten operas but is now known only for the Dance of the Hours from *La Gioconda*, is in need of a clean, and the grass in the middle of the piazza could do with a cut.

I had the area virtually to myself. I remembered a time when the square would have been crowded with mothers and their young children. When our offspring were babies I would regularly take time off from my work in the afternoons and bring them here with Caterina. We'd sit on a bench while they slept in their prams, or play with them on the lawns. You don't see many mothers and children now. The mothers are all out working to help pay the rent and their babies are being looked after by someone else. We'd been lucky, Caterina and I. We'd had time for our children, we'd been there for them. I can think of few better epitaphs for a parent.

Guastafeste came up from behind and slid on to the seat next to me. He was carrying a black fibreglass violin case.

'Sorry I'm late.'

'That's okay. I'm not in any hurry.'

He glanced around, his policeman's eye alighting on a lone man making his way towards the secluded, wooded area at the far end of the square which was notorious as a rendezvous for local drug dealers and their customers. Then he handed me the violin case.

'I think that's the one,' he said. 'It has Sofia's name on it.'

I opened the case on my knees and removed the violin inside. I recognised the maker's style, but checked the label all the same: *Antoniazzi Romeo Cremonese, fece a Cremona l'anno 1920.*

'This is it,' I said. I held the instrument up. 'The bridge

137

looks a little worn. The E string's been cutting into it, and the feet aren't a perfect fit. Did you have any difficulty getting it out?'

'It's not relevant to the inquiry. The investigating magistrate will never realise it's gone.'

I put the violin back into its case and refastened the catches.

'I rang Vincenzo Serafin,' Guastafeste said. 'He denied he'd ever spoken to Tomaso.'

'And Tomaso's phone call?'

'Serafin said he knew nothing about it. He checked his diary. The morning of the call he was out of the office – apparently. His secretary didn't remember it either.'

'You believe him?'

'I might have done – if you hadn't told me about him selling fakes. And if Tomaso's phone call – according to the phone company records – hadn't lasted six minutes. Who was he talking to all that time, if not Serafin? I think Serafin knows more than he's letting on. Problem is, I can't prove it.'

'And England?'

'I've talked to my superiors. They took some persuading, but they've agreed to let me go. They wanted to let the British police handle it for us – all for budgetary reasons, of course. Everything comes down to the bottom line. But I managed to convince them that it would take too long – putting in a formal request through the Ministry of Justice, all the bureaucracy. It would be months before anything happened. They can't pay for you though.'

'I didn't expect them to,' I said. 'I'll pay my own way.'

'You don't need to come, you know.'

'Is there a problem? Your superiors object?'

'I haven't told them about you coming. They don't need to know.'

'Do *you* want me to come?'

'Yes, I'd like you there. You're part of the team as far as I'm concerned. Besides, you speak English. I'm going to need you to interpret.' He paused, watching a second lone man heading for the trees across the piazza. 'But are you sure you want to do it? It won't be cheap.'

'The money's not an issue,' I said. 'I can afford it.' I looked at him. 'It's not the money you're worried about though, is it?'

Guastafeste smiled ruefully. I knew him so well I could guess his thoughts. He'd grown up in an apartment only a few doors away from ours. I'd met him first when he was only a couple of days old, seen him regularly throughout his childhood. His parents – his father was a salesman who was perpetually away from home, his mother a hairdresser who worked long hours – neglected him. Not wilfully, just carelessly. Their sins were ones of omission rather than commission. Wrapped up in their own lives, they simply seemed to forget about their son who, from an early age, began to gravitate towards me and my family, coming to my workshop after school with my son, Domenico, frequently coming home with us for meals that his own parents were unavailable to provide. I became a sort of surrogate father to him. I gave him his first cello – a shabby half-sized instrument I picked up cheaply at a local auction – and later made him the full-sized cello he still plays. He was a bright lad. He could have chosen any number of careers, but I think it was the chaotic, unsettled nature of his upbringing that made him opt for the police force – the most ordered, secure occupation he could find.

'I don't want to put you to any trouble,' Guastafeste said.

'Trouble?' I replied. 'Don't be silly. How can it be trouble, helping you track down Tomaso's killer? I want to be involved.'

'I'm taking you away from your work.'

'Hang my work. What does my work matter?'

'And there may be risks. Possible dangers.' He didn't look at me. 'Tomaso was murdered. So, I'm sure, was Enrico Forlani. Both were involved in the search for this violin, this Messiah's Sister. Somewhere out there is the killer: a desperate, very dangerous individual. If we get in his way . . .'

'You think I haven't thought about that?' I said. 'I know there are risks.'

'You know I'll protect you, Gianni. I just want you to be aware of all this before you get in any deeper.'

'I'm aware,' I said. 'And I want to help. For Tomaso. Not just to find his killer, that's your job. But to find the violin. I want to find the violin for him.'

'You think it really exists?'

'Let's see what we find when we get to England.'

My route back to my car took me past the building that had once belonged to my apprentice master, Bartolomeo Ruffino. It's a clothes shop now, a boutique full of chic blouses and expensive dresses, a far cry from the dilapidated workshop I remembered. I stood on the pavement on the opposite side of the street and gazed at the shop for a while. I'd spent nine years of my life in that building, from the age of fifteen to twenty-four when I broke away from Ruffino and set up on my own. I was married by then with a wife and young baby to support, but I'd seen my fair share of girls in the dark, secluded alley that ran down the side of the building. I could picture some of them now, recall the clumsy fumblings, the nervous giggles of adolescent courtship. I'd had my first sexual experience in that dingy alley; a hurried, awkward coupling up against the brick wall that had left me – and my partner, no doubt – wondering what all the fuss was about. Claudia Simeone, that had been her name. My first real love. We'd lasted less than six months, but I could still remember thinking at the time that I was going to marry her. I still saw her around occasionally. She'd filled out in her thirties; the breasts and thighs that I had so lusted after had taken on battleship proportions and she'd sprouted a moustache as black and downy as the one I'd attempted to grow during our juvenile affair. I'd had a lucky escape.

I thought about Ruffino. He'd been a cunning old rogue who'd always appreciated that the key to being a success-ful forger – apart from not getting caught, of course – was respectability. No one must suspect for even one second that you were not what you seemed. There had been nothing in either Ruffino's appearance or demeanour to indicate the true nature of his activities. He would come to his workshop five days a week and make violins, have an occasional glass of wine in a nearby bar at lunchtime and then go home to his wife and children in the evening. He was a leading member, and one-time president, of our local trade association; he exhibited at trade fairs, won medals at international violin-making competitions and even wrote a couple of well-received papers on the history of the violin trade in Cremona. As far as outward appearances were concerned, he was the model of a dedicated craftsman and family man.

The truth, however, was rather different. Yes, he made violins which bore his own label – and very fine violins they were too – but a good quarter of his time was devoted to crafting new instruments, or doctoring old ones, to pass them off as the work of greater, more sought-after luthiers. Yes, he was a loving husband and father who took his family out to a *trattoria* on a Saturday night, who played

141

football with his sons in the park and never forgot his wedding anniversary. But on Sunday mornings, returning home from Mass in his best suit and tie, he would stop off at his workshop and have sex with his mistress on the workbench. I know, because I caught them at it one day.

I had keys to the workshop – one of my duties was to open up every morning and have Ruffino's coffee ready for when he arrived – and on this particular Sunday I'd decided to go in and do some work on one of my own violins. I was in the storeroom when I heard them come in. By the time I peeked out they were already at it so it didn't seem wise to make my presence known. Ruffino's mistress, a voluptuous creature named Tiziana, was up on the bench, her blouse undone, her skirts spread to reveal her fleshy thighs. What did I do? I watched them, of course. Who wouldn't have? I was fifteen or sixteen years old. I couldn't take my eyes off them, Ruffino in his Sunday finery, Tiziana moaning softly as his fingers explored her.

It was pure accident that I happened to be there that Sunday. It was also an accident on the subsequent eight Sundays – or maybe it was nine – until, disgusted by my voyeurism, and terrified of being discovered, I kept away from the workshop on the Sabbath. But it taught me that a good forger, whatever he does in private, must always maintain the appearance of great respectability. The illusion of honesty must be created and carefully nurtured.

Ruffino would have appreciated the change of use to his old premises. Outside the workshop he had always dressed smartly and he had been something of a connoisseur of women's couture, spending wads of his spare cash on clothes for his mistress which he had taken as much pleasure in buying as he had later in removing. It was twenty-four years since he'd died but I still missed him – his cursing, his booming voice and theatrical gestures, his incomparable passion for violins. Somewhere in all the clutter of junk I keep at home I have a cutting of the local newspaper report of his death. I can remember most of it word for word. He'd died in his workshop one Sunday morning after he'd been to Mass, the article said. His body had been found by a friend, Miss Tiziana Ricci, who fortuitously happened to be passing and heard him cry out. He'd apparently overexerted himself and had a heart attack while sawing some new planks of maple. There are worse ways to go.

I heard the violin as I walked across the courtyard and stopped for a moment, entranced by the sound. It was some way off, muted by the barrier of the Conservatorio Giuseppe Verdi's thick walls, but it had a clarity, a purity that was arresting. I listened for a time before continuing on my way, the sound growing ever louder, ever more striking. There was something very special about it. It had a warmth to it, a depth that very few violinists manage to draw from their strings. The violin, to me, is the most profound of instruments. It is the only one – the viola excepted, but I'm a violinist so we don't count that – where your body, your skin is in direct contact with the instrument, where you can feel the vibrations in your head as you play. You are not detached from your instrument like a pianist, you are one with it.

Scientists will tell you that all materials, animal, vegetable or mineral, have a natural frequency – a point at which the atoms of which they are composed start to vibrate uncontrollably. So soldiers, when crossing bridges, are told to break step in case the rhythm of their marching feet sets the atoms of the bridge in motion, tearing the structure apart. The human body also has a natural frequency. That's why harmonic music pleases and discordant noise jars. We like sounds that vibrate at a frequency sympathetic to our internal structure – hence Mozart will always be more popular than Schoenberg – and the violin, of all instruments, produces that sound most effectively. It is perfectly in tune with the human soul.

That was how I felt as I listened to the music emanating from the recital hall. It was more than just music for my ears, it was music for my whole being.

I slipped inside the hall and waited silently at the back. Sofia was on the platform, clad in jeans and a tight T-shirt that exposed her midriff. As she played, her body swayed like a sapling and her long dark hair swung around her face, brushing the edges of her violin. She was playing the Bach D Minor unaccompanied partita with the poise and maturity of someone much older. I watched her, enraptured.

'No, no, what are you doing?'

A figure came forward from the side of the stage and the spell was broken. I recognised the distinctive aquiline profile of Sofia's teacher, Ludovico Scamozzi.

'The sound, no, it's all wrong,' he said sharply. 'This is Bach. You're making him sound ugly.'

Sofia lowered her violin and bow and stared at Scamozzi in bewilderment.

'Ugly?'

'Your tone, it has no beauty. You're digging in too much, your bowing is harsh. Here.'

Scamozzi stepped up to Sofia and stood behind her.

'Lift your arms.'

He reached over and took hold of her bow arm with his right hand while his left arm snaked around her waist. Sofia gave a shudder that was visible even from the back of the hall. I saw her stiffen and try to pull away. But Scamozzi was pressing in close behind her, holding on tight.

'Relax, Sofia, relax. You cannot play with so much tension in your body,' he chided her.

His face was in her hair, he was almost nuzzling the side of her neck. It seemed a very good moment to make my presence known.

I cleared my throat loudly. Scamozzi let go of Sofia abruptly and looked up.

'Who's that?' he barked, peering out into the hall.

I walked down to the front where he could see me.

'Oh, it's you, Castiglione.' We knew each other professionally. I'd done work for him on his violin. 'What do you want?'

I looked up at him, then at Sofia. She gave me a glance of relief and edged warily away from Scamozzi.

'I was admiring your playing,' I said to her. 'Most impressive. A beautiful tone,' I added in a deliberate contradiction of Scamozzi.

She smiled. 'Thank you.'

'We are having a lesson here,' Scamozzi said irritably.

'Ah, is that what it is, Signor Scamozzi?'

Any other teacher at the Conservatorio I would have graced with the title 'Maestro', but not Scamozzi. Respect you have to earn.

'You are interrupting us,' Scamozzi snapped.

'I have a violin here for Sofia,' I said. I held up the case. She reached down and took it from me. 'Try it out. I'll stay around for a bit in case it needs some adjustment.'

I sat down at the front of the hall and watched while Sofia changed violins and resumed her lesson. Scamozzi didn't touch her again, but he fussed around on the edges of the stage, interrupting her constantly, fiddling with his long hair – sweeping it back behind his ears, running his fingers through it, occasionally tossing his head back like a petulant pony and clutching clumps of it in his fists. He seemed unable to keep still and was clearly lacking in the primary quality a good teacher requires – the ability to listen.

But then he wasn't a teacher by choice or temperament. Once he'd been a celebrated prodigy who'd been hailed as the successor to Salvatore Accardo as Italy's leading virtuoso. He'd begun a career as a concert soloist that showed every prospect of being a glittering success. But in his late twenties it had all gone wrong. He'd always been a flashy player, with more technique than true musicality, in my opinion. Then his technique deserted him and there was nothing left. He could have recovered it with a bit of hard work, but he was lazy and arrogant. He reneged on a few bookings, let people down at the last minute and acquired a reputation for unreliability. Promoters stopped engaging him and he took to the bottle which only accelerated his decline. He still made infrequent appearances in the concert hall, but to all intents and purposes his career was over. He was pushing forty now, raddled with bitterness and resentment.

He'd hung on to his teaching post at the Conservatorio, though goodness knows how, for he was singularly unsuited to the job. All the great teachers I have encountered have believed in inspiring and encouraging their pupils. Scamozzi's philosophy – from what I was witnessing now – seemed to be the opposite: that only by terrorising his charges, by undermining their confidence and self-esteem, could he drive them to excellence. He was merciless in his relentless criticism. Perhaps with a mediocre violinist he might have had good cause for censure – though not in such an unnecessarily brutal

146

fashion – but Sofia was gifted. She could really play.

I squirmed with anger, suppressing a paternal desire to intervene, as I listened to Scamozzi tearing her to shreds. I loathed him for his cruelty, the envy in him that fuelled his bile. I knew why he was so harsh with her – he saw in her the same promise he had once had and failed to fulfil.

'Enough,' he said at the end of the lesson. 'I can do no more. Go away, go away and practise. All I can say is you had better pull yourself together before tonight.'

Sofia bowed her head over her case as she put away her violin. I could see she was close to tears. She came down off the platform, the case clutched under her arm, and almost ran out of the recital hall. I restrained myself from giving Scamozzi my opinion of his teaching technique – it was not my place to interfere – and hurried after Sofia. I saw her down the corridor, disappearing into the ladies' toilets. I waited for her to emerge. When she did so her eyes were bloodshot, the skin around them puffy. She'd obviously been having a good weep.

'Why don't you let me buy you lunch?' I said.

She hesitated. 'I have to practise.'

I took her by the arm and led her towards the exit.

'The last thing you need to do is practise.'

We found a cafe around the corner from the Conservatorio and sat on the pavement terrace under the shade of an awning. Sofia was preoccupied with her own thoughts, unable to focus on the menu, so I ordered us both a salad and a bottle of mineral water. I gave her a few moments, then said gently: 'Scamozzi is the wrong teacher for you, you know.'

'I know.'

'Why don't you change?'

'I would if I could, but . . .' She paused. 'It's not easy.

147

There are . . . personalities involved, a lot of politics.'

'Damn the politics,' I said. 'This is your career. You want to be a musician, don't you?'

She nodded. 'He's a very powerful man. If I cross him, he can make my life very difficult.'

'More difficult than it is now?'

Sofia shrugged, but didn't reply. The waiter brought us our salads. Sofia spiked a chunk of tomato and chewed it slowly. Her shoulders were slumped, despondent. I could see she needed a boost to her confidence.

'You sounded wonderful just now,' I said. 'You're really going to knock them out tonight.'

'I'm not. It's going to be a disaster.'

'Rubbish.'

'It is. There'll be people there, agents, promoters, important people, and I'm going to make a fool of myself.'

'Listen, Sofia, I've heard you play. I've heard a lot of violinists in my time and, believe me, you are not going to make a fool of yourself.'

She looked at me, biting her lower lip. I felt a need to protect her, to reassure her the way I used to do with my daughter when she was younger.

'Take no notice of what Scamozzi said. You play the music the way you think it should be played. That Bach partita, I've heard it played many times. I've heard Itzhak Perlman perform it. I've heard Menuhin and Oistrakh. And once, a long time ago, I even heard Heifetz play it. And what struck me most was that none of them played it the same. They were all great artists, but there is no right or wrong way to play a piece. There is only your own interpretation, Sofia. You cannot play it the way Scamozzi wants you to – indeed, you should not even try. You can only play it your way. And your way is as valid and as musical as Oistrakh's or Heifetz's, or anyone else's way. You are Sofia Vivarini, and this is your music.'

She looked up from her salad. 'You think so?' she said doubtfully.

'I think you know it. I can tell from the way you play it that you believe in your own interpretation. And you communicate that. That's the difference between a good violinist and an artist. All you young players have the technique, you can all play the notes. But you do more than that. You speak to an audience.'

'That's very kind of you to say so.'

'It's not kindness. It's the truth. Don't let Scamozzi destroy your individuality. Don't let him undermine your confidence. You play the way you did just now in your recital and you'll be fine. You'll be more than fine.' I smiled at her. 'I'm not a teacher, but I know something about violins.'

Some colour had returned to her cheeks. Her eyes had lost some of their hollow dullness.

'Will you be there tonight?' she said.

'Yes, I'll be there,' I said. 'Your family, your grandfather's friends, we're all coming. He was immensely proud of you, you know.' She flushed and glanced away. 'How was the violin?'

'The . . . oh, I'm sorry. How rude of me. It's perfect. Thank you. I'm glad to have it back. Grandpa's violin is good but, well . . .' She hesitated, trying to be tactful. ' . . . I prefer the Antoniazzi. It carries better in a hall like that.'

'You could do with a new instrument. The Antoniazzi is all right, but you're worthy of something better.'

'I don't have the money to buy a new one.'

'There are trust funds that lend out good instruments to promising players. The Conservatorio should put you in touch with them. I'll keep my eyes open too. You can't make a concert career with a violin like that.'

'It's served me well.'

'I'm sure. The tone, the volume of sound you produce from it is remarkable. But you need to move to the next stage now if you're to make the most of your talent.'

'Maestro Scamozzi says I don't have what it takes to make it to the top.'

I stared at her. 'He said that?' I was outraged. 'Well, you listen to me, Sofia. You listen to your heart, and to your audience, not to a malicious, embittered has-been like Scamozzi. How dare he say that to you! My God, the man is a cretin!'

Sofia laughed. It transformed her face. She really was a very beautiful young woman. She had a freshness, an innocence that was captivating. I feared for her when – there was no 'if' about it, in my view – she was signed up by an agent, a record label, all the sharks of the classical music world. She would need great strength of character to ensure they marketed her for her music, not her looks.

'That's better,' I said. 'You keep that in mind when you're playing tonight. It's *your* recital, no one else's.'

'I have to go back and do some practice. I'm having a run-through with my pianist later.'

'Not too much,' I said. 'Keep something back for this evening.'

'I'm scared as hell. There's a lot resting on this,' she said anxiously.

'Just remember the audience will be on your side. They want you to succeed. Just focus, play, communicate. That's what my teacher used to say to me. Focus, play, communicate.'

'I'll do my best.'

I squeezed her hand gently.

'I'm looking forward to it,' I said.

The office door was open. I could see a couple of students – a girl and a boy – standing by the desk. I couldn't see Margherita, but I could hear her voice explaining some abstruse point of economic theory. I stepped over the threshold. The students turned. As they pulled apart a little, I saw Margherita seated behind her desk, her reading glasses perched on the end of her nose. Her eyes met mine, opened wide in surprise, then she smiled.

'Gianni, come in.'

'Am I disturbing you?'

'Not at all, we're just finishing.' She made a few more remarks to the students, then came out from her desk to show them out, closing the door after they'd gone.

'How nice to see you,' she said, holding out her hand. 'You should have phoned.'

'I know. Is this a bad moment?'

'No, I've finished my classes for the day. How did you find me?'

'There's only one Margherita Severini teaching economics at the university.'

'Please, sit down.'

She went back behind her desk and resumed her seat, removing her reading glasses and tossing them carelessly aside. The desk was cluttered, covered with books and mounds of paper. Margherita lifted down a pile of files and dumped them on the floor by her chair to give us an uninterrupted view of each other.

'You've recovered from Venice, I hope,' I said.

She laughed. 'Venice, Part One, yes. But I fear there are many more instalments to come. My uncle's lawyers . . .' She grimaced. 'God, you've never met anyone like them. I thought there was only going to be one lawyer. There turned out to be four.'

'They hunt in packs,' I said. 'Like wolves.'

'Please, let's not be unkind to wolves. They claim it's a very complicated estate. My uncle – so they say – didn't like his legal affairs to be too transparent. There's money all over the place, apparently. Offshore, tied up in foreign companies, salted away in various tax havens. It's a nightmare. That's why it needs four lawyers – a probate specialist, a tax specialist, a corporation law specialist.'

'And the fourth?'

'He takes their expenses to the bank in a wheelbarrow.'

'And your uncle's violins?' I said.

'No one seems very sure about the violins. The lawyers are checking to see if Uncle Enrico made any separate pro-vision for his collection, or if it's just another part of his general estate. I was there for two days. I have to go back in a fortnight for more meetings with them.'

'You have my sympathy.'

'It's my lack of knowledge I can't stand. The lawyers could tell me anything they liked and I wouldn't know if it was true or not. I'd wash my hands of it now – God knows, I don't want his money – but I can't. I'm his closest living relative. I have an obligation to sort it all out.'

'Did Serafin bother you again?'

'Not in Venice, but he's telephoned me a few times since. He won't be put off. He must have the skin of a rhino. Mind, he's not alone. The others have been just as obnoxious.'

'Others?'

'Other dealers. A couple more have phoned, expressing interest in my uncle's collection. They're incredible. Polite, charming, but completely insensitive.'

'Do you remember their names?'

152

'One was Swiss, from Zürich. I think his name was Weissmann. The other was an Englishman, Christopher Scott. But you don't want to know about all that, it's very tedious. What brings you to Milan?'

I reached down on to the floor and picked up the violin case I'd brought with me.

'I thought your grandson might like this,' I said.

I opened the case on the desk and took out a quarter-size violin. Margherita gave an exclamation of delight.

'Oh, my, that is such a tiny violin. Let me see it.'

She took the violin from my hands and held it up.

'Stefano will love this. And it has a bow, too. It's like a toy, isn't it? How sweet. I can just see him playing it. Is this one of yours? I mean, did you make it?'

I shook my head. 'It's a factory-made import. The plates are pressed, not carved. They ink on the purfling, spray on the varnish. No luthier makes quarter-size instruments. For the amount of labour involved he'd have to charge such a ridiculous sum that no one would pay it. Not for a beginner's instrument like this.'

'Gianni, how kind of you.'

'Would you like it?'

'Of course I would. How much do I owe you?'

'Have it on loan,' I said.

'No, that's not right. I must pay you for it.'

'I won't take any money,' I said. 'Let your grandson try it, have a few lessons. He may not want to continue, in which case buying him an instrument would have been a waste. Even if he does keep it up, he'll have grown out of the quarter-size and be on to a half-size before you know it. When he's finished with it, just give it back to me.'

'Well, if you're sure. Thank you. But if I can't give you any money, let me pay you in some other way. Why don't I take you to dinner? Are you staying in Milan this evening?'

'I am,' I said. 'But I'm going to a recital at the Conservatorio. The granddaughter of an old friend is playing.'

'The violin?'

I nodded. 'I've heard her. She's absolutely stunning.' I looked at Margherita over the desk. 'I wondered if you might like to come. Do you like classical music?'

'I love it.' She paused, considering my invitation. 'You know, I'd be delighted to come – it's ages since I last went to a concert. But there is one condition. You must come home with me now and I'll make us something to eat.'

'With pleasure,' I said.

'You haven't tasted my cooking yet,' Margherita replied.

Her apartment was on the second floor of a modern block close by the university. It was small: kitchen, living room, bathroom and two bedrooms, one of which – I could see through the open door – Margherita used as a study. Her home was even more untidy than her office. There were books everywhere – on shelves on the wall, on tables and almost every available flat surface, even piled up on the floor. We picked our way through into the living room.

'Excuse the mess,' Margherita said. 'I don't know how it gets like this. I'm sure it's nothing to do with me. I'm really a very organised sort of person.' She picked up a bundle of what looked like dirty laundry from an armchair and took it away into the kitchen.

'Make yourself at home,' she called. 'Would you like some wine?'

'Let me get it,' I said, following her into the kitchen.

'In the cupboard in the corner,' she said. 'Corkscrew in that drawer there.'

'Red or white?' I said, opening the cupboard to discover a rack of some twenty bottles.

'Whichever you like, I don't mind.'

I poured two glasses of red wine and handed her one. The kitchen was what I call 'comfortably dirty', but I didn't mind. I have always found there is something deeply disturbing about people with tidy homes. The washing up from breakfast, indeed from the previous evening, was still untouched in the sink, the draining board was stacked with crockery which had yet to be put away and the cooker top was in need of a serious clean. But it didn't feel unhygienic, just healthy evidence of a woman with better things to occupy her time than domestic chores.

'I know it's a tip,' Margherita said. 'But at least it's my tip.'

'I could do the washing up,' I said.

'You'll do no such thing. Go and sit down with your wine. I hate being watched while I'm cooking.'

I went back into the living room. The furniture was good quality, but well used – a stained wooden sideboard, a settee and armchair whose upholstery was faded and wearing thin. Against one of the walls was an old Bechstein upright piano with a battered casing and chipped legs. A book of Chopin Nocturnes was open on the music rest.

'You're a pianist?' I said.

Margherita appeared in the kitchen doorway. 'Well, I'm not sure pianist is the right word. Not if you heard me play.'

'You can't be that bad if you're playing Chopin.'

'Chopin might not agree with you,' she said dryly.

She disappeared back into the kitchen and I continued my exploration of her living room. There were family photos on the sideboard: a couple of wedding pictures showing two young women who, from their likeness to Margherita, I was sure were her daughters; others of the same two women with their own children, a couple of little girls and a little boy with his grandmother's eyes. I picked up the photograph containing the boy and walked over to the kitchen door. Margherita was chopping tomatoes on a worktop.

'Is this Stefano?' I asked.

Margherita glanced over her shoulder. 'Yes, that's him.'

'He's cute. He looks like you.'

'You think so?'

'So do your daughters.'

'Yes, everyone says that.'

'Do you see much of them?'

'My daughters? Yes, we're close. They have their own busy lives, but I manage to see them perhaps a couple of times a month. We speak on the telephone, of course. Sometimes I babysit for them.'

'You enjoy that?'

'I do actually. I like being a grandmother. It took me a while to come to terms with it – it makes you feel so old – but I enjoy it now. I get the pleasure of my grandchildren without the responsibility – and noise – of having to look after them.'

'Do they come here, your grandchildren?'

'Not if I can help it. Three overexcited children in a flat this size? How about yours?'

'I've got more space for them. And fields outside they can play in.'

'I'm envious. I used to have more room, but we sold the house when we divorced and I bought this place with my share of the proceeds. As you can see, it's barely big enough for all my belongings.'

Margherita put the chopped tomatoes into a bowl with some lettuce and avocado, then spread pieces of Parma ham out on two plates.

'You couldn't cut some bread, could you, Gianni? The knife's somewhere – try the sink.'

'How long were you married?' I asked as I sliced the loaf of bread.

'Twenty-nine years. It sounds a long time, doesn't it? You'd think if you'd lasted twenty-nine years you could survive a few more. I suppose we were the typical cliché – a couple who'd grown apart without noticing it. Lorenzo, true to the script, had found himself another woman. Younger, of course. He said I'd stopped "looking after him". He said he needed a woman who was "more attentive to his needs".' Margherita smiled wryly. She didn't sound remotely bitter. 'A simpering doormat was what he meant. I'm afraid I don't do simpering doormat.'

She took some knives and forks out of a drawer and placed them next to the plates.

'Come and sit down. The funniest thing was, when I told my mother we were separating – she'd never liked Lorenzo – you know what she said? "I told you it wouldn't last."'

The Conservatorio concert hall was very nearly full – pretty good for a student recital. I saw Clara and Giulia and several other members of Tomaso's family as well as a few people from the Milanese music mafia I recognised – a couple of agents, record executives, a concert promoter. Down near the front of the hall I was surprised to see Serafin's sultry mistress, Maddalena.

Sofia's programme was an intriguing mixture of pieces: a first half comprising Beethoven's Spring Sonata and the Bach unaccompanied partita, the second a selection of lighter works by Saint-Saëns, Sarasate, Wieniawski and Paganini. It had an old-fashioned feel to it. It was the kind of eclectic programme that the giants of the early twentieth century would have tackled – men like Ysaÿe, Kreisler and

Elman – but which you don't tend to see so often nowadays. Soloists today tend to favour weightier programmes, a more earnest selection of music which they feel reflects the seriousness of their purpose, their perception of themselves as profound artists. Well, they are artists, but they are entertainers too and I was glad to see that Sofia was willing to take a few risks to show off the full range of her talents.

The Beethoven was warm and lyrical, a duet in which the violin and piano parts wove in and out of each other like courting eels, slipping coyly over one another in a seductive dance, breaking apart for a time then coiling back into another lubricious embrace before their final magnificent union. I exaggerate perhaps, I lose control of my metaphors, I know, but I am an emotional man and the performance was a delight to me.

Then came the Bach, and from the first notes I knew that Sofia had what it took to be a great musician. She played with an authority, an intensity, almost a wild abandon that was mesmerising. I could feel the bodies around me stiffen, senses awaken, our eyes and ears and thoughts focused on nothing except that spine-tingling sound. The hall ceased to exist, the world beyond it was a memory from a different life. There was just a girl on a platform with a violin.

No one seemed to move, no one coughed or rustled their programmes. And when she started the final Chaconne – perhaps the greatest piece of writing for the violin in the entire repertoire – I felt a prickle like a rash creep over my skin and knew unequivocally that there was not a single person in the audience who was not feeling the same. Tears came into my eyes. This piece had been such a part of my life. Hearing it now took me back fifty years to my youth when as a thirteen-year-old boy I used to struggle clumsily through the chords, searching for the notes, searching for a voice which this young woman was now finding with such a sublime, intoxicating ease.

At the end there was a full half-minute's silence, the last chords melting away into the ether, before anyone clapped. Then the applause was like an explosion. One person stood up, then another. Soon the entire audience was on its feet. Sofia stood petrified to the spot for a few seconds, then she smiled and her eyes flickered around the hall, taking in the golden approbation.

Five times she left the platform and five times she returned for yet another bow before – our hands sore from clapping – we allowed her to escape our enthusiastic embrace. The doors were opened and the euphoric atmosphere permitted to slip away.

We rose from our seats to stretch our legs.

'That was just incredible,' Margherita said enthusiastically as we walked out into the open courtyard next to the concert hall. 'I don't know much about violinists, but she was electrifying.'

'Wasn't she just,' I agreed. 'One to watch for the future.'

'And you know her?'

'She's the granddaughter of my old friend, Tomaso. The one I told you about who was killed.'

'Ah, yes, I remember,' Margherita said softly.

'If he'd been here tonight, he would have been so proud of her.'

'Rightly so. She was terrific. But she has other family here?'

'Oh, yes. Her mother, her father, grandmother, lots of support.'

'Don't let me keep you from them, Gianni. I'm just going to the ladies'. I'll see you back inside.'

I glanced around the courtyard. Sofia's family must still have been in the recital hall. I wasn't sure I wanted to see them just at the moment. There was something too painful about being here without Tomaso – for both them and me. But a couple of metres away I noticed Serafin's mistress talking to a woman with a mass of unruly jet-black hair. The woman looked familiar, though I couldn't place her. They broke apart and the dark-haired woman moved away to talk to another group.

'Good evening, Maddalena,' I said.

Maddalena turned and looked at me, surprised and haughty like a wealthy courtesan whose under butler has had the temerity to address her.

'*Ciao* . . .' She waved a manicured hand helplessly as if she couldn't recall my name.

'I didn't know you liked music.'

'But of course. I adore it.'

She looked around for someone more interesting to talk to, but there were no obvious candidates nearby. She was stuck with me. She fanned herself with her programme.

'Who was the woman you were talking to just a moment ago?' I asked.

'Magda? You mean Magda Scamozzi?'

Of course, now I remembered. Ludovico Scamozzi's wife. She'd been a concert violinist herself once, if my memory served me right. But she'd given it up after meeting Scamozzi. As so often when two musicians – two anything – marry, the husband's career had taken precedence.

'She used to play, didn't she?' I said. 'What was her name then, her maiden name? Magda . . .'

'Erzsébet. But it wasn't her maiden name. She had another husband, before Ludovico.'

'She was a talented player, I seem to recall.'

Maddalena shrugged. 'I didn't know her then. I met her only through Vincenzo.'

'Where is Vincenzo tonight?'

160

'He's gone to the country,' Maddalena said waspishly.

So he was visiting his wife and family. Poor Serafin, I thought. No, poor wife and family.

'He's back from Venice then?' I said.

'He's been back for days.'

'Do you know Venice at all?' I asked casually.

Her hard blue eyes came to rest on my face. 'Not well,' she said. 'It's a long time since I was there.' She glanced away, spying an escape route. 'Excuse me, I see someone I know.'

I walked back to my seat in the hall and waited for Margherita to join me. When Sofia returned to the platform with her pianist there was a brief burst of applause, then a hush of anticipation descended over the audience. She played Saint-Saëns and Sarasate and Wieniawski, bravura pieces which are regularly dismissed as shallow and lightweight. But there was nothing shallow about Sofia's performance. Her interpretation transcended the glittering fireworks, drawing out the soul of the music and scattering it profligately across the auditorium. Fritz Kreisler once said that if he could live his life over again he would ignore the great warhorses of the repertoire and devote himself solely to light music. Sitting there among the rapt audience, I knew what he meant. There was a joy in these pieces, a joy in the way Sofia played them, that made my spirits soar.

Then she moved on to Paganini, the Moses Variations and *Le Streghe*, The Witches' Dance, the piece that more than any other of his compositions gave rise to the speculation that Paganini was in league with the Devil. Indeed, at one performance several witnesses – of apparently sound mind – swore they saw Satan himself directing the virtuoso's bow arm and fingers. I've attempted the piece and, believe me, it would take more than the Devil at my elbow to enable me to play it. But Sofia was in need of no assistance, supernatural or otherwise. She was in her element, the runs and harmonics and all the other fiendish contortions executed as if they were no more difficult than a simple one-octave scale. This was stratospheric violin playing where technique wasn't in the fingers but in the mind, the difference between someone who played the notes and someone who played the music. Sofia went for it. She was herself and it was an exhilarating privilege to behold.

There was no respectful silence at the end. The applause and shouts of approval erupted before the final chord had died away. Then we were on our feet again, giving her another standing ovation which she acknowledged with a bow and a shy smile of pleasure. If the purpose of music is to make the heart sing, then she had transformed our cardiac organs into a heavenly choir.

'Do you want to come backstage with me?' I said to Margherita, leaning over to make myself heard above the noise of the applause.

She shook her head. 'I'd feel an intruder. I'll wait for you outside.'

I knew Sofia would have her family and friends with her, perhaps a few agents too, circling her predatorily. But after our conversation of the afternoon I felt I should congratulate her on her performance.

The door to the green room was open. As I came down the corridor, I could hear Scamozzi's grating metallic voice.

' . . . that's something you need to work on,' he was saying.

I paused on the threshold. Sofia was standing in the middle of the room looking tired and crestfallen.

' . . . some of the intonation was awry, you should watch that, and your bow arm tightened up near the end of the Saint-Saëns. Little things but they all make a difference . . .'

Sofia saw me and her face broke into a smile. Scamozzi turned and scowled at me, then swung back to continue his post mortem examination of her recital. I stepped forward, interrupting his flow.

'Magnificent,' I said. 'Absolutely magnificent.' I took Sofia's hand. In the process I may have trodden on Scamozzi's foot, but if I did it was purely accidental.

'That was a triumph,' I continued. 'You should be very proud.'

'As for the Wieniawski . . .' Scamozzi persisted, but Sofia was no longer listening. Somehow our positions had shifted so that Scamozzi was now talking to my back.

'You are going to go far,' I said warmly. 'In years to come I will boast that I was at your début recital.'

'Thank you.'

She was in a daze, lost for words. She would probably remember nothing of this, so overwhelmed was she by the response of the audience and her relief that the recital had gone so flawlessly. By tomorrow it would all seem a wash of smiling faces and murmured goodwill, the details lost in the warm flood of euphoric recall.

Other people were coming into the room now. A cascade of thick black hair brushed past me and I heard a woman's impassioned voice.

'Sofia, darling. So good, so good. Unbelievable.'

It was Magda Scamozzi, as fulsome in her praise as her husband was reticent. She threw her arms around Sofia and hugged her tight.

'What can I say?' she said, her Italian coloured with the inflections of Eastern Europe. 'You are a star in the making. They loved you. Didn't they, Ludovico?'

'Well, I don't think we should get too carried away . . .'

Scamozzi began, but was cut short by his effusive wife.

'Nonsense, of course we are going to get carried away. She was perfect, perfect. This is your night, Sofia. You float up into the clouds, enjoy the moment. You are young, full of promise. Wallow in your triumph. You will have many more in the future, but none of them will taste as sweet as this. The champagne, Ludovico. What did I do with the champagne? Ah, there it is. Fetch some glasses, we must celebrate . . . Ludovico, the glasses.'

Another wave of wellwishers enveloped Sofia. I saw Clara and Giulia. I took Clara's hands in mine. She forced a weak smile. Her eyes were moist. Neither of us said anything. We didn't need to. Our thoughts were the same. She turned away, reaching for her handkerchief. I blinked away my own tears.

'He should have been here,' Clara said indistinctly.

'He was here in spirit,' I replied. 'He always will be.'

She wiped her eyes and nodded. 'He would have been so happy.'

'I know.'

'I mustn't cry. It will upset Sofia. Wasn't she good?'

'She was superb.' I glanced around. 'She's waiting for you.'

'Come and see me, Gianni.'

'I will.'

I watched her go to her granddaughter and embrace her. I felt out of place. This was a family moment. I paused to compose myself and went back out of the room. Margherita was waiting for me in the courtyard. We walked out through the gates of the Conservatorio.

'Can I give you a lift home?' I said.

'Don't worry, I'll get a taxi,' Margherita said. She took a scrap of paper and a pen from her shoulder-bag. 'Give me your phone number.'

She wrote down my number, then stepped closer.

'Thank you for a wonderful evening, Gianni. We must do it again.'

She reached up and kissed me on the cheek. I inhaled her perfume, felt the touch of her lips, her body close to mine. Then she was gone, walking away down the street with her shoulder-bag swinging against her hip.

9

If anyone gave the lie to the notion that the English are a cold, reserved race it was Rudy Weigert. Rudy, admittedly, was perhaps not a typical Englishman. Though born in the country, his parents were Austrian Jews who had come to England before the war, and Rudy – in both appearance and temperament – had as many of the Central European characteristics of his ancestors as he did of his birthplace. But nonetheless I still thought of him as an Englishman, and a warmer, more demonstrative and emotionally open man it was difficult to imagine. He was standing now in the doorway of his office, his arms outstretched and a gleam of pleasure in his eyes.

'Gianni! Gianni, my old friend,' he cried. 'Why didn't you tell me? Come in, come in.'

I stepped over the threshold and felt Rudy's arms embrace me in a welcoming bear hug – if bear is the apposite description for someone of Rudy's diminutive height and gargantuan girth. I am not a particularly tall man, but the top of Rudy's head came to only just above my solar plexus. The wobbling expanse of his stomach between us made me feel as if I were being squeezed against a large balloon filled with warm water.

'You should have told me you were coming,' Rudy said reproachfully. 'How long have you been here?'

'I only flew in this morning. I came straight here from the airport.'

'It's good to see you. Come and sit down. You'll have a drink, of course.'

Without waiting for a reply, Rudy waddled over to the large cabinet behind his desk and filled – and I mean filled – two glasses with malt whisky. He handed a glass to me and beamed with a real, unconcealed affection.

'It's been too long, Gianni. You should come more often. Where are you staying? We've always got a bed for you, you know that.'

'I'm not on my own, Rudy.'

He leered at me. 'No? You're a dark horse, Gianni. Who is she?'

'It's not a woman. It's a friend from Cremona.'

'Well, where is he? I want to meet him.'

'He's trying to find somewhere to park our car.'

'Round here? He may be some time. You want a smoke?'

Rudy flipped open a humidor the size of a pirate's chest and extracted a couple of fat Cuban cigars. As a rule, I never smoke, but I'm always prepared to make an exception for one of Rudy's cigars. He gave me a light, then sat down on the sofa at the side of his office, gesturing to me to join him. I squeezed into what little space remained and settled back in the soft cushions.

'This has really made my day,' Rudy said. 'You're looking well. It must be all that sunshine and pasta. We're a little short on the sun here, but I'm doing my best with the pasta.'

He patted his stomach fondly and laughed, his face creasing into a squashy sponge of hollows and double chins.

'Your timing is perfect,' he continued. 'I've a fiddle you can look at for me. I'd value your opinion on it.'

I was flattered. Rudy was his auction house's principal string instrument expert, a world authority on violins.

'Of course,' I said. 'What is it?'

'Well, it's labelled Nicolò Amati, a good, authentic-looking label too. But I'm not sure. The date on the label is 1631. That makes me wonder.'

Violins from the early 1630s are extremely rare. Very few seem to have been made then, probably because the plague was sweeping across northern Italy. Nicolò Amati's father, Girolamo, himself a fine violin-maker, was killed in the epidemic in 1630 and two years later Maggini succumbed to the same disease. People were more interested in staying alive than buying violins.

'You think it's a fake?' I said.

'The violin's undoubtedly old. I think the label's been changed. From the purfling, the roughness of finish on the scroll, I think it may be an Andrea Guarneri, but I'd like your view. I'll show it to you later. How's your whisky?'

'Big,' I said.

'The way it should be.' He waved his cigar expansively. 'You're over for the sales, I assume. Something in the catalogue you've got your eye on?'

'No, we're on our way to the north. Derbyshire.'

'Nice. You'll like it up there. Wonderful countryside. Violins?'

'We're looking at some old letters. Just a sideline we're following up.' I paused. 'I wanted to ask you a favour, Rudy.'

'Fire away.'

'You've got databases you can check, sources of information that aren't available to me. I'm trying to find out something about a Maggini violin – the Snake's Head Maggini. You know the one I mean?'

'I certainly do. It was one of ours.'

I stared at him. *'You* sold it?'

'Five, six years ago. I remember it well. It was one of the best Magginis we've ever had. There was a lot of interest, I seem to recall, a lot of bidding. I'll check for you.'

Rudy went across to the computer on his desk and tapped a few keys.

'This is just a summary. I have the full file on paper somewhere. Here we are. Yes, autumn sales, 1998. It went for £120,000. Buyer – your old friend, Vincenzo Serafin.'

I started. 'Serafin?'

'You seem surprised.'

'No . . . well, maybe a little. But I shouldn't be. I know he goes to auctions for all sorts of clients.'

Rudy came back to the settee. 'He won't have been bidding on his own account. He'll have had a buyer lined up, a nice little commission arranged for himself.'

'Oh, he did,' I said. 'He was buying it for Enrico Forlani.'

Rudy exhaled a cloud of cigar smoke very slowly and raised one of his black caterpillar eyebrows.

'The *late* Enrico Forlani, you mean. This is starting to sound interesting.'

'The Maggini disappeared from Forlani's collection after he was killed.'

'Taken by the killer?'

'It's possible.'

'Just the Maggini?'

'Yes.'

'Even more interesting. And the rest of the collection? What's happening to that?'

I chuckled. 'I'm afraid a few other people are ahead of you on that one.'

'Serafin?'

'He's certainly keen.'

169

'Damn, the little shit.' Rudy pulled a face. 'A bit unseemly really. Not something a great auction house like ours would do.'

'No, of course not,' I agreed solemnly.

'We'd always allow a decent interval to elapse before we made an approach to the family.'

'How long is a decent interval?'

'Depends how long the body takes to cool,' Rudy said.

'Do you remember who else was bidding for the Maggini?' I said.

'Not on the floor. But I seem to remember there were a number of telephone bidders competing with Serafin.'

'Will you have any documentation on the phone bidders?'

'Of course. It might take a bit of digging out, but somewhere we should have a note of the instructions. How long are you going to be in Derbyshire?'

'I'm not sure. One, two days.'

'Call back in on your way home. I'll have the information for you then.'

'I'd like anything else you have on the violin too, if it's not too much trouble. Who was selling it, what its provenance was.'

Rudy gave a nod and sucked on his cigar.

'You think Forlani was murdered for his Maggini?'

'I don't know why he was murdered,' I said.

It was late afternoon when we began our ascent into the Pennines. I had visited England many times before – though only London and the south-east – but nothing had prepared me for the strange terrain we now encountered. The valleys and lower slopes of the hills seemed familiar, unthreatening – green meadows enclosed by dry-stone walls, copses of broadleaf trees, a reservoir gleaming in the evening light. But as we climbed the twisting road, the woods and fields gave way to dark swathes of coniferous plantations that seemed entirely alien to the landscape. The light began to change. Black clouds obscured the sun. A fine spray of drizzle spattered the windows of our hired car. Guastafeste turned on the windscreen wipers, then the headlights.

We climbed higher, the plantations far below us now. The road took a sharp turn, the gradient suddenly steeper, then we crested the brow of the hill and levelled out. There before us was a vast expanse of moorland, a sea of undulating heather and peat bog, its shores fringed by stark gritstone escarpments. The cloud was low and unbroken, smothering the horizon in grey mist. I could feel the wind buffeting the sides of the car, feel the damp, menacing atmosphere seeping in through the doors. I'd never seen such a bleak, inhospitable environment.

'She doesn't live up here, surely,' Guastafeste said. 'No one can live up here.'

I checked my notes, the directions Mrs Colquhoun had given me on the telephone when I'd rung her from London.

'It would appear she does,' I said. 'Look out for a turning to the left.'

The mist was closing in, drifting in skeins across the carriageway, creeping around the sides of the car like some malign spectre. Guastafeste slowed, leaning forward in his seat to get a better view of the road.

'Here,' I said.

We turned off on to a smaller, narrower road, still metalled but without white lines down the centre. The windscreen began to steam up. I turned on the fan to clear it.

'Right at these crossroads,' I said.

'I don't like this,' Guastafeste said. 'I can hardly see the road.'

'Just keep out of the ditches,' I said. 'We go in one of those and we'll never get out.'

Guastafeste turned the headlights on full beam, trying to penetrate the swirling fog, but the light just reflected back off the mist, making it even harder to see. He dipped the lights again and eased his foot off the throttle.

'We're looking for a sign,' I said. 'She said it was just before the track to the house.'

I saw a pool of peaty water in a hollow beside the road, its surface black and oily. Then a pole with a weathered board on top loomed up out of the haze. I could just make out the faded white painted letters: Highfield Hall.

'This is it.'

The track was unmade, full of deep potholes and ruts. Guastafeste took it slowly, negotiating the obstacles as if they were landmines. Tendrils of mist drifted across the bonnet of the car, clawing at the paintwork, at the windscreen, ethereal in the diffused light from our head-lamps.

'What the . . .' Guastafeste braked heavily as a sheep scampered across in front of us and disappeared over the heather.

We started to drop down off the plateau, the track descending into a shallow basin. The mist cleared for a second and ahead of us I caught a glimpse of a large house. Two rough-hewn stone pillars passed by on either side of the car – a gateway without gates – and then we were turning, following the track round to the front of the house. Guastafeste killed the engine and we sat for a moment, looking at the house through the sheen of rain on the wind-screen. It was an austere three-storey building constructed from blocks of the same orange gritstone as the escarp-ments up on the plateau. The roof tiles too were gritstone, thin slices of rock coated with moss.

'Just my idea of a cosy English country cottage,' Guastafeste said.

I pushed open my door and slid out, reaching back in for my raincoat. I buttoned it up tight against the biting wind. We'd left Rudy's house in high summer, yet somehow contrived to arrive here in what seemed like winter.

We climbed the steps to the front door. There was a palpable air of dilapidation about the house so intense that it felt as if it had long ago been abandoned, its walls and windows and roof left to crumble and return to the earth. Guastafeste glanced at me and gave a shiver.

'I wouldn't want to be here after dark,' he said.

He lifted the big brass knocker cast in the shape of a bear's head and hammered on the door a few times. We could hear the sound echoing in the hall on the other side. We waited. Guastafeste knocked again. Moments later a woman's voice called out faintly, 'I'm coming,' then the heavy wooden door swung open to reveal an elderly lady with a cat under each arm.

'I'm so sorry. Have you been waiting long? It's hard to hear at the back of the house. Do come in.'

She bent down and released the cats from her grasp.

'Off you go, Timmy. And no more mice tonight, remember.'

The cats poked their heads out of the door, took one look at the weather and scurried back into the house.

'Ah, well, who can blame them?' Mrs Colquhoun said sympathetically. She closed the door and turned to us. She was wearing a thick woolly cardigan and tweed skirt, both glistening with silvery cat hair.

We introduced ourselves, and Guastafeste showed his police identity card.

'How nice to meet you.' Mrs Colquhoun extended a

173

bony hand to each of us in turn. She looked frail, but there was nothing weak about her grip.

'You'll be wanting a cup of tea after your journey,' she said. 'Follow me.'

We went down a long, draughty corridor to a sitting room at the rear of the house.

'Make yourselves at home,' Mrs Colquhoun said and disappeared through a door.

We looked around for somewhere to sit. There were two large, threadbare sofas and three armchairs in the room, but every single centimetre of them was occupied by cats: black and white cats, ginger cats, tabby cats, grey and white cats, striped cats. There must have been twenty or thirty of them. They looked at us haughtily, as if to say, well, we're not moving, this is *our* house. We stayed on our feet.

Guastafeste glanced around, sniffing the air. Whatever scent of its own the room might have had was submerged beneath the sour, overwhelming feline odour. There were spreading patches of damp on the walls and ceiling, the wallpaper was peeling and green with mould in places, but we could smell none of that. All we could smell was cat.

I walked over to the windows. There were three of them – big bay windows with a view over a Yorkstone terrace. In the centre of the terrace was a raised stone pool with a statue of a woman on a plinth in the middle. There was no water in the pool, just a thick coating of moss and algae. Beyond the terrace were a couple of gnarled trees, twisted and stunted by the wind, then a lawn of yellowish grass, an incongruous man-made oasis in the moorland desert whose vegetation was already creeping in around the edges, threatening to reclaim the garden and absorb it back into the wilderness. All houses have a feeling of their own. This one seemed sad, an edifice eaten through with melancholy and decay.

174

'Now, isn't this nice?' Mrs Colquhoun had come back in with a tray of tea things. 'Please, sit down . . .' She looked around at the cats. 'Oh, I'm sorry.'

'We didn't like to disturb them,' I explained.

'Don't worry about that. They're only cats.' She moved towards the sofa, making shooing noises. 'Timmy, off you go. Go on. You too, Timmy. And you, Timmy.'

Three cats rose lazily to their feet, tilting their heads back with insolent pride, before slipping down from the sofa and sauntering away across the room.

'Are all your cats called Timmy?' I said.

'Oh, yes, every one.'

'Isn't that a little confusing?'

'Not to me. I used to give them all different names, but I could never remember which one was which so now I call them all Timmy. It's so much simpler. Please, sit down.'

The cushions were still warm from the cats. Already I could see hairs on the sleeves of my jacket. Mrs Colquhoun poured the tea and handed round the cups and a plate of buttered scones.

'I made them this morning,' she said. 'After you'd rung. Scones are so much nicer on the day they're baked, don't you think?'

'It's very kind of you,' I said.

'I don't get much opportunity to bake these days. It makes a change to have visitors.'

'Do you live all alone, Mrs Colquhoun?'

'Well, I have the cats, of course. But their conversation is very limited.'

'It's a big house.'

'Far too big. We used to have a small place in Castleton, over on the other side of the Peaks. Do you know Castleton? No, you wouldn't, of course, you're Italian.

175

Charming little village. It's famous for its caverns and Blue John.'

'Blue John?'

'It's a type of fluorspar – rock crystal. Very beautiful. The lead miners who first found it were French. *Bleu et jaune*, they called it, because the crystal is streaked with blue and yellow veins. The English weren't very good at French – *plus ça change* – so they called it Blue John.'

'Oh.'

Guastafeste was chewing noisily on a scone.

'What did you say these were called?' he asked.

'Scones,' Mrs Colquhoun said.

'They are very good.'

Mrs Colquhoun smiled. 'Thank you. Do help yourself to another. Then Edward – my late husband – inherited this place. That would have been about twenty years ago. It was falling apart then, but I'm afraid it's got much worse since. I simply can't afford to do anything about it.'

'It is . . .' I searched for something complimentary to say about the house,' . . . very old.'

'It dates back to the eighteenth century. So does the damp, I fear. And the ghosts.'

'There are ghosts?'

'Oh, yes. Long ago the mistress of the house had a baby. One evening the nanny accidentally dropped the child over the banisters from the first-floor landing and it was killed. Both the nanny and the mother are said to roam the house at night, calling for the dead infant. Sometimes I've heard the sound of a child screaming. More tea?'

She took my cup and refilled it.

'So don't worry if you hear strange noises later.'

'Later?'

'You're staying the night, of course.'

* * *

We remained in the sitting room for a further hour. Mrs Colquhoun – obviously starved of conversation – seemed anxious to make the most of our visit and we were happy to keep her company. Or at least I was. Guastafeste, struggling with his English, said very little. But he did his valiant best with the scones.

Then Mrs Colquhoun said, 'Shall I show you the letters now?'

We followed her down the corridor and up the oak-panelled staircase to the first floor. The smell of cat was less noticeable up here, but the damp was more pronounced. The high ceiling, decorated with ornate plaster mouldings, was black and mottled with fungus, the air tainted with a moist staleness that lingered in the nostrils.

The staircase to the second floor was at the back of the house, designed, I guessed, for use only by servants whose quarters would originally have been in the attics. It was steep and uncarpeted, flanked by grimy walls and a water-stained ceiling. Mrs Colquhoun led us up the stairs and along a dark, oppressive corridor to a room which was crammed with cardboard boxes and piles of junk.

'They're in there,' she said, indicating an old wooden chest.

'Signor Rainaldi,' I said. 'Did he know the letters were here?'

'Oh, no, how could he know that?' Mrs Colquhoun replied. 'I told him about them when he rang me. He was interested in any old papers I might have had, you see.'

'Did he say why? Or how he'd come to contact you?'

'Only that he was doing some historical research.'

'Research into what?'

'Something to do with violins, I believe he said. An Italian nobleman who had had a great collection.'

'Count Cozio di Salabue?' I said.

Mrs Colquhoun looked uncertain. 'That might have been it. I'm very bad with names. But didn't you say on the phone that he was a friend of yours? Why don't you ask him?'

I glanced at Guastafeste. I wasn't sure how to handle this. 'I'm afraid he's dead,' I said.

'Dead? Good gracious me. He was hardly very old. How?'

'An accident,' I said, deciding that the truth might be too upsetting for her.

'How awful. He was such a nice man. He brought me a box of chocolates, you know.'

'Yes, you mentioned that on the telephone.' I was annoyed with myself. I'd intended bringing her a gift but forgotten.

'There isn't much of value up here in the attics, but he was very interested in the papers in that chest. I don't know why, they're just old letters.'

'Do you know which ones he was particularly interested in?'

'Well, he photocopied one or two of them at the village shop, in Highfield. I went down with him. But I don't know which ones they were.'

'He returned the documents?'

'Oh, yes. I saw him put them back in the chest. I'll leave you to it, shall I? Dinner's at eight, will that be all right?'

'You don't need to give us dinner, Mrs Colquhoun,' I said. 'We can go out and find something to eat.'

'Nonsense, you are my guests. You've come all the way from Italy. The least I can do is offer you some good English hospitality.'

She went out of the room. Guastafeste knelt down and opened the lid of the chest. Inside it was almost overflowing with yellowing papers. Guastafeste lifted out one of the papers. It was brittle and brown at the edges and caked with dust. Guastafeste inclined the paper towards the window and squinted at it closely. It was almost dark outside. The window was small and smeared with dirt. There was nothing like enough light to work by. I stood up and switched on the overhead light, but the bulb blew immediately. The attic seemed dingier than ever.

'Tomaso probably went through the entire chest,' Guastafeste said gloomily. 'That's a hell of a lot of papers to check.'

'Let's try to narrow it down. Concentrate on those that look as if they've been recently examined. Maybe the ones near the top.'

Guastafeste rummaged delicately through the chest, taking out the bundles of papers one by one and placing them on the floor. They were very fragile, some so discoloured with age they looked like Biblical parchment. We divided them up into piles, separating out the loose documents. One piece of paper was so cracked and ancient it fell to pieces in Guastafeste's hand.

'Careful,' I said, collecting up the bits and trying to fit them back together like a jigsaw puzzle.

'What exactly are we looking for?' Guastafeste said.

'Letters, possibly in Italian. Particularly ones with a Casale Monferrato address at the top and Giovanni Michele Anselmi di Briata's signature at the bottom.'

We took a pile each. Sorting through the documents was harder than it sounded. They were all handwritten, of course, and some of the writing was so unclear it was next to impossible to work out what language they were in, never mind read the words. In addition, they were so faded and wrinkled with age that even the ones where the handwriting had originally been clear were now difficult to decipher.

Guastafeste held up a curling sheet which looked as if it had been rescued half-burnt from a fire.

'This is impossible, Gianni. We can't even begin to read them in this light. Why don't we take the chest downstairs?'

'Let's leave it till morning,' I said. 'It's late, we've driven a long way today. Let's look at them again when we're fresher.'

We made our way down the attic stairs which creaked disconcertingly as if they were about to collapse.

'Do we have to stay here?' Guastafeste whispered. 'Can't we find a hotel or a guesthouse instead?'

'We don't want to offend her. It's only for one night.'

The cats were back in their places on the sofa in the sitting room. We made a half-hearted attempt to evict them again, but they just twitched their whiskers disdainfully and went back to sleep. We left them alone and wandered off to explore the house. We found Mrs Colquhoun in the kitchen, a large, stone-flagged room with an enormous oak table and a blackened cooking range which emitted a welcome warmth. The house was distinctly chilly but there didn't appear to be any heating in the other rooms.

'Ah, you're just in time,' Mrs Colquhoun said. 'I've made you some fine traditional English cuisine.'

I caught the momentary look of horror on Guastafeste's face. If anything is guaranteed to make even the most robust Italian quake, it is the juxtaposition of the words 'cuisine' and 'English'. But the smell from the large casserole dish Mrs Colquhoun was removing from the oven was rich and inviting. Even more reassuringly, there were three bottles of red wine on the table. This was a good sign.

We ate in the kitchen, which was a relief. Guastafeste and I had found what appeared to be the dining room earlier and, leaving aside its glacial temperature, the smell of damp and cat pee from the rows of litter trays it contained would have been more than enough to put anyone off their food.

'The letters in the chest,' I said as we ate our hotpot and dumplings. 'Where did they come from?'

'My husband's family,' Mrs Colquhoun replied. 'They were up there when we moved into the house. We had a look at them once but didn't get very far. Edward was always intending to sort through them but somehow never got round to it. You know how things are. How is your hotpot?'

'Very good, thank you. We think there may be letters in the chest from a firm of cloth merchants in Italy. Why would your husband's family have correspondence with an Italian cloth merchant?'

'That was the family business. They were mill owners in Manchester. The wool trade at first, then later cotton. Edward's great-great-great – I forget how many greats – grandfather, Thomas Colquhoun, started the firm back in the eighteenth century. Made a fortune. He became very grand, built this house as his country retreat, to escape from the noise and grime of his factories.'

'Here?' I said. 'But it's so cold and bleak.'

'Thomas was something of a romantic, I believe. He liked the wildness of the moors.'

'And he did business with Italy?'

'With everywhere, I think. He was a very successful businessman. He filled his house with fine paintings and furniture, gave weekend parties, courted the aristocracy with his money. He was the epitome of the self-made English country gentleman.'

'The business still exists?'

'Alas, no.' Mrs Colquhoun waved an apologetic hand

181

around the kitchen. 'If it did, would I live like this? Unable to heat the place, to repair the leaking roof. No, the fortune disappeared long ago. Squandered by successive generations of idle young men. My husband made his own way in the world and when his father died inherited nothing but debts and this liability of a house.'

'Have you considered selling it?' I said.

'Oh, I couldn't sell it. It was Edward's family house. He would have wanted it to go to our son. Besides, who would buy a house as dilapidated as this?'

'You have a son?'

'In America. He rarely comes home.'

She took the lid off the casserole in the centre of the table. I sensed it was a distraction, a way of closing off a topic of conversation she did not wish to discuss. 'More hotpot, Signor Castiglione?'

'Thank you, but no.'

'And your friend?'

Guastafeste looked up from his plate.

'Would you like more?' I asked him in Italian.

'Well, if it's going . . .'

We stayed up late, listening to Mrs Colquhoun's reminiscences and drinking rather more of her wine than was good for us. Then she showed us to our room.

'I hope you don't mind, but I've put you in together. This is the only guest bedroom that's really habitable.'

I lay awake for a long time, listening out for the ghosts. But the only strange noises I heard were Guastafeste snoring.

10

We spent the next morning back upstairs in the attic, sifting methodically through the chest of papers. It was a strange, eclectic collection of documents. Some were business correspondence relating to the firm of Thomas Colquhoun and Sons, others were more personal family letters. Glancing at the contents of the papers, it was difficult to see why they'd been kept. They seemed very ordinary, mostly downright dull records of commercial transactions or mundane household matters. Perhaps this was all that remained of a larger, more interesting archive of documents that over the years had been misplaced or disposed of. What we didn't find, however, were any letters from Italy.

'They're not here, are they?' Guastafeste said despondently as he examined yet another dusty piece of paper.

'Don't give up hope,' I replied. 'There are plenty more to look at.'

At one o'clock Mrs Colquhoun came up to inform us that lunch was ready. We followed her back down the attic stairs and along the landing. It was then that I noticed the painting on the wall. I don't know how I'd missed it before. Something about its location maybe, something about the light on the landing that tended to obscure it. But I saw it now, a canvas about a metre square in a gilt rococo frame.

'That's one of my favourites,' Mrs Colquhoun said, seeing me pause to look up at the painting.

The canvas was old, its cracked surface badly in need of a clean and restoration. But despite its poor condition, the quality of the artist seemed to shine through the layers of accumulated dirt. It depicted a young man in a music room – from the man's dress and the furniture I put the date as somewhere around the beginning of the eighteenth century. There was an elaborately decorated virginal occupying one side of the painting, but the eye was drawn irresistibly towards the young man, who was standing before a music stand with a violin cradled in his arms. The neck of the instrument was gripped in his left hand, his right forearm curled comfortably around the lower bouts, a bow dangling loosely from his fingers. The attention to detail was striking. I could see the grain of the wood in the violin's belly, beneath the sheen of the varnish. There were flecks of rosin between the fingerboard and tailpiece, a trace of a gouge mark on the scroll. The whole thing was so perfect I felt as if I could have reached up with my hand and plucked the violin from the canvas.

'Who painted this?' I asked, trying to make out the illegible signature in the bottom left-hand corner.

'Cesare Garofalo,' Mrs Colquhoun replied.

I didn't recognise the name, but the painting was unmistakably Italian rather than English. The man's features, the colour of his skin were Mediterranean and through the window at one side of the music room was a view of cypress trees and a red-brick church that could only have been Italian.

'Do you know who the man in the picture is?' I said.

Mrs Colquhoun shook her head. 'I'm afraid not. Apart from the artist, I know almost nothing about it. It's always been on the wall here. Edward was very fond of it. He wasn't musical himself, but his ancestors all played.'

'The violin?'

'I believe so. Even Thomas Colquhoun, the founder of the family firm, made time to play chamber music. He was said to have been a rather fine violinist.'

'Do you still have his instrument?'

'No, his violins – he had several – were sold off long ago. Well before we inherited this house. It's very lifelike, isn't it?'

'Very.'

Guastafeste came up to my shoulder and peered curiously at the painting.

'You recognise the violin?' he said.

'The maker, you mean?' I said. 'Yes, it's a Guarneri "del Gesù".'

'How is your research coming along?' Mrs Colquhoun enquired over lunch.

We were in the kitchen eating sausages with hot English mustard and a potato salad sprinkled with chives from the Hall's herb garden.

'Slowly,' I said. 'Do you know why the papers are up there? Why they were kept?'

'Why do families keep anything?' Mrs Colquhoun said with a shrug. 'Sentimental attachment sometimes, but more often than not it's out of laziness or inertia. The Colquhouns have always been notorious for never throwing anything away.'

'But there must have been more at one time. The family business must have accrued thousands of documents over the years. Why does only one chest remain?'

185

'Pure accident, I would say. Most of the business correspondence was never kept here anyway, it was filed at the
firm's offices in Manchester. A lot of that was destroyed in
a fire back in the mid-nineteenth century. The chest upstairs
wasn't retained for any particular reason that I know of.'

'Have you ever heard of an Italian firm named Anselmi
di Briata?' I asked.

'No, I don't think so.'

'We have reason to believe that letters from the firm
were in that chest. We think it was those letters that Signor
Rainaldi photocopied. Yet we can't find them.'

Mrs Colquhoun gave a start of surprise. 'Well, they
should be there. I told you, I saw him put them back.'

'Are you sure they were the same letters?'

'What else would they have been? They were very old.
He handled them very carefully. I can picture them now, all
yellow and curling. Yes, he definitely put them back.'

We returned to the attic after lunch and resumed our
examination of the papers in the chest.

'Maybe Mrs Colquhoun's mistaken and Tomaso didn't
put the letters back,' Guastafeste said.

'Maybe.'

'If he had, they'd have been at the top, surely?'

'Who knows? This whole chest is a complete mess.'

We were down to the last layer of documents now, the
ones at the very bottom of the chest. Guastafeste lifted out
a pile and placed it on the floor between us. I picked up a
bundle of papers tied together with red ribbon. There was
a pale line across the outer document where the paper had
been protected from discolouration by the ribbon. But the
ribbon was no longer directly over that line.

'This bundle has been untied, and then fastened together
again,' I said. 'And fairly recently too.'

I undid the knot in the ribbon and carefully separated

the documents. There were four of them, as fragile as dried leaves. I saw the signature at the bottom of the first letter and felt a tingling sensation creep up my spine.

'Found them,' I said softly.

'Really?' Guastafeste leaned across and glanced at the letters. 'They're in English. You'll have to translate them for me.'

'If I can read them.'

I picked the letters up and carried them nearer the window where the light was better. Three of the letters were written in the same hand, the fourth in a different one. I peered more closely at them, trying to decipher the dates at the top. One looked like February 16, 1803. Another seemed to read July, 1803, though the exact day was unclear, and a third was dated September, 1803. The fourth letter – written in the different hand – was harder to read. The handwriting was spidery and untidy and in places the ink was badly smudged, making the words illegible. It appeared to have been written in 1804. All four letters were addressed to Thomas Colquhoun in Manchester and had Giovanni Michele Anselmi di Briata's address at the top and his florid signature at the bottom.

I started with the earliest of the letters, translating it into Italian as I went along.

'"*Distinguished Sir,*"' I read, '"*Please accept my most profound apologies for the delay in replying to your letter of December last. Events here, as you can imagine, have not been conducive to the proper arrangement of our business affairs. The state of uncertainty may continue for some months, so I would beg you to be patient . . .*"'

'What events is he talking about?' Guastafeste asked.

'The war between the French and the Austrians for control of northern Italy, I imagine. It would have disrupted most of the commerce of the time.'

The next few paragraphs of the letter dealt with mundane business matters – the ordering and transportation of bales of wool and cloth from England to Italy, banker's arrangements and so on – which had no relevance to our enquiries.

'Ah, this looks more interesting,' I said, and read aloud the next section.

'*"As to the delicate matter you addressed in your letter, I am instructed by His Excellency to express his regret that the situation has not yet been satisfactorily resolved, and to crave your indulgence in allowing him a little more time to set matters right. I have been instructed to write to Signor Carli, which I shall do with the greatest expedition, and I hope that in due course I shall have a more substantial reply for you. I remain, Sir, your most faithful servant, Gio Michele Anselmi di Briata."*'

I put the letter down on the top of one of the cardboard boxes that were under the attic window.

'What was interesting about that?' Guastafeste said. 'There wasn't a mention of any violin.'

'True,' I said. 'But look at the names. "His Excellency" and "Signor Carli".'

'And who were they?'

' "His Excellency" can only be one person – Count Cozio di Salabue.'

'And Signor Carli?'

'Carlo Carli, the count's Milanese banker, and incidentally a fine amateur violinist, good enough to play quartets with Paganini. When the Austrians and the French were fighting over Piedmont, Count Cozio had his violin collection removed for safekeeping from his country seat at Salabue, near Casale Monferrato, to Carlo Carli's home in Milan.'

I turned to read out the next letter. This was more specific. After the usual salutations and some discussion relating to the cloth trade, Michele Anselmi had written: '"*I must now address myself to the question of His Excellency's debts. I have been in communication with Signor Carli and regret to have to inform you that circumstances are but little changed since I last wrote to you. If anything, the situation has worsened. The confiscation of certain properties by the French military command has caused His Excellency much embarrassment . . .*"'

I paused. The next few words were difficult to read. I peered at the text. 'I'm not sure what comes next. *Regret*. It looks like regret. *I regret . . .* something. *I regret* something, something, *unable to repay.* No, the rest is too smudged.'

'Leave it for the time being and go on,' Guastafeste suggested.

I moved on to the next paragraph. '"*However, His Excellency, knowing your great interest in music, asks if you would be willing to accept an item from his collection in lieu of payment.*"'

I stopped reading. The rest of the letter was just a blur of ink. The paper was stained as if water had been spilt on it. But it didn't matter. We both knew that we'd just heard the most important bit.

'An item from his collection?' Guastafeste said excitedly. 'Now we're getting somewhere. What's next?'

It was the third letter that contained the real meat.

'"*I have made all the necessary arrangements to despatch the violin within the week,*"' I read out Michele Anselmi's words. '"*My son, Paolo, who is undertaking business on my behalf in France, will take the violin as far as Paris where he will arrange for a courier to transport the instrument to England. His Excellency asks me to express his gratitude for your understanding and patience in this matter, and feels assured that you will not find anything lacking in the instrument. It is one of the finest in his collection – indeed one of the finest the Master ever made – and has barely been touched since the day it left the workshop in Cremona. His Excellency is sorry to part with it, but he wishes you great joy in the playing of it."'*

'That's it,' Guastafeste said. 'That's the violin we're looking for. It was sent to England, to Thomas Colquhoun. Does it not say who the maker was? If it was one of the finest in Cozio's collection, it must have been a Stradivari surely. What do you think?'

'No, it doesn't mention the maker, just the words "the Master", which may mean Stradivari.'

'So Thomas Colquhoun had the violin. What if it's still here at Highfield Hall? I know Mrs Colquhoun said all his instruments were sold off long ago, but what if she's wrong? This house is full of junk. It could be hidden away somewhere in the attics.'

I shook my head doubtfully. It was a nice thought, that classic cliché of treasure-seeking lore – the dusty attic. But I knew it wouldn't be that easy.

'Why not?' Guastafeste said. 'Let's go and look now. Search the whole house. What do we have to lose?'

'Let's see what the last letter says.'

The handwriting of the fourth letter was the sloppiest and most difficult to read of them all. Either Anselmi had changed secretaries by this point – in which case he could surely have employed one with a rather more obvious talent for calligraphy – or he had written the letter himself. I was inclined to think it was most likely the latter.

Deciphering and translating the text was slow work. It began with a rambling exposition in which Anselmi enquired at length about Colquhoun's health. Then it moved on to more important matters.

'"I am continuing to make enquiries into the disappearance of the violin. My agent in Paris is endeavouring to trace the courier who was engaged by my son but has, so far, met with little success. It is impossible, at the moment, to be certain

whether the instrument ever left Paris or if it did, at what point in the journey to England it was stolen. As the months go by, I begin to fear that the violin will never be recovered and the thief will take the secret of its whereabouts to the grave with him."'

I looked up from the letter. Guastafeste, so animated only a few moments ago, now had an expression of bleak disappointment on his face. I turned back to the text.

'"I feel the loss very deeply. His Excellency entrusted to me the safe despatch of the instrument and in this task I have most manifestly failed to be worthy of his trust. As it was through my negligence that this unfortunate loss occurred, I feel honour bound to make due recompense to you. I am therefore enclosing a banker's order for the full amount of the debt owed to you by His Excellency. Knowing you as I do, I must override the objections I know you will make to this arrangement and insist that you present the order for payment. I value your good esteem too much to allow these events to mar our friendship. It is my fervent wish that this debt should be honourably discharged, for only then will my conscience rest easy. I remain, as ever, your most faithful servant, Gio Michele Anselmi di Briata."'

I put the letter down with the others. For a moment neither of us spoke.

Then Guastafeste said morosely: 'So that's it then. It's gone. Stolen two hundred years ago. What chance do we have of tracing it?'

His dejection was manifest but, strangely, I felt myself untouched by his dark mood.

'At least it confirms that there was such a violin,' I said.

'What use is that?' Guastafeste retorted tetchily. 'Who knows where it went? It might have resurfaced years ago and is now in someone's collection. Maybe some soloist is playing it and no one knows where it came from.'

'I don't think so,' I said. 'Not if it really was a Stradivari. Every surviving Stradivari instrument has its provenance

191

pretty well documented. If there was one that originated from Cozio's collection, but was stolen in transit through France, we would know about it.'

'So what are you saying?' Guastafeste asked. 'That it's still out there somewhere waiting to be discovered?'

'Either that or it's been destroyed.'

The contents of the letters were dispiriting in many ways, but I wasn't going to allow that fact to discourage me. They provided no simple route to the goal we were seeking, but they seemed to indicate that the goal existed – or had existed once – and that was important to me. I wanted to believe in it. I *had* to believe in it. Was I deluding myself? It was possible. The violin might well have been lost for ever, been chopped up for firewood or left to rot, but I would not let myself believe it. In some way, some powerful, inexplicable way that went to the very core of what I was, I needed this search. Not just for Tomaso, but for me too.

I looked out of the window. It was damp and overcast outside, but the mist of the previous evening had lifted. I could see sheep grazing on the moors, the silhouette of a strange weathered rock formation on the skyline.

'And this is all Tomaso had?' Guastafeste said. 'These are the letters he showed Forlani? He had nothing more?'

'These would have been enough for Forlani,' I said. 'He wanted to believe there was another Messiah out there. It was his dream. Tomaso offered him a way of making that dream come true.'

'But how? These letters are a dead end. The violin has gone missing on its way to England. No one knows where it is. In all likelihood it was never recovered.'

'That's possible.'

'So how could Tomaso have taken it further? Where could he have gone next in his search?'

'I don't know,' I said. 'Maybe Tomaso didn't know either. But what does a hunter do when his hounds have lost the scent?'

'He retraces his steps,' Guastafeste said. 'Tries to pick it up again somewhere.'

'And if he doesn't know where along the route to look, what does he do?' I said. 'He goes back to the beginning. He starts again at the source of the scent and follows it anew.'

I paused. 'We have to start with Cozio di Salabue and Michele Anselmi di Briata. And that means we have to go to Casale Monferrato.'

11

The Randolph Hotel, in Oxford, was the kind of place I could imagine Tomaso staying. Exclusive, expensive, discreetly luxurious, it would have appealed to his weakness for extravagance.

As we arrived, a coach was coming to a halt outside the hotel, disgorging a party of American tourists and their guide. We waited for the group to go inside and disperse to their rooms before we approached the reception desk and asked to see the manager. Guastafeste and I were not planning on staying there. Guastafeste's police expenses did not run to such an opulent establishment, and I have always been disinclined to waste money on ostentatious hotels when all I need for a night away is a comfortable bed and a washbasin.

The hotel manager, a soft-spoken, smiling man with the conciliatory manner of someone accustomed to dealing with wealthy – and demanding – customers, examined Guastafeste's police identity card carefully before handing it back and explaining – with the utmost regret – that it wasn't company policy to give out information about guests.

'This is important,' I said, interpreting for Guastafeste. 'Signor Rainaldi has been murdered. We are not asking for much. We are just trying to establish what he did while he was in Oxford.'

'Murdered?' The manager looked horrified, then reconsidered his earlier reluctance to help us. 'What was the date he stayed here again?'

The hotel records divulged very little we didn't already know. Tomaso had stayed for one night, had had dinner alone in the hotel dining room, the cost of the meal being added to his accommodation bill. The manager didn't remember him. One of the receptionists did – 'The large Italian gentleman with the beard' – but that was as far as it went. She didn't know where – if anywhere – Tomaso had gone during his stay. She certainly couldn't recall him asking for directions or information about any particular location.

We thanked the manager and the receptionist and left the hotel. On the pavement outside I paused, looking across the road at the impressive classical frontage of the Ashmolean Museum.

'I wonder,' I said.

'Wonder what?' Guastafeste asked.

'Maybe that's all Tomaso came here for. A stopover on his way back from Highfield Hall to London. An opportunity to see it.'

'See what? Oxford, you mean?'

'I'll show you,' I said.

I took him across the road into the museum, then upstairs to the Hill Music Room. There was nothing special about the room. It was unremarkable, scruffy even. My sitting room at home is bigger. The walls were a dirty off-white, the plaster cornice chipped in places. On the floor were polished cork tiles. Frosted-glass windows obscured by blinds kept out the sunlight so the room was illuminated by lights on a rail around the ceiling. In the midst of these drab surroundings, the violin in the centre of the room shone out like a beacon.

'*Le Messie*,' I said. 'The Messiah.'

It was on its own in a glass case, hanging at an angle from a brass bar, its lower bouts resting on a mat of light green felt. I have seen it many times before. On my infrequent trips to England I try to make a point of coming here to look at it – like a pilgrim on a holy trail. And never yet has it failed to move me. This is what violin-making is all about.

'The Messiah?' Guastafeste said. 'This is the Messiah?'

I wonder sometimes what others see when they gaze at the violin. Perhaps they simply regard it as an old fiddle – a piece of varnished timber, well made, aesthetically pleasing, but no more impressive than any other old violin. If so, I pity them their blindness, for *Le Messie* is one of the world's great works of art and like all masterpieces, though it can be appreciated by the layman, it takes a practitioner to fully understand its qualities. I know how hard it is to make an instrument like this. I can see the craftsmanship in the contours of the belly and back, in the purfling, the ribs, the scroll; and every time the perfection leaves me breathless.

I walked slowly around the case, my face almost touching the glass. The two-piece maple back had a distinctive curl in the wood, a pattern of light and dark stripes that reminded me of sunlight on a forest floor. The varnish had a lustre, a velvety sheen like oiled skin. Vaguely, as distant as a voice in another room, I heard Guastafeste – prosaic as ever – saying, '*That*'s worth ten million dollars?' But the words barely registered on my consciousness, I was so absorbed in my study.

The instrument is not as Stradivari left it, of course. Jean-Baptiste Vuillaume lengthened the neck and changed the bass bar and fingerboard. The pegs and tailpiece – ornately carved with a relief of the Virgin Mary and a baby Christ with a halo around his head, two cherubs above them playing the harp and trumpet – are also Vuillaume's work. But they are merely icing, decorations which, rather than detract from the rest of the instrument, seem to highlight the astonishing simplicity of Stradivari's genius.

'So this is the violin that was heard about, but never seen,' Guastafeste said. 'It seems a shame to shut it away in a glass case. Shouldn't it be out in a concert hall somewhere being played?'

'It should,' I agreed. 'Though I'm glad it's here. Just to be able to see it is a privilege.'

'What's all this?' Guastafeste asked. He was reading the printed notice on a stand next to the glass case.

'"The youngest ring on the front of the Messiah is 1682. If we allow for the removal of sapwood and ten years or so to season, this is perfectly consistent with the attributed date of manufacture by Stradivari in 1716." What's that all about?'

'The dendrochronological analysis of the wood,' I said. 'The case for the defence.'

'The defence?' Guastafeste said.

'Yes. You see, some people think the Messiah is a fake.'

In the silence, I heard the custodian sitting on a chair by the exit turn a page of the book he was reading. The rustle of paper seemed abnormally loud, reverberating disquietingly around the confines of the room.

'A fake?' Guastafeste said. 'The Messiah is a fake?'

'There are doubts as to its authenticity, yes,' I said carefully.

'Don't they *know*? Can't they be sure?'

197

'In the violin world, there is no such thing as absolute certainty,' I said.

'But isn't its provenance established?'

'To some extent. But not all the way back to Stradivari. We know for certain that this is the violin Vuillaume said was the Messiah. Its history since that moment can be proved beyond doubt. But what happened before that point is less clear.'

'Less clear?' Guastafeste said impatiently. 'What do you mean?'

'It's complicated,' I said. 'To explain it we need to go back in time, to early January 1855.' I paused. Guastafeste's gaze was fixed on my face. 'Have you ever played a party game called Fly on the Wall, when you have to choose a moment in history at which you would like to have been present? You know, to have witnessed the end of the dinosaurs, Vesuvius burying Pompeii, the birth – or Resurrection – of Christ, Hitler's last days in the Berlin bunker, to have stood at the window of the Texas Book Depository when Kennedy was assassinated. The list is endless. If you asked me, I would choose a moment only a handful of people have ever heard about, concerning two individuals who will never be more than footnotes in history.

'In late 1854, the great violin collector, Luigi Tarisio, died. The news of his death took a while to reach Paris, but the instant it did, Jean-Baptiste Vuillaume leapt on a coach and headed straight for Milan. He went to Tarisio's apartment in the Via Legnano, a small, squalid attic room Tarisio used for storing his treasures. I would love to have been there, watching from the wall as Vuillaume walked in and found Tarisio's violins – piled high on the floor, strung from ropes suspended across the room. Close on a hundred and fifty of them, including twenty-five Stradivaris.'

198

'The Messiah among them?' Guastafeste said.

'To be strictly accurate, no,' I replied. 'Vuillaume actually found *Le Messie* at Tarisio's family farm at Fontanetto. But we're talking myths here. It makes a better story if it was in the attic with all the other violins. Vuillaume bought the entire collection from Tarisio's relatives and took it back to Paris with him. The Messiah then passed through various hands before the Hill family acquired it and donated it to the Ashmolean.'

'So what's the problem?' Guastafeste said.

'The problem is the people who owned it before Vuillaume: Tarisio, Cozio di Salabue and Paolo Stradivari. Cozio is beyond reproach, but both Tarisio and Paolo had dodgy reputations. Vuillaume too is not entirely above suspicion. We have only his word for it that the violin he claimed was the Messiah was found at the Tarisio family farm.'

'But I thought Tarisio boasted for years about owning a perfect, unplayed Stradivari,' Guastafeste said. 'That's what you told me.'

'I know. But Tarisio is not the most reliable witness in this story. He was a dealer, a somewhat shady character who wandered northern Italy picking up old fiddles, no doubt not always honestly. He kept no records of any of his transactions, left no inventory of his collection. We know he acquired a number of Cremonese instruments from Count Cozio in 1827, but exactly which instruments is unclear. And we know Cozio bought some dozen or so Stradivari violins from Stradivari's youngest son, Paolo, in 1775, thirty-eight years after the Master died – and one of those was undoubtedly a magnificent violin of 1716 because Cozio kept detailed notes of his collection.'

'So we know Cozio owned the Messiah,' Guastafeste said.

'Yes, but was that 1716 violin he documented the same

Stradivari he later sold to Tarisio? And was it the same one Vuillaume found at Fontanetto?'

'You're losing me here,' Guastafeste said. 'There are too many names, too many owners.'

'I know,' I said. 'It's not easy to follow.'

'Are you saying the violin here, in the case, isn't the Messiah?'

'It may not be. In fact, it may not be a Stradivari violin at all.'

'What?' Guastafeste was frowning at me. 'If it's not a Stradivari, what is it?'

I glanced at the custodian by the door, but he was too engrossed in his book to be taking any notice of us.

'Stradivari supposedly made the Messiah in 1716, and never parted with it. That in itself is a little problematic. According to legend it was so perfect he couldn't bear to sell it. That doesn't fit with what we know of Stradivari. By 1716 he was a rich and successful luthier. He had far more commissions for instruments than he could possibly handle. Every minute of his time was taken up with making violins that someone had ordered. So why did he make a violin that he didn't sell? He wasn't a sentimental man. As far as we know, he didn't play the violin himself. Why did he make that violin and hang on to it for the next twenty-one years, until his death in 1737?

'In any case, this instrument here in the Ashmolean isn't perfect.' I turned to the glass cabinet and pointed at the belly of the violin. 'Up here, to the right of the fingerboard – it's difficult to see, but it's there – is a blemish in the wood, a sap pocket. That too is suspicious. Stradivari didn't use wood with defects in it. He was too much of a perfectionist and, besides, he didn't need to. He could afford the very best timber and his customers were prepared to pay for the very best.

200

'Now we move on a little. Stradivari dies, leaving behind a number of complete and incomplete instruments. His sons, Francesco and Omobono, finish the uncompleted violins and when they die the remaining instruments pass to Paolo who gradually disposes of them. But are the instruments he sells all his father's? Some are probably more Francesco and Omobono than Antonio. There are doubts about Paolo's probity, so much so that when Cozio di Salabue buys the final dozen violins he makes Paolo swear an affidavit that the instruments are truly all his father's work.

'Included in that dozen instruments is the violin of 1716. Cozio describes it in his records. Only there's another problem. There are inconsistencies between Cozio's records and the violin we know as the Messiah – inconsistencies that put a question mark over the authenticity of the instrument.'

'So if Stradivari didn't make this violin,' Guastafeste said, 'who did?'

'The finger points at Vuillaume,' I said.

'But it's been analysed.' Guastafeste pointed at the notice next to the glass case. 'It says it's consistent with the date of 1716.'

'That proves the age of the wood,' I replied. 'Not the age of the violin. In 1855 it was only a little over a hundred years since Stradivari had died. Vuillaume – if he *did* fake the violin – would have had no trouble in finding old wood, though not necessarily of the right quality. Maybe that's why the sap pocket is there on the belly. Because that was the only wood Vuillaume could lay his hands on.'

'Why would Vuillaume fake it?'

'Who knows? To fulfil his dreams, perhaps. He'd heard so much from Tarisio about this fabulous, perfect Stradivari. But Tarisio was a braggart, an embroiderer.

201

What if when Vuillaume went to Milan after Tarisio's death he found that the violin wasn't there? That perhaps Tarisio had been lying and the Messiah had never existed at all. Or that it had disappeared from his collection. Can you imagine Vuillaume's disappointment? So he decided to make a Messiah himself.'

'One good enough to fool all these experts since?' Guastafeste said sceptically.

'It was well within his powers. Vuillaume was a master copyist. On one famous occasion, Paganini took his Guarneri "del Gesù", *Il Cannone*, to Vuillaume's atelier in Paris and left it there. When he returned, Vuillaume had made not one, but two, copies of the instrument and Paganini couldn't tell which one of the three was the original – and this is the amazing part – from either the appearance *or* the sound of the instrument.'

'So how come Vuillaume isn't one of the great luthiers like Guarneri?'

'Because copying and original creation are two different things. There are artists who can take an Old Master and copy – or fake – it perfectly, but they couldn't have produced anything original of a similar quality themselves. Vuillaume was the same with violins. His own instruments are very fine, but his copies – and he made several of the Messiah – are in a class of their own.'

Guastafeste was walking around the glass case, taking in every detail of the violin.

'And what's your view?' he said. 'Do you think Vuillaume faked it?'

Did I? I've often wondered whether Jean-Baptiste and I had more in common than just our Christian names.

'I don't know,' I said. 'You must judge for yourself.'

Guastafeste stared at me pensively. 'Let me get this right,' he said. 'This violin might, or might not, be a fake.

202

This fellow Tarisio might, or might not, have owned a perfect, unplayed Stradivari. Am I correct so far?'

'Yes.'

'But we know for certain – and it's about the only thing we *do* know for certain – that Count Cozio di Salabue did own an outstanding 1716 Stradivari.'

'Yes,' I said. 'That fact is documented beyond doubt.'

'So if this isn't that 1716 Stradivari, then what happened to it? What if the violin Cozio gave to Thomas Colquhoun – that went missing somewhere on its journey to England – was the 1716 Stradivari?'

'That's possible.'

Guastafeste's eyes were gleaming with suppressed excitement.

'So what we're looking for . . . might not be a sister to the Messiah. It might be the Messiah itself.'

12

Violin auctions are not overtly exciting events – you'd probably see more explicit passion in a village cattle sale – but it is their very restraint that, to me, makes them so gripping. On the surface everyone is so controlled, so reticent, so perfectly well-mannered, yet underneath I know the emotions are seething away, a cauldron bubbling over with the basest human impulses. I love that charged atmosphere, the sense of anticipation, the smell of desire and greed in the air. It is one of life's most intoxicating experiences.

The room was almost full. There were one or two empty seats scattered around the floor, but then a great crowd of people standing up at the back, talking in low murmurs, waiting impatiently for the auction to begin. We were five minutes past the scheduled start time, but that was all part of the game – keep the audience waiting, build up the heat until the pressure cooker was ready to explode.

I could see Rudy Weigert at the front, pink-faced and spruce in a dark suit and red bow-tie. He was chatting to one of his colleagues. I saw him glance at his watch, gauging the moment at which to make his entrance, then he stepped up on to the podium and the whole room fell silent. Rudy checked his lapel mike. Above his head the digital electronic display lit up to show the lot numbers and the prices in sterling, US dollars, Swiss francs, euros and Japanese yen.

'Good morning, ladies and gentlemen . . .' Rudy rattled off his opening patter, smooth, relaxed, putting us at our ease. He announced a couple of withdrawals, outlined the rules of bidding, then the show began.

'Lot 1, a violin by Giuseppe Zamberti. I'll start with twelve hundred pounds. Twelve hundred with me . . . thirteen hundred . . . fourteen hundred . . . fifteen hundred . . . with you, sir, at fifteen hundred . . . fifteen hundred . . . do I have any more bids?' Rudy's gavel banged down. 'Sold to you, sir, for fifteen hundred pounds. Could I see your paddle, please?'

The successful bidder held up his numbered paddle and Rudy moved swiftly on to Lot 2, a violin by Otto Moeckel. The early lots were mostly the cheaper instruments, interspersed with groups of bows, scraps thrown out to get the buyer's salivary glands going before the real meat came out and Rudy – he hoped – stepped back to watch the feeding frenzy. He went through the lots at a lick – a hundred in just over an hour. It was a pleasure to watch him in action, the master of ceremonies playing to the crowd, his innate showmanship to the fore.

'Have I missed anything?' a voice whispered beside me.

I turned my head to see Vincenzo Serafin slipping into the adjacent empty seat.

'Not much,' I said.

'Good.'

He adjusted his trousers to preserve their knife-edge creases and opened his catalogue. I could smell his aftershave lotion, hear the faint hiss of his breathing as if he'd had to hurry to get here and overexerted himself in the process. It must have been a long walk from the taxi to the kerb.

'What lot are we on?' he asked, though the number was prominently displayed at the front of the room.

'Lot 109,' I said. 'Carlo Loveri.'

Serafin flicked through his catalogue without haste. He hadn't come all the way to London to buy a Carlo Loveri.

'Now, Lot 110,' Rudy said. 'A violin *circa* 1900, labelled *Josephus Cerutti filius Joannis Baptistae Cremonensis fecit anno 1825*. Who will give me two thousand? Thank you, sir. Two two . . . two five . . . two eight . . . three thousand.' The bidding went up steadily. 'Do I have four five?' Rudy asked. 'Four five, thank you, sir . . . four eight . . . five . . . five five on the telephone . . .' Rudy turned his gaze to the side of the room, to the row of telephones manned by the thin-lipped thoroughbred women all the London auction houses seemed to employ. 'Five five with Emily on the phone . . . six thousand, thank you, sir . . . six five on the phone . . . seven . . . seven five?' Rudy looked to the phones. Emily shook her head. 'Do I have seven five? Seven five at the back there . . . eight . . . with you, sir, for eight thousand pounds . . . eight . . . eight five . . . nine, with you, sir . . .'

The bidding kept going. 'Ten . . . eleven . . . Do I have twelve? Twelve . . . thirteen.' I felt the change in the atmosphere. The people in front of me began to turn round in their seats, looking to see who was bidding so much for such an apparently undistinguished instrument. The catalogue estimate was only £2,500 to £4,500, but the bidding kept going up. Someone obviously knew more about the violin – or thought they did – than the rest of us. I twisted round too, watching the two men at the back vying with each other, upping the ante like guys in a bar staring each other out to see who would blink first.

'Twenty-two thousand,' Rudy said finally. 'With you, sir, at twenty-two thousand pounds.' The gavel came down. 'Sold!'

I turned back to the front, shifting a little in my seat. The steel-framed plastic chairs were uncomfortable and so hard I was starting to lose all sensation in my buttocks. I looked down at my catalogue. The supporting acts were all over. It was time for the leads to come out centre stage.

'Lot 111,' Rudy announced. 'A viola by Giovanni Battista Gabrielli . . .'

I caught a movement out of the corner of my eye – a man walking down the aisle and taking one of the unoccupied seats two rows in front of me. It was Christopher Scott. I sat up abruptly, staring at his sandy hair, his freckled cheek as he turned to look across to the table beside the podium where an attendant in a navy-blue apron was holding up the next instrument to be sold. I heard Serafin suck in air between his teeth, as if he'd bitten on a lemon. I glanced sideways. He was glaring at Scott with undisguised loathing.

'I've had some interest in this. We'll start at seventeen thousand pounds. Who will give me eighteen? Thank you, sir, I have eighteen here at the front . . . nineteen . . . twenty . . . twenty-two . . .'

I watched Scott as the lots were knocked down one after the other. The Gabrielli went for £38,000, a Tomaso Balestrieri for £75,000, a Vuillaume for £42,000. He bid for none of them, though I could see he had a numbered paddle on his knee.

Then came the real star of the show – a 1698 Pietro Guarneri of Mantua which had an estimate of £200,000 to £250,000. Pietro Guarneri was the uncle of the great 'del Gesù'. He made outstanding violins, but not many of them for – unusually for a luthier of the time – he also held an appointment as a violinist in the orchestra of the Gonzaga court at Mantua.

Rudy started the bidding at £140,000, going up in intervals of £10,000. Scott came in early, registering his interest with a bid of £170,000. This was the violin he'd told Guastafeste he'd been engaged to acquire for Enrico Forlani. He certainly wasn't bidding for Forlani today.

'One eighty,' Rudy said, looking at Serafin who'd nodded at the rostrum. Scott turned his head to see whom he was up against and his mouth curled at the corners. Serafin avoided his eye, his gaze fixed on Rudy.

'One ninety? Do I have one ninety?'

Scott swivelled back to face the front and held up a finger.

'One ninety, thank you, sir.'

Serafin bid two hundred thousand.

'Two hundred thousand,' Rudy said. 'I have two hundred thousand . . . two ten . . . two twenty . . . two thirty . . .' I watched the red glowing numbers on the digital display change as the price went up. There were only two bidders in the race – Scott and Serafin. 'Two forty . . . two fifty . . . with you, sir, at two hundred and fifty thousand pounds.' Rudy looked expectantly at Serafin. I was tempted to put in a bid myself – though I hadn't registered for a paddle – just to annoy Serafin.

Serafin gave a nod. Then Scott raised his finger. I wondered for whom they were bidding. I doubted it was on their own accounts – they were vying against each other with the casual enthusiasm of men spending someone else's money.

The bidding reached £300,000 – fifty thousand above the upper end of the estimate – and kept going. Scott bid three ten, Serafin three twenty. I glanced at Serafin. His expression was unnaturally calm, but there was a fine sheen of sweat on his brow. Scott bid three thirty, Serafin three forty.

'Three fifty? Do I have three fifty?' Rudy said, looking at Scott.

Scott seemed to hesitate. I could sense everyone around me willing him to continue. Keep it going, I thought. Let's see how high this can go.

Scott raised his finger.

Rudy looked at Serafin.

'Three fifty. I have three fifty. Do I have three sixty?'

I could hear my own heartbeat, thought – impossibly – that I could hear Serafin's too, racing away next to me. He was holding his breath – *that* I could hear. Waiting. Thinking. Maybe praying. Rudy kept looking at him.

'I have three hundred and fifty thousand pounds. Do I have any more bids?'

Serafin was in agony. I could see it in his face. Did he have a ceiling? Everyone has a ceiling, even someone like Serafin. What was it?

'Do I have any more bids?' Rudy repeated.

Serafin didn't move. His features were set rigid, his mouth a tight line. He still hadn't breathed. His eyes were staring at the rostrum, cold, unblinking. Come on, Vincenzo, I urged him silently. *Do* something.

Serafin inhaled sharply, the sound audible throughout the room. With an effort that seemed to take every last remaining ounce of his energy, he shook his head and looked at the floor, grimacing as if he were in pain.

Rudy's gavel hammered down. 'Sold! For three hundred and fifty thousand pounds.'

Christopher Scott held up his paddle, then turned round in his seat and gave a thin smile of triumph at Serafin.

Rudy came towards me across the crowded lobby, manoeuvring his way around the clusters of people – the dealers huddled together in conspiratorial groups, the long line of successful bidders waiting to settle their bills at the sales counter.

'Gianni,' he said. 'My apologies for not speaking to you earlier. You know how it is.'

'Of course I do,' I said. 'Don't let me get in your way now. I know you're very busy.'

'Not at all. I've done my bit. Others take over now. So how was your trip to Derbyshire?'

'Good.'

'Where exactly did you go?'

'A place called Highfield Hall.'

'Never heard of it. You must tell me all about it. What are you doing for lunch? I know what you're doing, you're having it with me.'

'My friend, Antonio . . . he's meeting me here any moment,' I said. 'He couldn't face sitting through the auction.'

'Then you're both coming for lunch,' Rudy said. 'I know a little place around the corner.'

He took me by the arm to lead me towards the exit. As I turned, I almost bumped into a figure who had been standing right behind me. It was Christopher Scott. I wondered how long he'd been there. He gave me a hard stare, his pale blue eyes cold and hostile, then he nodded brusquely at Rudy and pushed past us to the sales counter.

Rudy's 'little place around the corner' was an expensive French restaurant which specialised in the kind of rich, high-cholesterol food that provided so many English heart specialists with their second homes in Tuscany.

We had barely sat down before Rudy ordered two bottles of red wine – 'I can't stand the wait while they bring out the second' – and a plate of hors d'oeuvre. He waited for the wine to arrive and drank down his first glass in two long gulps.

'That's better.' He sighed deeply and relaxed back in his seat. 'How do you think it went?'

'The auction?' I said. 'I think your job's secure.'

'Quite a few lots unsold.'

'There always are. The important ones all went. Were you surprised by the Guarneri? A hundred thousand above the upper estimate.'

'It was a very good violin.'

'Serafin was livid that he didn't get it.'

'He should have kept bidding then. I'm surprised he didn't. Especially against Christopher Scott. Losing to Scott must have been especially galling.'

Guastafeste looked up, frowning. He'd been struggling to follow the conversation in English, but he'd caught the mention of the name.

'Christopher Scott?' he said.

'He was at the auction,' I replied in Italian. 'Snatched the prize lot from under Serafin's nose.'

Then, reverting to English, I said to Rudy, 'Why especially galling?'

'You must have seen,' Rudy said. 'There's not exactly any love lost between them.'

'They're dealers, what do you expect?'

'It's more than professional rivalry. I know a lot of dealers. They compete with each other, but most of them are realistic about the business. If they lose a violin, they shrug their shoulders. They know there'll be another one along at the next sales. Scott and Serafin are different. There's a real personal animosity there.'

'Based on?'

'Well, this is just trade gossip, you understand,' Rudy said. 'I probably shouldn't be repeating it.'

'But you will,' I said.

'Why break the habit of a lifetime? You know that

woman of Serafin's – the coiffeured stick insect? What's her name? Marietta?'

'Maddalena.'

'Yes, Maddalena. Expensive little piece to run. She was here with Serafin for the spring sales. Not that I saw very much of her. Complete shopaholic, she seemed. Must have almost cleaned out Harrods, not to mention Serafin. Well, they say – and this, of course, is unsubstantiated rumour – that Scott had a fling with her.'

'In the spring?'

Rudy nodded.

'And Serafin found out?'

'I'm not sure about that. But relations between the two men have been somewhat frosty ever since.'

'Maddalena and Serafin still seem to be together.'

'Perhaps it's all wrong then.' Rudy helped himself to a couple of stuffed olives.

'You know Scott well?' I said.

'Well enough.' Rudy pulled a face. I could tell he didn't like him, and there aren't many people Rudy dislikes.

'You've had bad experiences with him?'

'Let's just say he's not the most pleasant person I've ever had dealings with.'

'But he's big.'

Rudy nodded. 'And getting bigger. Does a lot of business, buys a lot, has good contacts . . .'

'But . . .'

'He's a little too aggressive, too nakedly ambitious for my liking.' Rudy refilled his glass with wine. 'There are others like him. Brash young men in a hurry. He's bright, educated, the type who could have gone into the City. You know, been a commodity broker or an investment banker. But he chose violin dealing instead – saw it as a way to make a fortune. He knows his stuff all right, jets around the world doing deals. Breakfast in Hong Kong, dinner in LA, that kind of thing. But he's not . . . well, my type. He has no graces, no manners. Everything is up front, take it or leave it.'

'So he's simply more honest than other dealers,' I said. 'The one shark in the pool who doesn't trouble to hide his teeth.'

Rudy chuckled. 'You could say that. You know how the business works, Gianni.' He picked up the menu. 'Now what do you fancy?'

I usually get by with just a light lunch, but Rudy insisted we work our way through starter, fish, meat and dessert courses, a culinary marathon that made me feel as if I'd been force fed like some *foie gras* goose.

'You don't do this every lunchtime, do you?' I asked.

'Good God, no,' Rudy said. 'Only three, four times a week. I'm on a diet, you see.'

My mouth was empty or I would have choked.

'A diet?'

'Ruth's insisting. So's my quack. He says I'm in line for a massive coronary if I don't cut down on the food and drink. What he doesn't realise is that that's the whole bloody point. I want a massive coronary.'

'You're not serious?'

'Seems a good way to go, if you ask me. I don't want to end up some doddering old fool in an armchair, or get Alzheimer's or a horrible lingering cancer when they pump you full of chemicals which don't do a damn thing except make you wish you were already dead. No, a heart attack seems a pretty merciful end. A couple of glasses of good claret and a Tournedos Rossini, then bam! Lights out. That'll do me fine.'

Rudy polished off what was left of the second bottle of wine and smiled contentedly. 'I'm making a bit of an effort, for Ruth's sake really, but lunch is my *raison d'être*. It's the only reason I bother getting up in the mornings and going to work. And I don't have so many lunchtimes left that I can afford to waste any of them on cheese sandwiches.'

'And are you losing any weight?'

'Oh, yes. I lost a couple of pounds last month. I'm being very disciplined. Within reason, of course. Now how about a brandy?'

'How on earth does he do any work in the afternoon?' an already half-asleep Guastafeste asked me when Rudy had excused himself to go to the Gents'.

'He doesn't,' I replied. 'He works for an auction house.'

'Now,' Rudy said, settling himself back down in his chair and adjusting his jacket over his bulging stomach. 'The Maggini you asked about.'

He took a piece of paper from his pocket and unfolded it on the table.

'November sales, 1998. Violin by Gio Paolo Maggini. Excellent condition, known as the Snake's Head. We put an estimate on it of between seventy and ninety thousand pounds. In the end it went for a hundred and twenty thousand. Buyer, as you know, Vincenzo Serafin. Now, as I told you before, there was a lot of interest in it on the floor. I obviously don't have any records of those bidders, but we had written instructions from six telephone bidders – three in America, one in Japan and two in Europe.'

He gave me their names. I recognised all six of them: all well-established dealers who would have been bidding on their own account or perhaps – like Serafin – for some wealthy collector who preferred to remain anonymous.

'Did Scott bid for it?' I asked.

'I couldn't tell you. He'd have been on the floor, not the phone. He may well have done, I don't remember.'

'What about the provenance?'

214

'It has an interesting history,' Rudy said. 'Unlucky. A bit like the Bott.'

'Really?' The Bott was a Stradivari violin reputed to be cursed because so many unfortunate – and tragic – things had happened to successive owners.

'There appears to be reliable documentation going back to the middle of the nineteenth century when George Hart, the London dealer, acquired it,' Rudy continued. 'The seller was the widow of a man who had been murdered by footpads – muggers to us – while on his way home from the theatre one evening. Hart later sold it to a London financier who went spectacularly bust in 1875 and had to sell all his belongings, including the Maggini. The violin then passed through various hands until in 1906 it was sold to a buyer in Bulgaria named Stoiko Lalchev. He held on to it until 1920 when, in the aftermath of the First World War, he sold it to someone called Imre Borsos, in Oradea, Romania. The instrument then seems to have disappeared for the next sixty or so years, resurfacing at an auction in Zürich in 1984.'

'Resurfacing from where?' I asked.

'The Soviet Union, it would appear. It was bought by a Swiss collector who held on to it until 1995 when he was found dead in Lake Thun after apparently falling from his sailing boat.'

'Any suspicious circumstances?'

'I gather there was a police investigation, but it concluded that the death was probably accidental.'

'I see what you mean about it being unlucky,' I said. 'Two previous owners dead in unusual circumstances, then Forlani. I don't think I'd want to acquire that fiddle.'

'No,' Rudy agreed. 'It does have a somewhat chequered past.'

'Anything else?'

'That's it. I hope it helps you.'

'Thanks, Rudy.'

'I have bad vibes about that violin. Sometimes it's better to leave things well alone, you know.'

'I'm just curious.'

'Well, be careful, Gianni.'

13

Casale Monferrato is known as the cement capital of Italy. Need I say more? Actually, the title is rather unfair, for on a visit to the town there is nothing obvious to indicate its industrial status: no clouds of smoke over the suburbs, no looming factory chimneys, no coatings of limestone dust on trees and buildings. Rather it is a quiet, not unattractive little settlement on the banks of the Po, its centre dominated by a castle, one of the finest synagogues in Italy and innumerable elegant sixteenth-century palaces dating from the time when it was the fief of the Dukes of Mantua.

It was early evening when we arrived, but we didn't linger. We headed south-west from Casale, along the road to Asti. The countryside was flat to start with, but very soon we were driving through low wooded hills, the red roofs of scattered farms, the tower of a church, half hidden in the trees. There were fields of maize beside the road and neat rows of vines higher up. This was wine country, home of the Barbera and the Nebbiolo grapes.

After twenty kilometres, we turned off the main road, over a level crossing, and began to climb into the hills, the road twisting between more fields of maize and vines.

Through the open car windows came the scent of wood-smoke. We turned a corner and ahead of us, on the summit of a steep peak, we saw the Castello di Salabue, the ancestral home of Count Ignazio Alessandro Cozio di Salabue, the greatest, most celebrated collector of violins in history. The Castello – which was more a country villa than a true fortified castle – was illuminated in the setting sun, its stucco walls glowing pink and orange. Next to it, the bell tower of a church stood out clear against the powder-blue satin of the sky.

We drove through rusty iron gates and up a rough, winding drive fringed by trees. Beyond the edge of the drive the forested hillside dropped away steeply into the valley. The barking of dogs close by told us that our arrival had been noted.

It was the Weimaraners who came out to greet us first, three bouncing good-natured animals with sleek, shining coats. Behind them came a tall, bespectacled figure with a pipe clamped between his teeth.

'Giovanni Davico,' he said, extending his hand. 'Welcome to Salabue.'

He led us through another gate and across a gravelled forecourt, the dogs bounding along beside us. We ascended a covered stone staircase to a terrace garden, then went through a door into the house.

'I'll show you around later,' Giovanni said. 'First, you must have a glass of wine.'

He took us into the library where his wife, Marie-Therese, was waiting with a tray of drinks.

'From our own grapes,' she said, handing out the glasses. 'Nothing special, I'm afraid. Just an ordinary table wine.'

There were shelves of books on the walls – old leather-bound volumes which had seen better days – but the room was clearly a living room as much as a library. The centre of it was occupied by a long wooden dining table and at one side, in front of an open fire, were armchairs and settees, a coffee table overflowing with magazines and a television and video player on a wooden cabinet. Family photographs were spread around the bookcases and mantelpiece, the furniture and rugs on the stone floor were worn and well used. There was an air of comfortable dilapidation about the place – a historic house that was lived in, not just preserved for the guided tour.

We drank our wine around the hearth. One of the Weimaraners came and rested its head on my knee, waiting to be stroked. Giovanni called it away.

'I don't mind,' I said. 'I like dogs. These are handsome creatures.'

'You keep dogs yourself?' Marie-Therese asked.

'No. They're gun dogs, aren't they? Do you hunt with them?'

'These three? They're too soft and pampered. They'd run a mile if they saw a wild boar.'

'You have wild boar nearby?' Guastafeste said.

'In the woods. White gold too – truffles.'

'They can sniff out truffles?'

'No, the good truffle hounds are mostly mongrels. I wish they could. A truffle hound is worth a fortune around here.'

'Or a pig,' Giovanni said. 'We had a pig once who could sniff out a truffle better than any dog. But he was hell to house train.'

I laughed and drank some of my wine.

'You were too modest about this,' I said. 'It's a little more than an ordinary table wine.'

'It's only Barbera,' Marie-Therese said. 'For the really good stuff – the Barolos and Barbarescos – you have to go closer to Alba.'

'You have a lot of vines?'

'Very few,' Giovanni replied. 'The land that once belonged to the house has mostly been sold off. We have only a small area on the hill below the drive now. Enough for a few litres of wine for our own consumption, but no more.'

'And in Count Cozio's day?'

'Things were different then. There was land, farms, a town house in Casale.'

'The town house has gone?'

'Long ago. Like the violins.'

I looked around the room. 'Where did Cozio keep his violins? In here?'

'I don't know,' Giovanni replied. 'There seems to be no record of exactly where the collection was stored. The house is not big. Only four reception rooms. Perhaps he used more than one room.' He got to his feet. 'I'll show you.'

We went out of the library into the adjoining room – a larger, more formal salon containing gilt-framed paintings, elegant gold furniture and an antique Pleyel grand piano. From there we continued into the dining room which had a huge faded mural of the surrounding countryside painted on to the walls.

'Was this how it was in Cozio's day?' I asked.

Giovanni shook his head. 'When Cozio died he left only a daughter, Matilda, who had no children. On her death, the house was inherited by the Marquis dalle Valle, one of my ancestors, who was related to Cozio's wife. The estate then passed out of the family for many years, falling into ever greater disrepair until my parents managed to buy it back in 1935. It was virtually derelict, just a shell with holes in the walls and roof. My parents restored it. It was my mother who had these paintings done in the classical style.'

The fourth reception room – the darkest, gloomiest of all – was almost entirely taken up by a large billiards table. On one of the walls was a portrait of Count Cozio himself.

'I've seen this in the Museo Stradivariano, in Cremona,' I said.

'The one in Cremona is the original,' Giovanni said. 'This is a photographic reproduction. It's quite good, but it's not the same as a painting. It has no texture, no depth to it.'

I moved closer to study the portrait. It showed the count as an old man, in white wig, wing collar, ruffled shirt, frock-coat and white bow-tie. His left hand was resting on the head of a walking stick. In his right hand, dangling down so that the surface was revealed, was a blank piece of white paper. There was something incongruous about the piece of paper – an expanse of plain white paint in the midst of all the fine detail of the count's dress. Guastafeste noticed it too.

'That's strange,' he said. 'Why didn't the artist paint something on the paper? It surely wouldn't have been blank.'

'It is a little odd,' Giovanni conceded. 'I don't know the answer. Maybe it had something on it originally – the count's name perhaps – and it was thought prudent to remove it. Piedmont was occupied by the French after the Revolution. It wasn't wise to advertise your membership of the aristocracy.'

'Did Cozio have trouble during the Revolution?' I asked.

'It would appear not. He kept his lands, and his head, which was something of an achievement. It doesn't seem that he was hated by the locals in quite the way the French nobility were. Perhaps the piece of paper had "Citizen Cozio" inscribed on it and someone – some counter-revolutionary – later erased it. Who knows?'

'Are any of Cozio's papers still here?' I said.

'A few,' Giovanni replied. 'Most are in the Civic Library in Cremona. His *Carteggio*, the detailed descriptions of his violins, are certainly there, but you probably knew that already.'

I nodded. I'd read some of the *Carteggio* – not in the count's original notes, but in the transcriptions the scholar Renzo Bacchetta made in the 1950s. They made dry, very dull reading, even for a luthier.

'But you say there are some still here?'

'Not a great number, and they are in a very poor condition.'

'You've read them?'

'I tried a couple and gave up. They're very faded and Cozio's handwriting was atrocious. I keep meaning to ask the museum in Cremona if they would like them, but I don't think they're very significant. All the important stuff was taken from here years ago. I'll show you them in the morning.'

We had dinner in the dining room, our voices echoing around the high reaches of the ceiling. Marie-Therese had made *agnolotti*, plump little pasta half moons stuffed with meat – a local speciality – followed by pork and fresh fruit. Afterwards we took our glasses of Barbera back into the library. I wandered around the perimeter of the room, studying the paintings and photographs on the walls.

'Was this a library when Cozio lived here?'

'No one knows,' Giovanni replied. 'There are no records, no pictures of what it was like then.'

I took in the plain stucco walls, the high windows, the mosaic floor, imagining what the room must have been like two hundred years ago. Was this where Cozio had kept his fabulous collection of violins? Was the room big enough to accommodate them all? I pictured him here at his desk, writing by candlelight with a quill pen, one of his violins beside him as he measured its dimensions, as he recorded the details of its appearance for posterity.

Very little is known about Cozio. He inherited his title and the Salabue estate when he was a very young man and showed an already obsessive interest in violins from his late teens when he began commissioning instruments from Giovanni Guadagnini who was then an old man, living in Turin and struggling to make ends meet. The count was only twenty when he bought Stradivari's last remaining dozen or so violins from Paolo Stradivari and for the next quarter of a century Cozio applied himself – as only an enthusiast of independent means could – to building and documenting an unsurpassed collection of instruments.

However, as with most passions, there came a time when his interest began to wane. At the end of the eighteenth century Piedmont was invaded by French, Russian and Austrian armies. When Cozio sent all his violins to the banker Carlo Carli in Milan for safekeeping perhaps that was the point when the fire of his enthusiasm started to die a little. With his precious violins out of sight he turned his attentions to other matters – to the collection of local history papers which he transcribed and catalogued with the same meticulous care he had once devoted to his violins.

There is no evidence that the violins ever came back to Salabue. We know that in 1817 Carlo Carli sold one of Cozio's Stradivaris to Paganini, and we know that a number – including, ostensibly, the Messiah – were sold to Tarisio in 1827. But that still left a large number unaccounted for. The question that tormented me, gnawing away relentlessly at my mind, was: what happened to those other violins?

* * *

I shared a room with Guastafeste that night, down below the main part of the Castello in some old storage buildings that had been converted into a bedroom and bathroom.

I slept badly, kept awake by the noise of heavy rain on the roof and the incessant hooting of an owl in the woods. When I emerged next morning, Guastafeste still buried beneath his sheet, I found the hillside draped with thick mist, the houses and fields in the valley lost from sight. The ground was damp, the trees dripping. There was a ripe mustiness in the air, an earthy scent like the smell of rotting wood or mouldy mushrooms. I strolled out on to the terrace and met Giovanni coming back from walking the dogs. The Weimaraners – emerging like grey ghosts from the fog – were hot and panting. I could see the vapour rising from their velvety coats.

'You're up early,' Giovanni said. 'Would you like breakfast?'

'I'll wait for Antonio.'

'Let me show you the church then. Cozio's tomb.'

We went through a door at the far end of the courtyard and came out at the side of the church whose open bell tower was almost built into the walls of the Castello.

'Was this Cozio's private chapel?' I asked.

'No, it's always been the village church. But the family has had strong links with it for centuries.'

The main doors of the church were open. One or two people were drifting inside, exchanging greetings.

'Is there a service?' I asked.

'Early morning Mass. But not for ten minutes. Come in, no one will mind.'

I followed him into the church. It was a small, very simple place of worship – just a handful of pews in the nave, no transepts to speak of. The main altar was marble and gold, but on the left was another much plainer altar, next to which was a marble headstone embedded in the wall of the church. The inscription on the headstone was in Latin, the name and date standing out as if they'd been freshly carved: Ignazio Alessandro Cozio di Salabue, December 15, 1840.

I gazed at the modest, unadorned tomb for a long time, wondering about Cozio, about his violins, about the secrets he had taken with him when he died.

The papers were in a cardboard box-file in Marie-Therese's office in one of the turrets of the Castello. They were yellowing and fragile, stained so badly by damp and mould that the writing on them was almost impossible to read.

'You see what I mean?' Giovanni said. 'There's not much you can do with them.'

I spread the documents out on the desk and leafed through them anyway, examining each one in turn in case there were a few legible passages, then passing them across to Guastafeste for a second opinion.

'Where did you find them?' I asked.

'In the basement,' Giovanni said. 'There's an underground chamber beneath a wooden trapdoor. My wife calls it a dungeon, but I think it was most probably used as an ice house in the past. They were dumped in a corner under a pile of junk. Some were just blackened pulp. We had to throw most of them away.'

'So this is all that was left?' I said.

'Yes.'

'There are no unexplored nooks and crannies in the Castello? No secret hiding places?' Guastafeste asked hopefully.

'If there were, we would have found them. I've been over every part of the house and all the outbuildings.'

'What about Casale?' I said. 'Are there any papers in the archives there?'

Giovanni shrugged. 'There may be. I've never looked.' He lit up his pipe and sucked on the mouthpiece, smoke leaking out between his lips.

Guastafeste was examining the last of the documents. 'There's something,' he said. 'Not very significant. It's clearer than all the others, but that's not saying much.'

I took a closer look at the document. It was a letter to Cozio. The address at the top and the opening words, 'My Dear Cozio', were reasonably clear, but after that the text was completely illegible until you got to the signature at the bottom of the page.

'What's the name of the sender?' Guastafeste said. 'It's hard to make out. Federico? Federico something. Marinelli?'

'Marinetti,' I said. 'Federico Marinetti.' I looked at Giovanni. 'Does that name mean anything to you?'

'Not a thing.'

I'd been overoptimistic. I'd hoped that the Castello di Salabue might reveal some hitherto undiscovered secret, something to put us back on the scent of the violin we were seeking. But once again the trail had gone cold.

'How about the name Giovanni Michele Anselmi di Briata?' I asked.

'That means nothing either,' Giovanni replied. 'Who is he?'

'He was a Casale cloth merchant, Cozio's agent in the purchase of Stradivari's last remaining violins from Paolo Stradivari. He also acted for the count in at least one transaction with an English cloth manufacturer named Thomas Colquhoun to whom Cozio, apparently, owed money. Why would an Italian nobleman owe money to an English factory owner?'

Giovanni pursed his lips, then lifted his pipe pensively, tapping the stem of it lightly against his teeth.

'No one in the family has ever been absolutely sure

where Cozio's money came from,' he said. 'There have been rumours that he engaged in trade of some kind – always using an intermediary, of course. A nobleman of his time would never have done anything so distasteful openly.'

'The cloth trade?'

'It's possible.'

'That would account for him knowing Anselmi,' Guastafeste said. 'Perhaps the firm still exists. Maybe they have records we could look at.'

Giovanni took down a local telephone directory from a shelf and leafed through it. 'It doesn't look like it, I'm afraid. There is no entry for any Anselmi, business or residential.'

'So what now?' Guastafeste said.

'We try the library in Casale Monferrato,' I replied. 'See if there's anything in their archives.'

14

The River Po, in Cozio's day, would have been a thriving waterway, its banks cluttered with jetties and wharves, heavily laden barges waiting two and three deep to unload. Stevedores would have been moving to and fro, their backs bowed beneath sacks and crates and barrels, horse-drawn carts lined up to transport their cargoes to the merchants in Casale and beyond. It was here that Stradivari's last few violins arrived in 1775, brought upstream from Cremona by a bargemaster named Gobbi. Packed carefully in wooden boxes, they were transferred to one of Count Cozio's carriages for the final twenty-kilometre journey to Salabue.

Sadly, there is no sign of this vibrant history today. Now the Po seems detached from Casale. The bustling, noisy waterfront is gone, so too are the barges, their role long ago usurped by the roads and railways. There are no buildings along the riverbank, just a crescent of pale shingle on the north side where the course sweeps round in a long curve, and a swathe of wild grassland on the town side, deserted this morning except for a courting couple kissing beneath one of the trees.

We left the car in the sprawling parking area just above the river and walked into the centre of the town, along colonnaded streets overlooked by imposing stone palaces. Out of interest – mine more than Guastafeste's – we made a short detour to the Via Mamelli where Cozio had once had his town house. The building had long since been converted into apartments and offices. There was no indication, no sign or plaque on the wall, that the count had ever lived there. Unless you are a luthier, the name Cozio – even in Italy – is virtually unknown.

The civic library was only a short distance away. The librarian in the archives section was one of those classic public servants who loathed both the public and any idea of service. When we explained what we were looking for she rolled her eyes behind her thick spectacles and gave a long, peppery sigh of irritation.

'Anselmi di Briata, we don't have anything on him,' she said.

'How do you know without looking?' I said.

'I know.'

'Perhaps we could look?' I suggested.

I made a move towards the stack of filing drawers next to the desk, but the librarian – reacting with the speed of a choleric rattlesnake – interposed herself between me and my goal.

'I said we don't have anything on him. Someone was asking only the other week.'

Guastafeste and I exchanged glances.

'Asking about Anselmi?' Guastafeste said sharply. 'Who? Who was asking?'

'I'm afraid I'm not at liberty to divulge that,' the librarian replied primly.

Guastafeste took out his police ID card and held it up in front of the librarian's face.

'This is a homicide investigation, signora. We'd appreciate a little cooperation.'

The librarian screwed up her nose as if Guastafeste's warrant card were tainted with a noxious smell.

'I don't know who he was,' she said. 'He didn't give a name.'

'Was he an Englishman?' I said.

The librarian started and stared at me, then recovered herself.

'I couldn't say. Perhaps.'

'And you told him you had nothing on Anselmi, is that right?' Guastafeste said.

'We don't have anything on him.'

'I'd like to look for myself.'

Guastafeste walked across to the filing cabinets. The librarian scurried after him.

'The files are for staff use only,' she snapped.

'This is a public archive,' Guastafeste said coolly. 'I have a right to look.'

Guastafeste pulled open one of the drawers and leafed through the cards inside – computer databases, like other aberrations of the modern age, not yet having made it to Casale. The librarian glared at him, but made no attempt to stop him.

Guastafeste pulled out a filing card and held it up, reading out the heading on it. '"Anselmi di Briata. Cloth merchants, Casale Monferrato, 1726–1870." Is this what you mean by nothing?'

The librarian didn't respond for a moment. I could tell she was regrouping, gathering her resources for a counter-attack.

'They're uncatalogued documents,' she said with a smug hint of triumph in her voice.

'Meaning?' Guastafeste said.

'Meaning they've never been sorted out and given a proper filing reference.'

'So?'

'They're probably in boxes in the basement. It could take me a long time to find them. And I don't have that time right now.'

'You don't have to find them,' Guastafeste said. 'If you'll show us the way, we'll find them ourselves.'

There were fifteen large boxes full of dusty documents. Guastafeste looked at them in dismay.

'Maybe this wasn't such a good idea. Do we have to go through them all?'

'The earlier stuff, before 1775, we can probably ignore,' I said.

'How do we know which is the earlier stuff?'

'We don't.'

I opened the first box and tipped the contents out on to the table. A thick cloud of dust gusted up into my face and I turned away, coughing.

'How did you know it was Scott?' Guastafeste asked.

'It was just a guess.'

I took off my jacket and draped it over the back of a chair. It was hot and oppressive down here in the basement. The stacks of shelves were all around us, blocking us in. There was no daylight, just a naked bulb above the table, casting a harsh yellow aura over the documents below. I sat down and picked up the first paper. I could tell this wasn't going to be an enjoyable experience.

An hour later and I knew more than I'd ever wanted to about the eighteenth-century cloth trade, but I'd seen nothing at all – not even a passing mention – about violins. All I'd read so far were dull requests for bales of cloth, invoices for payment and other commercial trivia. I wasn't surprised that no one had bothered to catalogue this stuff. It was a miracle they hadn't taken one look at it and dumped it in a skip.

We were on box five before anything of interest surfaced. Guastafeste held up a letter he'd been perusing. 'This is about a violin.'

'What does it say?'

'Take a look.'

Guastafeste handed me the letter which I saw was dated June, 1787. The writing was clumsy and childish as if the sender were only poorly educated, a conclusion reinforced by the Italian which was basic and full of grammatical errors.

'Gracious Sir, I thank you much for interest you show in violin left me by my mother. It very good thing. Nothing bad about it. Price you say is good. I send it you now.'

The signature was printed in capital letters, making it easy to read.

'Elisabeta Horak,' I said. 'An address in Bohemia.'

'Who was she?'

'I have no idea. Just someone selling a violin to Anselmi.'

'For Cozio's collection?'

'Most probably.'

'Does that take us any further?'

'I don't see how,' I replied, but I put the letter to one side anyway. It sat on its own in a corner of the table, insignificant and rather pathetic. It wasn't much to show for three hours' concentrated work.

We took a break for a brief lunch in a bar at around 3 pm, then returned to the archives, refreshed but hardly raring to go. Guastafeste fingered the pile of documents on his table unenthusiastically.

'Do we have to do this?'

'You have a better way of spending the afternoon?' I said.

'Well, yes.'

'Having a few beers in the square doesn't count.'

'It would probably be as productive as sitting here chewing dust.' He looked at my expression. 'Okay, okay, I'll get down another box.'

It was two more hours before anything else of any significance emerged from the mountain of moribund papers. This time it was I who found it.

'Federico Marinetti. There's a letter from him,' I exclaimed.

'Saying what?'

'Let me finish it . . . well, not a lot, I'm afraid,' I admitted. 'Listen. "*My dear Anselmi, you must excuse my silence these past two weeks, but I have been confined to my bed with a fever that left me unable to sit up, much less attend to my correspondence. I am now, thank the Lord, fully recovered from the illness and looking forward to resuming our musical diversions. I am having guests from Milan at the end of the week. Bring your fiddle over on Saturday and we will amuse ourselves with some quartets.*"'

Guastafeste gave a snort. 'Is that it? Not exactly a breakthrough, is it?'

'Don't give up hope,' I replied. 'There are still another four boxes to go.'

'Wonderful. Two each.'

'Got it!' Guastafeste jolted upright so fast he nearly toppled over backwards on his chair. He grabbed the edge of the table to steady himself. 'A letter to Anselmi from Thomas Colquhoun. It's in English. Here.'

He passed me the letter. It was stiff and wrinkled like a piece of hide. I studied the faded text for a time.

'Well?' Guastafeste said. 'What does it say?'

'Nothing,' I replied with a heavy sigh. 'Absolutely nothing. It's a thank you letter for that painting.'

'What painting?'

'The one on the wall at Highfield Hall. The Garofalo. The man with the violin.'

'It was a gift from Anselmi?' Guastafeste said.

'So it would appear.'

I read out the relevant section of the letter, translating it into Italian. '"*The painting is truly magnificent, the brushwork on the violin of exceptional quality. I confess that I would have much preferred His Excellency's instrument – and indeed I have not yet given up hope of it being recovered – but your painting goes some way towards consoling me for my loss. I am indebted to you for your kind consideration and unfailing generosity. The riddle to which you allude escapes me for the moment, but I have grown accustomed to your love of japes and I will endeavour over time to attempt to solve the puzzle. Without your assistance, however, I fear I may not be successful . . .* "'

Guastafeste frowned. 'What's he saying. What riddle? I'm confused. Is the violin in the painting the one that went missing?'

'It's not clear from the text. Maybe.'

'But at Highfield Hall you said it was a Guarneri "del Gesù."'

'It was.'

'So it wasn't a Stradivari that Cozio sent Colquhoun?'

'I don't know,' I said. 'I'm confused too. I don't know what to make of it either.' I looked at the date at the top of the letter – June, 1806. 'It was written two years after the last of the letters we found at Highfield Hall. It would appear that the missing violin – whatever it was – had still not been found by then.'

'It never was found,' Guastafeste said despondently. 'It

disappeared for ever. That's the truth of the matter, isn't it?'

I put the letter on the pile with the other two we'd saved. I felt deflated. The poison of defeat was seeping into both of us.

'I'm right, aren't I?' Guastafeste said. 'It's gone for good.'

'Yes,' I said. 'I fear it has.'

15

We left Casale that evening. There didn't seem much point in remaining any longer. We drove to Cremona in a heavy thunderstorm, sheet lightning breaking over the horizon, the road swimming with rainwater. Guastafeste dropped me off at my house. I opened the car door to get out, but Guastafeste put his hand on my arm.

'I've been thinking,' he said. 'A couple of things bother me. Well, more than a couple, but these two in particular have been nagging away at me. First, how did Tomaso track down Mrs Colquhoun? What made him go all the way to England, to that isolated house in the hills, in search of old documents? Something must have put him on to the scent. I'm going to talk to Clara about that. Second, that painting at Highfield Hall. I want to know more about it. The riddle Thomas Colquhoun mentioned in his letter to Anselmi. What was he talking about? Would you ring Mrs Colquhoun, Gianni? I'd do it myself but you know how bad my English is. Ask her if she can recall anything more about the history of the painting, ask her to look at it for us, check the back for marks, see if there's anything striking, anything peculiar about it. I'll call you later.'

I went into my house. The rain had stopped, but the air felt damp and clammy. I opened a few windows and made myself some pasta for supper, then phoned Mrs Colquhoun. An hour later, as I was preparing to go to bed, Guastafeste rang.

'You get through to her?' he asked.

'Yes. She wasn't much help. She didn't know any more about the painting than she'd already told us.'

'Did you ask her to look at it?'

'I gave her fifteen minutes, then called her back. The picture was too heavy for her to lift down, but she swung it out from the wall and had a look on the back of it. Nothing. She didn't know anything about a riddle either. How about Clara?'

'She didn't know how Tomaso got on to the Colquhoun-Anselmi connection. But she did say that Tomaso had been spending a lot of time in the Cremona public library recently.'

'Looking at what?'

'I don't know, but I intend to find out. You interested? I might need a bit of help.'

I sighed. It had been a long, tiring day. I was growing weary of libraries and old documents, but I knew we had to follow up every lead, track down every missing piece in the jigsaw.

'When do you want to meet?'

'First thing tomorrow,' Guastafeste said. 'Outside the Palazzo Affaitati.'

The Palazzo Affaitati is quite a handsome sixteenth-century building, though you wouldn't know it from the exterior which has been virtually obscured by scaffolding for many months and will no doubt remain so for years to come – almost as if the architect in charge of restoration has

237

incorporated the planks and rusty poles into his 'concept'.

You enter through an arched gateway and porticoed foyer which opens on to a courtyard dominated by three large magnolia trees, then go up a broad marble staircase to the first floor. On one side of the landing is the city art gallery and Museo Stradivariano, on the other the Cremona public library and historic archives. Guastafeste and I went through into the archives.

The librarian in charge was, fortunately, rather more cooperative than the one in Casale.

'Yes, I remember Signor Rainaldi,' she said. 'He came here a lot. Sat at that table over there. We were sorry to hear about his death. And in such horrific circumstances.'

'Do you have any record of what he looked at when he was here?' Guastafeste asked.

'Of course. Every reader has to fill in a request form, then the material is brought up from the archives.'

'You still have the forms?'

'They are kept for twelve months.'

Thank God for Italian bureaucracy, I thought, that pathological need to hoard old bits of paper.

The librarian disappeared into her office and returned a few minutes later with a thick wad of request forms. Guastafeste and I spread them out on one of the tables and studied them.

'He must have spent weeks here,' I said.

'He did,' Guastafeste replied. 'Look at the dates: April, May, June. That was serious research.'

Tomaso had visited the archives, and requested material, some twenty times over that three-month period. Each time he'd asked for the same collection of documents, or rather parts of the same collection – the *Carteggio* of Cozio di Salabue, the extensive, painstakingly detailed record that the count kept of his violin collection.

238

'Let's take a look at some of these,' Guastafeste said and I gave him a sceptical glance.

'You know how many pages there are? Cozio was an obsessive. He measured every tiny bit of his violins – the height of the archings, the width of the purfling, the dimensions of the scrolls. It took him years of meticulous work. The *Carteggio* runs to thousands of pages. Cozio kept everything. Not just his own notes, but copies of letters he wrote to musicians, to violin-makers, to other collectors. He was constantly dealing, trying to enlarge his collection, selling off instruments he didn't want, buying others.'

'You think Tomaso found some mention of Thomas Colquhoun in the *Carteggio*?' Guastafeste said.

'It's quite possible. But to find it will take us as long as it took Tomaso – weeks, months. Are you sure there was nothing in Tomaso's workshop? No notes of his research?'

'Not a single sheet. I've checked. There were bills, invoices, all that sort of thing, but no notes, nothing at all from the public archives, at least none that . . .' Guastafeste broke off. 'Wait a minute. Wait a minute.' He put his thumb to his mouth, chewing pensively on the nail. 'Stay here, I'll be right back.'

I sat down at the table and waited. A good half hour elapsed before Guastafeste returned. He was holding a clear plastic bag stamped with the words 'Cremona Police Department'. There was a white label on the bag bearing a serial number and a description of the contents. Guastafeste placed the bag on the table. Through the transparent plastic I could see a rectangular piece of paper about ten centimetres by eight. It was bright orange with the printed heading 'Comune di Cremona Sistema Museale', and beneath that the words 'Biglietto Cumulativo' and four black ink drawings of a boy with a dog, a plough, a violin-maker and a violin.

239

'You know what this is?' Guastafeste said.

'A ticket for the Museo Stradivariano,' I said.

'It was in the waste bin in Tomaso's workshop. No one has got round to checking it out yet. You have friends over there, don't you?'

I followed Guastafeste out of the library and across the landing to the Stradivari Museum. The museum used to be around the corner on the Via Palestro – a scruffy little place with a few violins hanging up and a collection of grubby glass cases containing the Master's tools and forms. But in the last couple of years the city council – under pressure from various citizens, myself included – had refurbished the Sala Manfredini in the Palazzo Affaitati to provide a setting worthy of Stradivari's place in the history of the city.

'What is it you want to do here?' I asked Guastafeste.

He pointed at the bottom left-hand corner of the ticket in the plastic bag. 'There's a serial number here – 4578. I want to know on what date it was issued.'

I gave the young girl on the ticket counter my name and asked her to call the director of the museum. A few minutes later, Vittorio Sicardo came out through a door behind the counter and shook hands.

'Gianni, how nice to see you.'

'I want to ask a favour,' I said.

We went back a long way, Vittorio and I. I'd sold him one of my violins – at a big discount – thirty years ago when he was still a fine-arts student at the University of Milan and we'd maintained our friendship ever since, through his early days in museum posts in Brescia, Turin and Parma until his return to Cremona as assistant director and then director of the civic museums. He was an art and sculpture man by training – specialist subject, Italian painters of the fifteenth century – but he was a keen amateur violinist and champion of Cremonese cultural history. I'd been a member of the committee that had pressed for this new, improved museum in honour of Stradivari, but we would never have succeeded without Vittorio's tenacity, commitment and political cunning.

'That shouldn't be a problem,' Vittorio said when I'd explained who Guastafeste was and what he wanted. 'Just let me check through the counterfoils.'

Vittorio unlocked a drawer in the desk behind the ticket counter and examined a thick black ledger.

'It was issued on June the sixteenth,' he said, looking up. 'A couple of weeks ago.'

I glanced at Guastafeste. He was keeping his expression resolutely neutral.

'Thank you,' he said politely. 'I'm grateful for your help.'

'Is that all?' Vittorio said.

'Would you mind if we looked around the museum?'

'Not at all. Feel free.'

I thanked Vittorio and exchanged a few words of small talk with him, though I could sense Guastafeste was impatient to move on. Then we shook hands again and Vittorio returned to his office.

'June the sixteenth,' Guastafeste said to me, knowing I was only too aware of the significance of that date. 'The day he was killed, Tomaso came here. Why?'

We walked through into the museum complex, passing first through the city art gallery and its hundreds of worthy but dull examples of the Fleshy Women and Naked Cherubs school of painting. Then we reached the Museo Stradivariano.

The first room we entered was half taken up by a display showing the various stages of making a violin, and half by a group of chairs lined up in rows before a television screen where you could watch a video about violin-making. I looked around blankly.

'Why would Tomaso have come here?' I said. 'A museum. He was hardly likely to find an undiscovered violin.'

'He must have had a reason,' Guastafeste said. 'Just keep your eyes open. See if anything strikes you.'

In the next room were violins in glass cases by various nineteenth-century luthiers whose names are unknown outside violin-making circles – and some within it too. But what was interesting was the painting hanging on the wall, the original portrait of Count Cozio di Salabue by Bernardo Morera from which the photographic reproduction we'd seen at the Castello di Salabue had been taken.

I paused in front of the painting and studied it for a time. It wasn't a great work of art, but it was competently executed like most portraits of obscure noblemen of the time. It had more life than the copy at Salabue. You could see the texture of the oils, the colours were more intense, the expression in Cozio's eyes more striking.

'What do you think?' Guastafeste said, coming up to my shoulder.

'I don't know.'

'That blank piece of paper in his hand still looks peculiar to me. I'm not convinced by Giovanni Davico's theory about it.'

'The French Revolution, you mean?'

'Look at the date. It was painted in 1831. That was almost half a century after the Revolution. Why would anyone worry about being identified as an aristocrat?'

I mused on that as we moved on through the other rooms of the museum, ending at the most impressive of them all, the Sala Manfredini which contains the collection of Stradivari's tools, moulds and forms which Paolo Stradivari sold to Cozio di Salabue in 1776. The room has a high ceiling with a crystal chandelier in the centre and walls painted with fake pillars and classical scenes of ancient ruined buildings. There is a background hum of air-conditioning and humidifying equipment and the softer, more attractive sound of violin music being piped in through speakers.

By the first of the illuminated glass cases I bumped into two of my students – a German and a Swede – from the International School of Violin Making; there, presumably, seeking inspiration from Stradivari's legacy. I am an occasional visiting professor at the school which is housed in the shabby splendour of the Palazzo Raimondi – an apposite preparation for the impoverished gentility the students will face in their subsequent careers as luthiers. Young men and women come from all over the globe to study here in Cremona. All are talented and enthusiastic but I fear for their futures. There are too many violin-makers in the world, too many old violins around. The new artisans will struggle to compete in such a crowded marketplace.

I had a brief conversation with the students, then continued my slow perambulation around the room.

'I've never been in here before. Now I can see why. This is the most boring museum I've ever been in,' Guastafeste said witheringly from across one of the cabinets.

'You're such a philistine sometimes,' I replied.

'But there's nothing here except a few old planes and chisels and lots of meaningless bits of paper.'

'These are historical treasures.'

'Treasures? To whom? They've got all these security cameras in here but, really, what thief in his right mind is going to want to steal any of this junk?'

'There are the violins in the other rooms,' I said.

'But none of them are Stradivaris. This is a Stradivari Museum that doesn't contain a single violin he made.'

I had to concede that that was true. The city's small

collection of great violins – by Stradivari, Guarneri and Amati – is in the Town Hall, in a locked room which is opened only when someone wants to view them, and then only under the watchful eyes of two security guards.

'This is a valuable part of our heritage,' I began defensively. Then I saw the expression on Guastafeste's face. 'What's the matter?'

'*Cameras*,' he said.

'Take as long as you like,' said Vittorio Sicardo. 'I think the tapes are all there. Let me know if you need anything else.'

We were in one of the museum offices, a small room made even smaller by all the clutter on the floor – boxes of broken pottery, a stack of tatty gilt frames and a disembodied marble head with a chipped nose which had somehow strayed in from the restoration workshops. On the desk in front of us was a television and video cassette recorder. Guastafeste inserted the first of the tapes Vittorio had dug out for us.

'This is the camera covering the entrance to the Museo Stradivariano,' he said. 'The first tape of the day for June the sixteenth, immediately after the museum had opened to the public.'

Guastafeste played the recording back. There was nothing on it for the first few minutes, just a deserted vestibule, then a man in the uniform of one of the museum attendants came in from the art gallery. He glanced around briefly before moving out of shot into one of the adjoining rooms. Guastafeste let the tape run for a few more minutes, then pressed the 'fast forward' button on the remote control. According to the time code in the bottom corner of the screen it was another half an hour before anyone else entered the museum, and then it was another uniformed attendant.

'Popular place,' Guastafeste said sarcastically. 'They're really packing them in, aren't they? What's he doing?'

The attendant was pushing a trolley bearing a number of plastic canisters. He stopped by the piece of apparatus in the corner of the room and removed its lid.

'Changing the reservoirs on the humidifying machinery,' I said.

Guastafeste fast forwarded the tape again, the speeded up image still on the screen so we could see if anything happened. We'd been lucky. The museum stored the tapes from the CCTV cameras for only a fortnight. If we'd been a couple of days later, the tapes would all have been wiped.

'There,' I said. 'What's that?'

Guastafeste pressed the 'play' button. A man had entered the vestibule and was pausing to take his bearings. But it wasn't Tomaso. We kept going. A few more people came into the museum during the course of the morning, but none of them was Tomaso. I started to get restless. I stood up and stretched. I'd have paced around the office only there was no room.

'There he is,' Guastafeste said quietly.

He froze the picture. Tomaso had just stepped into the vestibule. It brought a lump to my throat to see my dead friend brought back to life.

Guastafeste started the tape again. After only a few seconds Tomaso moved out of shot into the adjoining room. Guastafeste made a note of the time code, then stopped the tape and searched through the pile of tapes on the desk for the one covering the next room. It was a relatively simple task to fast forward to the point at which Tomaso came through from the entrance vestibule. He stopped, glancing perfunctorily around the cabinets of violins, before turning his attention to the portrait of Cozio on the wall. It seemed to interest him. He gazed at the painting for a long time, changing his position to gain different angles on the image of the count. Then he moved closer, leaning forward to examine a portion of the painting in more detail. He lifted a finger and – so quickly it was easy to miss – ran the tip over the blank sheet of paper in Cozio's right hand.

'He's noticed something,' Guastafeste said.

'That's more than I did,' I said, peering intently at the screen.

We followed Tomaso through the next few rooms, but he didn't linger in any of them. Then Guastafeste inserted the tape from the Sala Manfredini and played it back from the moment Tomaso entered. He didn't seem in a hurry. He glanced at his wristwatch, looked slowly around the room, then moved to the first of the waist-high glass cabinets and studied the exhibits inside it – his gaze distracted as if he had time on his hands to kill.

His attention passed to the next cabinet, but it soon started to wander. He began looking around casually. He seemed bored. At one point he even yawned. There was still no real purpose to his movements. It was as if he'd come to the museum in the hope of finding something, but wasn't sure exactly what.

'He doesn't know what he's doing there,' Guastafeste said.

'Fishing, perhaps,' I said.

'Fishing for what?'

'Inspiration. Like my students. He'd told Forlani that he could find him a second Messiah. He had some old letters to indicate that the violin might once have existed but had gone missing. But that's all. I suspect he had no idea where to go next. He needed a new lead to get him on the right track. So he came here to the museum hoping that something – anything – might strike him and provide that lead.'

'It doesn't look as if he found it,' Guastafeste said.

'Hang on a moment, what's this?'

Another figure had come into shot – a taller, younger man with thin wispy hair swept back from his freckled face. He was wearing an open-necked shirt and a fashionable light-coloured linen jacket. Tomaso seemed to know him. The two men exchanged a few words, their lips moving soundlessly on the screen. Then Tomaso gave a nod, as if agreeing to something, and followed Christopher Scott out of the room.

I stepped closer to the painting, aware that the camera high up in the corner of the room was recording my every move. I could see nothing particularly interesting in the portrait, nothing I hadn't seen when I'd examined it before. I took a pace to my right. The angle of the light changed, casting a sheen over the canvas and obscuring Cozio's face and the front of his frock-coat. I moved back to my original position, then kept going left. The light changed again. This time the count's face was brought into sharper relief. I could see the artist's brush strokes, the way he'd painted the fine detail of Cozio's shirt, the wrinkles on the skin of his fingers and hands. And I saw something I hadn't noticed before – a subtle change in the texture of the oils along the edges of the blank sheet of paper. I touched the join, expecting to feel a minute ridge, but of course I felt nothing except the smooth layer of varnish over the paint.

'Anything?' Guastafeste asked.

'I don't know. But there's a way of finding out.'

'This is really very irregular, Gianni,' Vittorio Sicardo said. 'If the curator of pictures gets to hear of it, he'll blow a fuse.'

'Who's going to tell him?' I said. 'It'll only take a couple of minutes. It's important.'

Vittorio sighed. 'You go back upstairs. I'll bring the equipment up.'

Guastafeste was still standing in front of the portrait of Cozio di Salabue.

'It's all fixed,' I said.

A few minutes later, Vittorio arrived with the ultra-violet lamp, an extension lead and three pairs of tinted goggles. He called in one of the museum attendants and told him to keep visitors out of the room, then plugged the extension lead into a socket in the wall and handed out the goggles.

'Which area are you interested in?'

'The blank piece of paper,' I said.

Vittorio switched on the lamp and shone the ultra-violet beam on to the painting. Through my tinted goggles I could see the image of Cozio glowing with a strange bluish luminescence. The blank piece of paper in the count's hand was darker than the rest of the canvas, almost black in fact.

'See that?' Vittorio said. 'Areas of overpainting always fluoresce black. It seems you were right, the picture has been altered.'

He switched off the UV lamp and we removed our goggles.

'Is there any way of seeing what was overpainted?' I said.

'What do you think might have been there?'

'I don't know. Words, perhaps. Something written on the piece of paper. Can't you see images beneath the paint with infra-red light?'

'You can use infra-red photography to detect images on the ground layer, yes. The chalk or graphite lines the artist used to sketch out the portrait would be visible. But if there were words on the piece of paper, Morera, the artist, would never have put them in at the ground stage. Details like that would always be in the paint layer, and infra-red

248

photography can't distinguish between different layers of paint.'

'So there's no way of finding out if there *was* anything written on the paper?'

'Not without stripping away the varnish and then the overpaint,' Vittorio said. He saw what was coming. 'And no, Gianni, I am not going to allow that. This is a precious painting.'

I gave a weary nod. 'Thanks, Vittorio. It was worth a try.'

Vittorio unplugged the extension lead and wound it into a coil around his arm. 'You could always look at Morera's sketches, if you like,' he said.

'You have his sketches? For this portrait?'

'I'm not absolutely sure about that, but we have a collection of his drawings in the basement. You want me to have them brought up?'

The drawings were in three A1-sized portfolios, fastened shut with faded black ribbons which looked as if they hadn't been untied for decades. Vittorio had to use a letter opener to prise apart the knotted ends of the ribbons, then he spread open the first portfolio on his desk. He was wearing white cotton gloves to prevent any soiling of the drawings.

He went through them slowly, removing the pieces of paper one at a time and placing them to one side for us to study. There were rough sketches of landscapes, of fields and gardens and grand country houses; there were still-life drawings, charcoal outlines of nudes, both male and female, and numerous studies of faces, the outlines of the portraits which formed the greater part of Morera's artistic output.

'There,' Vittorio said, pulling out another sketch from the portfolio. 'That looks like Cozio.'

It did indeed. It was a chalk outline of the count's head, his features drawn in some detail. His torso and arms were missing, but I had no doubt that this was a preliminary sketch for the portrait hanging on the wall in the museum.

Vittorio lifted out another drawing of Cozio's head alone, then a larger, less detailed sketch of the full portrait, with Cozio seated, his left hand resting on his walking stick, his right holding a piece of paper – a piece of paper with a few words scribbled carelessly across it.

Vittorio peered closer. 'You guessed correctly, Gianni. That looks like a coat of arms at the top, Cozio's family crest.'

'And below it?' I leaned over the desk, trying to discern the words.

'They're hard to make out, the chalk is very smudged. I can see a figure here, a number. A seventeen, then more digits. It looks like 1716 – a date.'

I glanced at Guastafeste. 1716, the year the Messiah was made.

'I'm afraid the rest is very faint,' Vittorio said. He took a magnifying glass from his desk drawer and held it over the drawing. I can see an S followed by an L – no, I think it's a T. The next few letters are illegible. Then maybe a V, then an I. I'm not sure.'

'Could it be Stradivari?' I said.

Vittorio took his time replying. 'It might be,' he said eventually without looking up from his magnifying glass. 'Then there's another couple of words. Federico . . . Federico something.'

'Marinetti?' I suggested.

'Yes, that's possible. There's something that looks like an old-fashioned lire sign, but the figures after it are too blurred to read.' He straightened up. 'It's intriguing. It doesn't look as if it's a letter the count is holding. From the pattern of the words, the layout, the fact that there are so few words, I'd say it was more like an invoice or a bill of sale; a commercial document of some sort. That date puzzles me though: 1716. The painting was done in 1831. Why would Cozio be holding a document dated 1716?'

'It's not the date of the document,' I said. 'It's the date of a violin. A Stradivari of 1716. A Stradivari violin that Cozio sold to Federico Marinetti.'

16

The three letters we'd found in the public archives in Casale Monferrato were spread out on my kitchen table – not the originals, of course, but photocopies we'd been allowed to take. I looked at each in turn: Thomas Colquhoun's letter about the painting at Highfield Hall – an intriguing missive, but still a puzzle to us; the letter from Elisabeta Horak about her mother's violin – I wondered about that. Was it of any relevance? I could not see at the moment how it might be. And who was Elisabeta Horak? Finally, I turned to the letter from Federico Marinetti to Michele Anselmi. I read it through again. The first thing I noticed was that it wasn't, in fact, addressed to Michele Anselmi, as we'd thought before, but to his son, Paolo.

'Does it matter?' Guastafeste said when I pointed out the discrepancy. 'All we want is Marinetti's address.'

That was when I noticed the second thing. 'Ah. The address.'

'It's there, isn't it?'

The address at the top of the letter, I now realised, was so badly stained as to be completely indecipherable.

'Can you make anything out?' I said.

Guastafeste took the letter from me. 'Not a word.'

'The other letter from Marinetti – at Salabue – did that have an address on it?'

Guastafeste shrugged. 'I don't remember. We didn't think he was significant then. Let's call them and ask.'

I rang Giovanni Davico. He went away for a couple of minutes and returned with the letter.

'Yes, there's an address on it,' he said. 'Faint and smudged, but I think it says Villa Magenta, Frassineto Po.'

Frassineto Po was five kilometres east of Casale Monferrato, one of those nondescript, insignificant settlements that are almost too small to be flattered with the title 'village' – a one-horse town where the nag has long since keeled over and been consigned to the dogmeat factory.

We asked in a bar and were given directions away from the river and up into the rolling hills on the southern bank of the Po. The Villa Magenta was a couple of kilometres away, perched on the side of a low hill, copses of trees and open pastureland on the slopes below it. We sped up a steep, twisting drive from the road and came out on a gravel forecourt in front of the house – a large, three-storey seventeenth-century villa that had been built in three distinct sections: a long central segment with a turreted wing on each end. The near and middle sections looked occupied, but the furthest wing was derelict – its roof had gone completely and the windows were devoid of glass, the stucco around them blackened with soot and peeling off in sheets. Parked in front of the main entrance was a yellow Lamborghini sports car. Guastafeste turned in next to it.

The man who answered the door was in his early thirties. He was casually, but expensively, dressed, a pair of reflective sunglasses concealing his eyes. Guastafeste showed him his police identity card.

'I hope we're not intruding,' he said. 'You are Signor Marinetti?'

'No, my name is Ferrucci.'

'But this *is* the house where Federico Marinetti lived?'

'It was.'

'You are descended from him?'

'No, the house passed out of the Marinetti family . . . oh, a hundred and fifty years ago. They went broke. What is this?'

Guastafeste explained why we were there. Ferrucci pulled off his sunglasses and squinted at us.

'A violin? I don't know anything about that.'

'Could we come in for a moment?' Guastafeste said.

Ferrucci hesitated. 'Well . . . I suppose so.'

He led us across the hall and into a drawing room which was furnished more for show than comfort. The chairs and sofas – all rococo curves and silk upholstery – looked too fragile to sit on and the walls were overcrowded with gloomy paintings in heavy gilt frames that gave the room an oppressive atmosphere.

'You say the Marinettis went broke?' Guastafeste said, sitting down on one of the sofas.

'Yes,' Ferrucci replied. 'Gambling debts. Federico Marinetti was a compulsive gambler. He inherited this house and a vast estate from his father and blew it all away on extravagant living and the gaming tables. You don't know the story?'

'I'm afraid not,' Guastafeste said.

'It was quite a scandal at the time. Federico was something of a character. He liked to throw huge parties, invited friends, dozens of friends, to stay. He'd hire an orchestra for a week at a time – he was a great lover of music – and party day and night until he collapsed of exhaustion. He ran up such large debts that gradually the estate was sold off piece by piece. But that didn't stop him. He went on one final, mad gambling binge and blew what was left of his inheritance. Then he came back here to the Villa Magenta, shut himself away in the west wing with his mistress and set fire to the place. Both he and his mistress perished in the blaze.'

That explained why the words on the piece of paper in Cozio's portrait had been painted over. Who would have wanted to publicise any association with a man like Federico Marinetti?

'The wing has never been rebuilt then?' I said.

'No, it was left derelict after the fire. The servants managed to extinguish the blaze before it took hold in the rest of the house, but the west wing was gutted.'

'And after Marinetti's death?' Guastafeste said. 'What happened?'

'I believe everything was sold to pay his debts.'

'So nothing of Marinetti's is left here today?'

'Not in the main house.'

'And in the west wing?' I said, still hopeful that our visit might not be entirely wasted.

'Well, it's pretty much the way it was left after the fire,' Ferrucci replied. 'The floors and roof have gone. It's just a pile of rubble. No one's bothered to get rid of any of it.'

'Do you mind if we look?'

Ferrucci shrugged. 'Be my guests.'

'Are you sure it's safe?' Guastafeste asked, peering up into the empty shell of the building.

'Well, there's nothing above to fall down on us,' I replied. 'And the walls must be pretty secure to have sur-vived intact for all these years.'

255

I stepped through an opening which must once have been a door and looked around, my heart sinking. Perhaps I'd been guilty of deluding myself, of allowing my common sense to be overridden by an unrealistic optimism that we would eventually find the violin we were seeking. If so, this was the moment of my awakening. There was no way any degree of optimism could have remained intact when faced with the scene of absolute destruction that was now before me. The walls were bare stone, their surfaces still stained by the marks of the fire, by soot and ash and scorching blisters. The roof, of course, was gone, but fragments of the rafters remained embedded in the tops of the walls, great stumps of charred timber that had burnt like kindling in the ferocious inferno. What little was left of the roof tiles and the collapsed upper floors of the building now lay in a heap on the ground, their origins almost invisible beneath the dense tangle of weeds and grass that had colonised them over the intervening years.

I picked my way around the mound of rubble, looking for gaps in the vegetation. There was sunlight, blue sky above me, but down here all was shadow. Was it my imagination, or could I really smell the sulphurous residue of smoke? I grasped hold of a tall clump of weeds and wrenched it out, then another, clearing a patch in the debris. With the toe of my shoe I scooped out some of the looser material, eating into the side of the mound.

'A violin is made of wood,' Guastafeste said. 'It would have been one of the first things to be destroyed.'

I caught a glimpse of a thin filament of wire half buried in the earth. I bent down and pulled it out. Was it a violin string? I knew it wasn't. The strings would have been made of gut that would have burnt as easily as the instrument itself. This was just a piece of rusty wire. I tossed it away and gazed around. Guastafeste was right – no violin could have survived such an all-consuming fire – but a part of me still hoped I might find some trace of its existence: a charred peg, a piece of scroll, perhaps even a brittle fragment of paper bearing the words, '*Antonius Stradivarius Cremonensis Faciebat Anno 1716* . . .'

'Leave it, Gianni,' Guastafeste said gently. 'It's over.'

17

Disappointment is like a disease, a debilitating fever that saps your energy, drains your willpower and leaves you frail and feeble. If left untreated, it can eat away at the mind, depressing the body's immune system and eventually producing physical symptoms as painful and genuine as any bacterial or viral illness.

I was despondent. So too was Guastafeste. We'd been to England, to Salabue, to Casale Monferrato and now Frassineto Po, but had yet to arrive at the destination we craved.

'Sleep on things,' Guastafeste said when he dropped me off outside my house. 'I'll call you in the morning.'

It was late, I was tired after our drive, but I didn't go up to bed immediately. I put on a CD of Bach and sat in my sitting room, thinking back to the night Tomaso had been killed, of everything that had happened since. The murder investigation was the province of the police. They had resources, specialist personnel, powers that were way beyond anything I could command. I could give Guastafeste no assistance in that area. But violins – violins were *my* province.

In the excitement of tracing the 1716 Stradivari to Federico Marinetti, then the bitter disappointment of discovering that it had most probably been destroyed, we had temporarily lost sight of the other instrument – the violin that had gone missing on its way to England two hundred years ago. And we had lost sight of the painting that I was sure held the key to that violin's fate. Mrs Colquhoun had not known any more about the portrait on the wall of her house, but there were other ways of alleviating my curiosity. In the morning, as soon as the museum opened, I telephoned Vittorio Sicardo at the Palazzo Affaitati and told him what I wanted.

'Just let me find a pen,' Vittorio said. 'What was the name again?'

'Cesare Garofalo,' I said.

'This kind of stuff's easy to track down on the internet, you know.'

'I'm old-fashioned,' I said. 'I still have a touching faith in books and libraries. Besides, I don't have a computer.'

'I'll see what I can find and call you back. It might take me some time, I've meetings all morning.'

'Whenever, that's fine.'

I went into my workshop and diverted my troubled mind by finishing off the repairs to the damaged Stradivari for Serafin. Nearing eleven o'clock, Guastafeste called and we had a brief conversation. He told me that the British police – who had been officially asked to locate Christopher Scott – had been unable to find the dealer, at either his home or business address. He seemed to have disappeared.

I was having lunch in the kitchen when the phone rang again. It wasn't Vittorio, as I'd expected, but Margherita Severini.

'How busy are you this afternoon?' she said.

'Nothing that can't wait.'

'Can I come and see you?'

'But of course. Come for dinner.'

'No, I won't do that – I have to be back in Milan this evening – but thank you.'

'See me about what?'

'I'll tell you later. Now where are you, and how do I get to you?'

I took her out on to the terrace when she arrived and we sat in the shade under my pergola, the trellis of vines above our heads protecting us from the heat of the sun. She was wearing a sleeveless blue summer dress and just a trace of make-up. I brought out a jug of iced tea with lemon and poured her a glass. She looked at me and smiled.

'I could have done this on the phone,' she said. 'But I thought it would be better face to face. I had no classes this afternoon and I felt like getting out of Milan. I often feel like getting out of Milan.' She looked across the terrace. 'You have a lovely garden. Do you do it all yourself?'

I nodded. 'It was already pretty mature when we bought the house. The previous owner planted most of the trees, but I've added a lot of shrubs, made a vegetable patch down at the bottom.'

'You have such a lot of space. I can smell fresh air, not petrol fumes, see the sky, not a line of traffic.'

'Well, if you will live in the city,' I said.

Margherita made a wry face. 'I know, it's my own fault. Is your workshop here too?'

'Over there. I'll show you it later, if you like.'

She sipped some of her iced tea. I waited.

'I've heard from my uncle's lawyers,' she said. 'He made no separate provision for the disposal of his violin collection, so it would seem that I inherit it, along with the rest of his estate.'

'It was a formidable collection,' I said.

'More than a hundred instruments,' Margherita said. 'Not all of them on display. He kept some in a bank vault. He was not a great one for paperwork, Uncle Enrico. Apparently he kept no proper record of the violins he acquired. There are no invoices, no receipts. No one knows exactly what violins he owned, by what makers, when they were bought or what he paid for them. It's all a complete mess.'

'Weren't they insured?'

'Some, but by no means all. Uncle Enrico didn't seem to be too worried about insurance. The end result is that there's no full inventory of the collection. And the lawyers need one. So will the tax man. Which is where you come in, Gianni. You've seen the collection, you know about violins. Would you be willing to identify, catalogue and value the instruments? For a fee, of course.'

'I'm not a dealer,' I said. 'I don't have up-to-the-minute knowledge of the market.'

'I don't want a dealer. My experience of dealers leaves a lot to be desired. They'd only cheat me, I have no doubt about that. I've made a few enquiries, asked around. Your name keeps coming up. You want someone who knows his stuff *and* has integrity, Gianni Castiglione is your man, they all say.'

'I'm flattered.'

'Could you do it? Would you?'

'Certainly I could do it. I do valuations for insurance purposes all the time. But an insurance valuation is not the same as a market valuation.'

'What's a market valuation?' Margherita asked rhetorically. 'A figure some crooked dealer has pulled out of a hat to swindle some unsuspecting client. No, I'll settle for your figures, Gianni.'

'Yes, I'll do it,' I said. 'Where are the violins? Still in his house?'

'The lawyers had them moved to a bank vault. You'll have to go to Venice, of course, but all expenses will be paid. Just name your fee.'

I waved a hand. Talking money has always made me uncomfortable.

'We can agree a fee later,' I said.

'No, I won't have you do it for nothing. This is business. I'm paying for your time and expertise. It's not my money. It will come out of my uncle's estate and – believe me – the estate can afford to pay you properly.'

I glanced away across the garden. The borders were daubed with vibrant colours – scarlet fuchsias, deep purple buddleias, a vivid yellow climbing rose. Butterflies, their wings as striking as the flowers, fluttered over the foliage like petals drifting in the breeze.

'I don't want money,' I said.

'Gianni . . .'

'No, let me finish. I'd like something else. When I visited your uncle in Venice, he showed me all the violins he had on display. He played a little game with me, asking me to identify the violins. It was an awesome collection – certainly the finest I've ever seen. Every instrument was of the highest quality, its pedigree unquestionable – except for one. One of his violins was a fake.'

Margherita stared at me. 'A fake?'

'I didn't tell him, of course. He was immensely fond of that particular instrument. It's a good fake, good enough to fool most experts, but it's a fake nonetheless. For my fee, I'd like that violin.'

'The fake?'

262

'Yes.'

'Why?'

'There are reasons. It has curiosity value, but its monetary value is slight – a few thousand euros perhaps. Would you regard that as an excessive fee?'

'Not at all. Which violin is it?'

'A Guarneri "del Gesù", dated 1740. Your uncle believed it had once belonged to Louis Spohr, but he was deceived.'

Margherita regarded me curiously. 'I'm intrigued. It's a strange request, but I sense your reluctance to tell me more.'

'This isn't some devious way of getting my hands on a priceless "del Gesù",' I said. 'You have my word on that. But I don't want to say any more at the moment. Will you accept that?'

'Of course. And I accept your terms. I'll contact my uncle's lawyers. They'll be in touch to arrange for you to go to Venice to examine the collection.'

'Is it urgent?'

'They're lawyers,' Margherita said dryly. 'To them, nothing is urgent – except the settlement of their bills.'

We finished our iced tea and I took her into my workshop. There is nothing particularly interesting about a luthier's bench, his tools and forms and moulds. But I wanted her to see it, I wanted to share with her the place in which I spent my working hours, the place which more than anywhere in my house I consider my true home.

I showed her one of my finished violins, then others in progress, some in the white, some just a promise of things to come, mere rough-cut tables and half-assembled ribs. I explained to her the process, how the raw planks of spruce and maple that were stacked to the ceiling in my wood store were transformed into the rich, varnished instruments of the concert hall. She listened quietly, attentively, and when I looked up I saw she was smiling at me.

'What?'

'You love your work, don't you?' she said.

'Yes, I do.'

'It's good to find a man with such a passion – such a talent – for creating something beautiful.'

'All I do is make violins,' I said. 'I know it seems a little absurd to get so worked up about a few bits of wood, but I can't help it. These things have been my life. All I hope is that my instruments have made a few people happy, have given music and joy to many others. That seems to me a worthwhile achievement.'

'And to me.'

'Now let me show you my garden, my other enduring passion.'

We went back out on to the terrace and for half an hour we explored the pathways and shrubberies, my apple and plum orchards, my herb and rock and water gardens which for the past seven years, with Nature's help, I have tended with the love and patience of a doting father.

Then we grew tired of the heat of the afternoon and went inside the house. Margherita noticed the piano in my back room.

'You play the piano too?'

'No, my wife was the pianist.'

Margherita ran her fingers lightly over the keys, then looked at the piles of sheet music on the lid.

'You like Brahms?' I said.

'Yes.'

'Perhaps some time we could try a duet together.'

'Perhaps.' Her hand touched my arm. 'I really have to be going now.' She kissed me on the cheek. 'I'll be in touch, Gianni.'

That kiss stayed with me long after she'd gone. I had grown accustomed to being alone, to spending the dark hours of the night – and often the day – in quiet contemplation of my own end. I prepared myself for it long ago. The whole of life, I suppose, is a preparation for death, but when we are young it is easier to forget that fact. Only in middle age, when my mother died, did the chilling realisation of my own mortality really hit me. I started then to count the years, to dwell a little more on eternity. There were distractions – my wife, my children, my work – that gave some form, some purpose, to my life. But when my wife died everything seemed to disintegrate around me. I was overwhelmed by a feeling of desolation, of guilt – that Caterina was gone while I, such a worthless creature in comparison to her, was still alive. Then when the grief subsided I began to feel a strange sensation of relief, almost of comfort that I would not have to endure many more years alone. That sounds morbid, despondent, but it is perhaps a misleading description for I had not been unhappy all that time. Rather I had found an equilibrium, a contentment that in some ways had been fulfilling. I believed that if my life ended tomorrow, I would not much mind.

But that equilibrium had now been disturbed. The reassuring routine of my life had been thrown out of kilter and I was feeling confused and disorientated. This was not supposed to happen. Not at my age. I found the experience bewildering. Bewildering, yet somehow liberating.

It was evening before Vittorio Sicardo called me back.

'Cesare Garofalo,' he said. 'Not a name I was very familiar with. I'm afraid I couldn't find out all that much about him.'

'Just an outline will do,' I said.

'Well, he was born in Cameriano, near Novara, in 1642 and died in Casale Monferrato in 1704, aged sixty-two. He was believed to have been a pupil of Francesco Cairo, in Milan, somewhere around the 1660s, then later moved to Turin and finally Casale where he spent the last thirty years of his life. I've only managed to find a couple of illustrations of his work – both portraits of minor noblemen – but they're remarkably good. I'm surprised he isn't better known. If you want more, the city art gallery in Casale might be able to help you.'

'What was the year of his death again?'

'1704.'

'Thanks, Vittorio.'

'I'm sorry I couldn't be of greater assistance.'

'You've given me exactly what I needed.'

I broke the connection without replacing the receiver, keeping my finger on the button for a moment. Then I called Guastafeste.

'Remember this?' I held up one of the photocopied letters from the archives in Casale. 'From Thomas Colquhoun to Michele Anselmi, thanking him for the painting.'

Guastafeste settled himself down in the armchair by the piano. 'I remember. What of it?'

'Let me read you a bit.' I translated the section into Italian. '"The riddle to which you allude escapes me for the moment, but I have grown accustomed to your love of japes and I will endeavour over time to attempt to solve the puzzle."'

'Yes?'

'I think I know what the riddle was. The painting at Highfield Hall is by Cesare Garofalo. If you recall, it shows a man in a music room with a violin in his arms. A Guarneri "del Gesù" violin, to be exact.' I paced across the room to the French windows. I was too excited to sit down.

'I've done some research. Cesare Garofalo was a Casale artist so it's quite possible that Michele Anselmi knew his work, perhaps owned some of his paintings. There's just one problem. Garofalo died in 1704.'

'So?'

'Giuseppe Guarneri "del Gesù" was born in 1698. When Garofalo died, Guarneri was just six years old. So how was it possible for Garofalo to incorporate a "del Gesù" into the painting?'

'The painting's a fake?' Guastafeste said.

'It has to be.'

'Maybe you're wrong about the violin. Maybe it's not a "del Gesù", but a violin by some earlier maker. It's a painting, after all, not the real thing. What if Garofalo didn't reproduce it very accurately?'

I shook my head. 'It's a "del Gesù" all right. I'd stake my life on it.'

'Why would Anselmi send Colquhoun a forged painting?'

'I don't know,' I said. 'But I think we ought to take another look at it.'

Guastafeste's superiors at the *Questura* baulked at the idea of him returning to England to examine an old painting, so he took a couple of days' leave and paid for the air flight himself. At Manchester airport I noticed a Thornton's chocolate shop and we bought the biggest box they sold before picking up our hire car and driving to Highfield Hall. Mrs Colquhoun was wearing the same tweed skirt and cardigan as before, though with the addition of a few more silvery cat hairs, and her feline friends were still in smug occupation of her sitting room. We went into the kitchen, where only a couple of 'Timmies' were ensconced in front of the stove, and Mrs Colquhoun made us tea.

'You shouldn't have,' she said, opening the box of

chocolates we'd brought. 'Oh, how wonderful. You must have one. These ones, with the dusting of sugar, are particularly good. Go on, I can't eat them all myself. Well, I can, but it would be very naughty.'

An hour later we were still there, on our third pot of tea, the chocolate box looking severely depleted. I decided it was time to make a move if we were to get away by the evening – neither Guastafeste nor I being particularly anxious to spend another night in the house.

'The painting,' I said.

'Oh, yes, of course. I'm so sorry, I'm talking too much. Let me show you.'

'No, please. Don't trouble yourself. We know where it is.'

We went upstairs by ourselves and studied the painting on the landing. I ran my eyes slowly over every centimetre of the canvas, taking in the man holding the violin, the virginal to one side, the detail of the walls and floor, the trees and church tower beyond the window of the room.

'You're still sure it's a "del Gesù"?' Guastafeste asked.

'There's no doubt about it. The painting has to be a forgery.'

Guastafeste touched the gilt frame of the picture. It looked original.

'Is that the only riddle?' he said reflectively. 'Or is there something more? Help me get it down.'

It was a big painting, the frame thick and heavy. We lowered it carefully to the floor and turned it round so we could examine the back. A protective cloth covering was stretched across the frame. I'd hoped for some writing, a significant mark or two, but the cloth, beneath its coating of dust, was completely blank. I took out my pocket knife and cut a slit along the top edge of the cloth, then slid my hand in and felt around in the gap between cloth and canvas. There was nothing there.

'Maybe there's something on the back of the canvas,' Guastafeste said.

I hesitated. That would mean removing the cloth covering entirely.

Guastafeste saw me pause. 'She'll never know. We can borrow some tape on some pretext or other and stick it back.'

I nodded. Now we were here, there was no sense in having too many scruples. With my knife I cut away the piece of cloth to expose the canvas back of the painting itself. We both crouched down and examined it closely.

'You see anything?' Guastafeste asked.

'No.'

'Me neither.'

I felt around the edges of the frame with my fingertips, hoping to find . . . what? Some piece of paper, some conveniently hidden clue that would lead us to the violin? I was dreaming. There was never going to be anything so simple.

'It must be in the painting itself,' Guastafeste said. 'The picture, the subject matter.'

We turned the painting round and propped it up against the landing wall. I studied it again.

'Maybe it's the man holding the violin?' I said.

'We don't know who he is.'

'But if we did, perhaps he's the key.'

'Mrs Colquhoun didn't even know who he was. How are we supposed to find out?'

The man was staring directly out from the canvas. He was young – maybe in his mid twenties – with a fresh complexion. The painting was dirty, but I thought I could detect a slight flush on the young man's cheeks. A flush of what? Embarrassment? Good health? . . . Guilt? I moved back a little to get a better perspective, taking in the whole

269

of the young man's person. The expression in his eyes, the set of his mouth, seemed troubled. Or was I simply imagining it all, seeing things that weren't there?

I scrutinised the rest of the painting, going backwards and forwards over the oils, peering minutely at every detail in case there was something I'd missed. The virginal to one side of the music room was beautifully captured. The lid was raised to reveal a scene of bucolic tranquillity painted on its underside. In the centre was a lake overhung with exotic trees while around the edges were figures – a couple out for a stroll, the woman holding a parasol; two men in earnest conversation; another man on horseback; a family sharing a picnic with a group of ducks loitering nearby for titbits. The sides and front of the instrument were decorated with an inlaid pattern of ivory and different coloured woods and on the panel behind the keyboard was a marquetry rose surrounded by intricate fretwork like handwriting. *Handwriting?* I stared at the fretwork, hoping to make out words amidst the curlicues and arabesques, but I sought in vain.

'Well?' Guastafeste said.

I shook my head. In Italy I'd been so sure there would be something in the painting. Now we were here before it, I could see nothing.

'Just move aside, Gianni.'

Guastafeste had brought a digital camera with him. He crouched down and took several shots of the painting.

'I'll get them blown up in the lab,' he said. 'We can study them when we get home.'

I was still looking at the painting. It *had* to be there. Why couldn't I see it?

'Gianni . . .'

I nodded and tore my eyes away from the picture. There was no point in lingering.

Mrs Colquhoun tried to persuade us to stay longer, but we politely declined. We drove away from the house in silence. In stark contrast to our previous visit there was no mist on the moors. The heather and the sandstone crags were illuminated in brilliant sunshine, but neither of us was interested in the scenery. We dropped down off the plateau, past the coniferous plantations, the reservoir, the enclosed fields of grazing sheep. We passed under a railway bridge, the outskirts of a village closing in around the road. I saw a pub, rows of stone houses, the tower of a church on the hillside in the distance . . . and it came to me suddenly, as if a magnesium flare had erupted inside my skull.

'Pull over . . .'

Guastafeste turned his head. 'What?'

'Stop the car.'

'Here?'

'Anywhere.'

Guastafeste slowed, pulled in to the kerb. A driver behind sounded his horn and overtook us with an angry rev of his engine. Guastafeste looked at me. I was trembling, my stomach gripped in a tourniquet of sickness and excitement.

'I know what it is,' I said, my voice little more than a croak. 'The riddle, the clue. And the violin. I know where it is.'

18

For a long time neither of us moved. I stared straight ahead through the windscreen, listening to the racing beat of my heart. Cars went past in both directions. I was aware vaguely of their shapes, the noise of their engines, but my gaze was focused intently on the hillside beyond the village; on the tower of a church just visible above a line of trees.

'I'm waiting,' Guastafeste said calmly.

I blinked and turned to look at him. Then I slid my hand into the inside pocket of my jacket and pulled out an envelope containing the photocopies of the letters we had found at Highfield Hall and in the archives at Casale Monferrato. I unfolded the last of the letters from Michele Anselmi to Thomas Colquhoun, dated some time in 1804 – the letter revealing that the violin Cozio had sent to Colquhoun in lieu of his debt had disappeared en route to England.

'Let me read you a few passages,' I said.

'"It is impossible, at the moment, to be certain whether the instrument ever left Paris or if it did, at what point in the journey to England it was stolen. As the months go by, I begin to fear that the violin will never be recovered and the thief will take the secret of its whereabouts to the grave with him."*

'Then later in the letter, Anselmi writes, *"As it was through my negligence that this unfortunate loss occurred, I feel honour bound to make due recompense to you. I am therefore enclosing a banker's order for the full amount of the debt owed to you by His Excellency."* That was a noble, generous act on Anselmi's part. It was Cozio who owed Colquhoun the money, yet Anselmi paid it in full.

'He was clearly a man of great integrity. At the end of the letter he writes, *"It is my fervent wish that this debt should be honourably discharged, for only then will my conscience rest easy."* He uses the word honour at least twice in one paragraph and is clearly very troubled by the loss of the violin. Perhaps a little too troubled.'

'Why do you say that?' Guastafeste asked. 'He undertook to send the violin to England, but it never got there. Wouldn't you feel troubled by that?'

'Certainly I would. But I wonder whether there was more on his conscience than just the disappearance of the violin.'

'More? What do you mean?'

'That by the time he wrote this letter, Michele Anselmi knew what had happened to the violin, and it was that knowledge that weighed so heavily on his conscience.'

I paused. Was I right? Was the evidence really there to support me, or was I simply deceiving myself?

'I think his son stole it,' I said.

'His son?' Guastafeste frowned at me.

'Paolo Anselmi. His father gave him the job of transporting the violin to Paris and finding a courier to take it on to England. But Paolo didn't find a courier, he may not even have taken the violin to Paris. We know from Marinetti's letter that Paolo was a violinist himself. I think he saw the violin, was overcome by the desire to possess it, and kept it for himself.'

'You have some foundation for this theory? Or is it just guesswork?'

'It's guesswork,' I admitted. 'But I know how powerful is the urge to own a fine violin. I've seen it many times in the course of my career. It can override a man's reason, his principles, even his sanity. Sometimes it's frightening. Sometimes the consequences – as for Tomaso and Enrico Forlani – can be fatal.'

'But if Anselmi knew, why didn't he simply say the violin had turned up and send it on to Colquhoun?'

'I don't know. Shame perhaps. His son had disgraced him. Maybe he didn't want to open that particular can of worms. Who knows what might have come out? Maybe he preferred to pay the money and forget about the violin. The painting tells the whole story. It's all there. The young man holding the violin was Paolo Anselmi – made to pose for the artist by his angry father who was determined to humiliate his son, to punish him for what he'd done. Paolo's guilt is there in his face, in the way he's holding himself.'

'And the violin?' Guastafeste said. 'What happened to it?'

'There's another clue in the painting,' I said. 'Where's your camera, the pictures you took?'

Guastafeste leaned over into the back of the car and brought out his digital camera. He switched it on, holding it between us so we could both see the image of the painting on the tiny display screen on the back.

'Just here,' I said, pointing with my finger. 'Through the window at the side of the music room. You see the cypress trees, the tower of a church? That distinctive brick tower with an open belfry? I knew I'd seen it somewhere before. It's in the trees on the hillside just outside Casale. We saw it when we drove to Salabue.'

'The violin is in the church?' Guastafeste said.

'Not the church. Anselmi gave it away in his letter. *"The thief will take the secret of its whereabouts to the grave with him."'*

Guastafeste stared at me. 'You think the violin is in a grave? Buried?'

'In a grave, yes,' I replied. 'But I don't think it's buried.'

The road to the Sanctuary of St George climbed up the hillside in a series of tight hairpin bends, the slopes on either side cloaked in dense woodland. In the dark there was something sinister about the trees, the headlights of our car playing over their trunks, emphasising the deep shadows behind them, the hidden glades shrouded in the night. The church was on the summit of the hill. It was small and unostentatious, its bell tower silhouetted against the moonlit sky. I suppressed a shudder as I saw it. This was not a task I was looking forward to undertaking.

Guastafeste slowed and pulled off the road on to the tiny parking area in front of the church.

'You all right?' he said. 'You can stay in the car, if you prefer.'

'No, I want to be there.'

We climbed out. Guastafeste clicked on his torch, keeping its beam low, focused on the ground. There were no houses nearby, but there was a village across the valley where, even at two o'clock in the morning, someone might just be awake and wonder what a light was doing at the sanctuary.

We crossed the parking area to the wall around the churchyard. It was just over head height, covered with an uneven layer of whitewashed stucco. Guastafeste cupped his hands in front of him and gave me a leg up the wall, then scrambled over after me.

We set off across the churchyard. We'd been there that morning to reconnoitre, but everything looked different in the dark. The church was to our right, and on our left, perhaps fifty metres away, was a long wall of marble tombs stacked one on top of the other like drawers, the fronts inscribed with names and dates and sometimes an enamelled photograph of the deceased. In between, the ground was crammed with other graves, some with vertical headstones and crosses, some covered by horizontal stone slabs. Slowly we picked our way through them, following the narrow gravel paths that criss-crossed the whole area.

From the ranks of tightly packed graves it was easy to get the impression that the churchyard was full to overflowing, but as we came out of the shelter of one of the tall cypress trees that were planted at intervals along the paths, we almost stumbled into a freshly dug hole in the ground.

'Careful,' Guastafeste said, shining his torch along the edges of the pit, the mound of excavated soil piled up on the far side.

The atmosphere was unnerving. The graves were all around us, the moon hidden by clouds. Guastafeste's torch beam picked out the shape of another cypress tree next to the path, then a white marble headstone so smooth and polished it reflected the light like a mirror. I could feel my flesh tingling, a tremor of foreboding on the back of my neck.

At the lower end of the churchyard were the grander tombs, the large family vaults that stood in their own plots of land like miniature temples, their marble pillars and turrets and towers emphasising the fact that even in death not all men are equal. The Anselmi family vault was one of the more modest in the enclave, reflecting their position as prosperous merchants rather than landed gentry. It was built in the shape of a marble cube, four sculpted angels standing vigil at each corner and the name 'Anselmi' carved above the door. A short flight of marble steps led up to a pair of heavy wrought-iron gates which protected the entrance to the tomb. The gates were fastened in the middle by a padlock and chain.

Guastafeste swung the rucksack he was carrying off his shoulders, unfastened the flap and took out a pair of bolt-cutters and a crowbar. He grasped hold of the boltcutters and glanced quickly around the churchyard. What we were doing was not only sacrilege, but a criminal offence. Guastafeste had considered applying for a court order to open up the tomb, but had decided against it. No judge, on the basis of a few cryptic sentences in an old letter and some tenuous guesswork, would have granted permission. Maybe we were wrong. Maybe this was all a mistake. But we had to know.

Guastafeste placed the jaws of the boltcutters around the chain and snapped through the links. The severed chain and padlock clattered to the floor. Guastafeste pulled open the gates. I put my hand on his arm.

'Ssssh,' I hissed. 'I hear something.'

Guastafeste clicked off the torch. We waited in the dark-ness, listening. Faintly, in the distance, was the sound of a car engine drawing nearer. It was in a low gear, coming up the road from the valley. I could see the dim reflection of headlights in the trees beyond the perimeter wall of the graveyard. The glow grew brighter, the engine note louder. The car changed gear, nearing the summit. It slowed. I listened, waiting for the noise of tyres on gravel as the vehicle pulled into the parking area and stopped. But instead it accelerated, went straight past the sanctuary, dropping over the summit and away down the other side of the hill. I started breathing again.

We stepped inside the vault. Guastafeste's torch flickered

over the marble interior, illuminating the individual tombs that were stacked against the three walls. There were twelve in total. I inhaled. The air smelt fresh, no hint of damp or mustiness.

Guastafeste shone the torch beam over the inscriptions on the tombs. The oldest – in the lowest tier – dated from the early seventeenth century, the latest from the mid-nineteenth when either the vault had become full or the Anselmi family line had petered out. I saw the name Giovanni Michele Anselmi di Briata.

'That's the father. Where's the son?' I whispered. There was no one within earshot, but the very fact of being inside a vault made me lower my voice.

'Over here,' Guastafeste said. 'Paolo Anselmi di Briata, 1778–1851.'

It was the very top sarcophagus in a stack of four. We examined it with the torch.

'Do you think we can get the lid off?'

Guastafeste reached up and ran his fingers under the rim of the stone lid. 'There's a small gap just here.'

Guastafeste lifted the steel crowbar and jammed the tip under the lid of the sarcophagus. He pulled down with all his strength. The lid didn't budge.

'Give me a hand, Gianni.'

I took hold of the crowbar and we pulled together.

'Again,' Guastafeste said. 'Pull!'

I applied all my weight, every iota of power I could muster, to the crowbar.

'And again,' Guastafeste gasped.

I gripped the steel, felt my muscles knot, my feet almost leave the ground.

'It's going,' Guastafeste breathed. 'Don't stop.'

There was a sharp crack as the seal around the lid broke. Then the crowbar dipped down suddenly, sliding out from

278

beneath the stone rim and slipping from our grasps. It fell heavily to the floor, narrowly missing our feet. In the enclosed vault, the noise of steel hitting marble was like a grenade going off. Neither of us moved. My ears were ringing.

Then Guastafeste said, 'You all right, Gianni?'

'Yes, I'm okay.'

I picked up the torch and directed the beam upwards on to the sarcophagus. The lid had slid a little to one side, the corner jutting out above our heads. We looked at it, reluctant to make the next move. Finally, I turned my gaze to Guastafeste and he gave a slight nod. He knew it had to be him.

The wall of tombs wasn't smooth. Each individual sarcophagus had a lip of marble around the base and another where the lid overhung the sides. Using the protruding lengths of stone as steps, Guastafeste clambered up to Paolo Anselmi's sarcophagus and pushed one end of the lid away from him, opening up the marble casket.

'Pass me the torch.'

I watched him examining the inside of the sarcophagus, leaning over, his head almost below the level of the sides.

'Anything?' I said, unable to contain my impatience.

Guastafeste looked down at me, his face in shadow so that I couldn't see his expression.

'Well?' I prompted.

'I'm sorry, Gianni,' Guastafeste said gently. 'It's not there.'

I refused to believe it. I'd been so sure.

'Look again, it has to be there.'

'I've looked,' Guastafeste said. 'There's no violin, nothing that resembles the remains of a violin.'

I felt my legs give way suddenly. I reached out and grabbed hold of one of the tombs to support myself.

'Gianni, what is it?' Guastafeste said in alarm.

I let out a gasp. 'Nothing. Honestly, I'm fine.'

I straightened up, keeping my hand on the edge of the tomb. My legs were shaking, my pulse racing. I wondered fleetingly if I'd experienced a minor heart attack, but I knew it was nothing so serious. I was in mild shock, that was all; a shock induced by shattered expectations, by mental rather than physical trauma. I waited a moment, letting my breathing get back to normal. Guastafeste was sliding the lid of the sarcophagus back into place, jumping down next to me.

'You need a drink,' he said. 'Let's get out of here.'

He took hold of my arm, guiding me towards the exit. I kept my hand on the tombs just in case my legs went again. The cold marble under my palm was solid, comforting. I ran my fingertips over the smooth stone as we headed out of the vault. Then a gust of fresh air caught me in the face, reviving me. I paused, inhaling deeply.

'I can manage,' I said, easing my arm from Guastafeste's grasp.

There was a waist-high marble plinth just by the exit, tucked away in the corner of the vault. I gripped the edge of it for a moment to steady myself before we went out through the wrought-iron gates. My thumb slid into a hole in the stone. I extricated it and rubbed the grazed knuckle, then stepped forward over the threshold of the vault, seeing the night sky above me, the moon obscured by cloud.

I came to an abrupt halt. A *hole*? Why would there be a hole?

'Let me have the torch,' I said to Guastafeste.

'It's all right, I'll lead the way.'

'No, I'm going back inside.'

'What? Gianni, look . . .'

'The torch.'

I took the torch from his fingers and went back into the vault, shining the beam on to the marble plinth. It was perhaps a metre long and half that in width. It struck me as incongruous. The vault in every other respect was symmetrical, yet there was no corresponding plinth on the opposite side of the entrance. I examined the top. It overhung the sides by four or five centimetres and cut into its underside was a series of holes. I crouched down and shone the torch upwards, sliding my forefinger into one of the holes. It seemed to go right through into the inside of the plinth.

'The crowbar,' I said.

'Gianni, it's not there. Don't torture yourself,' Guastafeste said.

'Let me have it.'

Reluctantly, Guastafeste handed me the crowbar. I jammed one end under the top of the plinth and levered it downwards. The lid started to give a little. I forced the crowbar further in and pressed down on it. With a sudden jolt the marble slab broke free of the sides. I heaved the slab aside and shone the torch down into the hollow interior of the plinth. Only it wasn't completely hollow. There was a small casket inside it, a rectangular box of what looked like lead. I tried to lift it out, but it was too heavy.

'Antonio, help me.'

'Help . . .' Guastafeste peered inside the plinth. '*Dio.* What is that?'

I grasped one end of the lead casket, Guastafeste the other and together we lifted it out and placed it on the floor. I noticed that, like the marble plinth, the casket had air holes cut into one of its sides. It was locked. I knelt down and broke open the lock with the crowbar. I paused, preparing myself. Then I took hold of the lid and slowly raised it. Inside was another box made of wood – a long, tapering box about the size and shape of a violin case. Guastafeste came closer, looming over my shoulders.

'Open it,' he said.

Then another voice said, in English: 'Yes, why not?'

Christopher Scott was standing in the entrance to the vault. Guastafeste straightened up, twisting round, but Scott was ready for him. The length of timber he was holding in his hand came hammering down on to the side of Guastafeste's head. Wood and skull connected with jarring force. Guastafeste grunted and crumpled to the floor. Scott leaned over him and with one slick movement removed Guastafeste's police revolver from the holster under his arm. Scott pointed the revolver at me.

'Give me the box.'

I ignored him and crawled over to Guastafeste. He was stunned rather than unconscious.

'Antonio? Antonio?'

Guastafeste groaned, one hand going to the gash on the side of his head. I helped him up into a sitting position. There was a thin trickle of blood on his cheek.

'You okay?' I said.

Guastafeste nodded weakly.

I looked up at Scott. He was edging round us, trying to get to the violin case. He was too dangerous for me to risk tackling him on my own. I needed to distract him, to give Guastafeste time to recover.

'How did you know?' I said. 'Did you follow us?'

Scott paused. He gave a contemptuous laugh. 'Highfield Hall. I was there just after you. The old lady told me about the painting. I'd already been to Casale, seen this church on the hill. I worked it out.'

'And Tomaso Rainaldi? Why?'

282

'He was stupid, naïve. He was in the way. An obstacle that had to be removed.'

Scott bent down and picked up the violin case. I felt the rage bubbling up inside me. I knew Scott was going to kill us too. I groped around on the floor and my fingers closed around the stem of the torch. Scott was turning away, moving back towards the door of the vault, his gaze momentarily distracted. I pushed myself to my feet and swung the torch round in a vicious arc. Scott was un-prepared, slow. The torch smashed into the side of his head. He reeled and stumbled against the marble gatepost. His right wrist caught on the sharp edge of the post. The revolver fell from his grasp and skittered away across the floor. I hit him again. Scott lost his footing and fell over backwards, tumbling down the steps outside the vault. I heard a thud as his body hit the ground.

Guastafeste was standing up now. He pushed past me and staggered to the entrance of the vault.

'Antonio?'

'I'm all right.'

He steadied himself for a second, then stepped out. I went after him. Scott was kneeling up on the gravel path at the bottom of the steps, the violin case beside him. He looked up and saw us emerging from the vault. His face was pale in the moonlight, his mouth twisted into a savage snarl. He picked up the violin case and stood up, turning to run. Guastafeste didn't wait. He pushed off from the top of the steps, hurling himself out into space. His outstretched arms grabbed hold of Scott's legs and the two men crashed to the ground. Scott rolled over, kicking out with his foot. His shoe caught Guastafeste on the side of the head. Guastafeste shook it off and threw himself on top of Scott. Scott twisted sideways, writhing like a snake. One of his fists scythed round into Guastafeste's face.

283

Guastafeste's head snapped back and he lost his grip on the dealer.

Scott grasped hold of the violin case and slithered away. Guastafeste groaned, one hand going to his temple. He had a nasty wound. He was losing blood. I had to do something. Then I remembered Guastafeste's revolver. I stepped back into the vault and picked up the torch. The beam lanced around the marble tombs. Where was it? I saw the dull gleam of gun metal in a corner and bent down. I hurried back outside. Scott was stumbling across the graveyard, Guastafeste a few metres behind him. The revolver clutched in my hand, I ran after them.

Scott was weaving between the gravestones, a shadowy figure in the darkness. Guastafeste was pursuing him doggedly, but losing ground. Scott was uninjured, younger, more agile. He was getting away.

'Antonio!' I yelled. 'Your gun.'

I saw Guastafeste pause, turning in my direction, then continue running. He couldn't afford to wait for me. I was out of breath, slowing. My lungs and knees were feeling their age. I lost sight of both Scott and Guastafeste as they disappeared behind a cypress tree. Then I heard a distant cry. A sudden, sharp exclamation, more surprise than pain. Whose voice had it been? I couldn't be sure. I came round the bend by the cypress tree and stopped abruptly. Guastafeste was standing on the path in front of me, looking down. Of Scott there was no sign.

'Antonio.'

I held out the revolver. Guastafeste took it from me and let it dangle down by his side.

'He slipped,' he said.

Only then did I realise where he was looking. By his feet was the freshly dug grave. I moved forward, directing the torch beam into the hole. Sprawled in the

mud at the bottom, still clutching the violin case, was
Christopher Scott. From the unnatural angle of his neck,
the empty glaze over his eyes, there was no doubt that he
was dead.

19

'What are we going to do?' I said.

Guastafeste didn't reply. He walked over to a waist-high rectangular marble tomb and sat down wearily on the edge of it. He took out his handkerchief and held it to the gash in his head.

'You need a doctor,' I said.

'Later.'

'Let me see it.'

'It looks worse than it is.'

I examined his head in the torch light. 'It will need stitches. We'd better get you to a hospital.'

'I'll be okay. There are other, more pressing matters.'

I nodded and waited for him to continue. He looked at me. 'This is more complicated than we expected. How far are you prepared to go?'

'You don't think the truth will do?'

'We've broken into a tomb illegally. Robbed a grave, I suppose. Someone has died. I can keep you out of it, Gianni, say I came here alone. But it will be the end of my police career, perhaps any career.'

'That's too high a price to pay,' I said. 'Scott was a killer.

His death was accidental. We should have nothing on our consciences.'

'Or I can make something up,' Guastafeste said. 'Wipe our fingerprints from the vault. Say I followed Scott here, caught him breaking into it. There'll be a storm ahead, but I think I can weather it.'

'And the violin?'

'Who's to say Scott found anything in the vault?'

'You mean we keep it?'

'It has no legitimate owner. Cozio di Salabue gave it away to pay a debt. Paolo Anselmi stole it. Thomas Colquhoun was paid the money he was owed. Who does the violin really belong to? Technically you might say it ought to go to the State. But do you want a bunch of politicians in Rome to have it?'

I shivered. It was getting cold in the graveyard. I didn't want to remain there much longer.

'I know what we have to do with it,' I said.

It was almost dawn when Guastafeste returned to our hotel room from the *Questura* in Casale. I was waiting up for him, still fully dressed. There hadn't seemed much point in going to bed. Guastafeste had a dressing over the gash on the side of his head.

'How does it feel?' I said.

'Sore, but not too bad.'

I opened the door of the mini bar and took out a miniature bottle of cognac. I poured the brandy into a glass and handed it to Guastafeste. He took a sip.

'Thanks.'

'How was it?' I said.

'Tricky.'

'Did they believe you?'

'For the time being. I'm one of theirs. They want to

believe me. The hard bit will come later when the investigating magistrate gets involved. By then I hope there'll be other developments.'

He drank some more cognac. 'I've asked for a sample of Scott's DNA to be sent to Cremona. There was a spot of blood on the workbench in Tomaso's workshop which wasn't his. If it turns out to be Scott's, neither the Casale police nor my colleagues in Cremona will give a damn about the Anselmi vault or any violin.'

Guastafeste looked around the room and saw the violin case on my bed. 'You haven't opened it?'

'I was waiting for you.'

I went across to the bed and stared down at the case, unable to bring myself to touch it. This was the moment we'd been waiting for – for how long? Was it really only a couple of weeks? It is a cliché, I know, but I felt as if I had been waiting a lifetime. And perhaps I had. My mouth was dry. There was a sickness in my stomach: the nausea of anticipation, and maybe of fear, for I did not know what this moment would bring.

'Come on, Gianni,' Guastafeste said. 'This is your honour.'

It was an old-style violin case, of the type they used in the seventeenth and eighteenth centuries when the instrument was inserted lengthwise into the end of the case rather than – as today – being placed under a hinged lid. My fingers found the fastening, fumbled with it, unable to open it. Guastafeste leaned past me and undid the simple metal catch. I murmured my thanks and took hold of the flap covering the opening. I glanced up. Guastafeste was utterly still, his gaze fixed intently on the case. I was almost paralysed by nerves. It might be empty, it might contain nothing but sawdust. I had to find out.

Closing my eyes, I lifted aside the flap and slid my hand inside the case. Just a short distance in I encountered something soft and yielding. It felt like a bag. I pulled it out and opened my eyes. It was indeed a cloth bag. I undid the drawstring and peered inside. It contained grains of rice, now swollen with moisture – protection from the damp and humidity that can destroy an instrument.

I closed my eyes again and slipped my hand back into the case. I felt more cloth, then something harder beneath the cloth. My fingers closed around it and pulled. The object came slowly out. I used my other hand to guide it. I could feel its shape, the curve of the bouts, then the waist, then more curves and finally the neck and scroll. I opened my eyes. All I could see was a length of yellow silk, a parcel with something inside it. I placed the parcel carefully on the bed next to me and unwrapped the silk sheath. As the folds fell apart, I heard a gasp of astonishment, of awe, and realised it had come from my own lips. For one brief moment my whole body seemed to shut down. I stopped breathing, my heart ceased beating. Beneath the silk was a violin. A violin unlike any other violin I'd ever seen. Unlike any violin anyone alive had ever seen.

It was perfect. Absolutely perfect – in near mint condition despite its century and a half in a vault. Only the gut strings were damaged, all four of them snapped in two. I picked the violin up and gazed at it. The back was made of two pieces of maple, cut on the quarter, with a fine, well-marked curl in the wood. The belly was an even, open-grained spruce, the waist quite long, the f-holes rather pointed – all classic signs of its maker. And the varnish . . . even in the unflattering light of our hotel room the varnish glowed like molten rubies.

'My God,' Guastafeste breathed. 'That is beautiful.'

I tilted the belly so the light shone through the bass f-hole, revealing the label inside the instrument. '*Joseph Guarnerius fecit Cremonae anno 1743'*, followed by the mark of the cross and the cipher IHS.

'Look at the fingerboard, the tailpiece, the bridge, the neck,' I said. 'They're all original, exactly the way Guarneri made them. Nothing has been changed.'

'That's special?' Guastafeste said.

'Very. Even the Messiah is not as Stradivari made it.'

'So it's not a sister to the Messiah?'

'In one way it is,' I replied. 'The Messiah is a perfect, unplayed Stradivari. This is an even more perfect Guarneri "del Gesù". They don't share a maker, but they are sisters all the same.'

'And its value?' Guastafeste said, practical as ever.

'It is beyond valuation,' I said. 'How can you put a price on something like this? It's like putting a price on a new-born child, or a sunset over the mountains. Some things are too precious to think of in terms of money.'

'You're such a romantic, Gianni,' Guastafeste said. 'It's only a violin.'

'Only!' I exclaimed. 'Only a violin! Are you blind? Can you not see perfection when it's before your eyes?'

I stood up, the violin still in my hands.

'If only I could play it for you. If only you could hear the sound, then you would realise what I mean. This is not just an old violin. Not just an old violin by a maker who – in terms of tonal beauty – is the greatest who ever lived. This is a living, breathing thing. This can sing, make your heart soar, move you to the depths of your soul.'

I looked at him. His face was blurred by my tears. Guastafeste held out his arms and embraced me.

'We've found it,' he said. 'We've found it.'

20

I put the violin case down on my workbench and carefully removed the instrument. It seemed more beautiful than ever. In the warm evening sunshine its varnish burnt with the scorching intensity of red-hot lava.

Guastafeste pulled out a stool and watched while I strung the 'del Gesù'. The pegs were stiff and swollen after their years in the vault. I let the sun warm them for a bit, then removed the remains of the old broken gut strings and lubricated the pegs with a bit of dry soap to make them turn smoothly. Before I put on the new strings I checked the bridge and soundpost which, amazingly, was still in place.

'It looks remarkably good for a violin that's been in a tomb for a hundred and fifty years,' Guastafeste said.

'Whoever put it there knew what they were doing. The marble plinth, the lead casket, would have protected it from extreme fluctuations in temperature. There were air holes to keep it well ventilated, to stop the wood rotting, and grains of rice to soak up the excess moisture.'

'Are you sure you wouldn't have preferred it to be a Stradivari?'

I shook my head. 'A "del Gesù" is much rarer, much

more interesting. There is something restrained, almost clinical about Stradivari's perfection, his consistency. Guarneri was a wilder character, more erratic in his life and craftsmanship. But that passion is in his violins, and what a passion it was. And what a sound!'

I tightened the strings one at a time and fine-tuned them. Then I went back into the house and returned with one of my bows. I slid the violin under my chin.

'What are you waiting for?' Guastafeste asked.

'I don't know whether I can do this.' My throat felt constricted, my stomach fluttering with nerves as if I were about to perform before an audience of thousands. 'I don't know whether I can cope with my expectations. With the disappointment if it fails to live up to them.'

'Just go for it, Gianni.'

I touched the bow to the strings, running it lightly over each one in turn. The sound sent a shiver up my arm and all the way down my spine.

'Properly,' Guastafeste said.

I played a G major broken chord, letting the bow dig into the strings.

'Wow, that is some sound,' Guastafeste said in amazement.

'Imagine what it would be like in the hands of a real player.'

'Play some more.'

I played Bach from memory, the slow Sarabande from the D Minor Partita. A shudder went through me. I had never heard a sound like it, never heard myself play like this. For a hundred and fifty years the violin had been shut away in the darkness, entombed among corpses who would never hear again. Now it was back in the light and it seemed to me as if during all those years of silence the violin had been storing up its voice for this one moment when it would be allowed to sing again. The power was overwhelming, the resonance rich and dark, one moment full of passion, the next sobbing out in anguish, then crying out in joy, every element of human emotion encompassed in that wondrous, uplifting sound.

I couldn't get enough of it. Not just the music, but the violin too. I wanted it for my own. The music alone was not sufficient, I had to possess the source of that music. I began to see in myself the greed, the lust for ownership I'd observed, and so despised, in wealthy collectors – men who cared nothing for the voices of their possessions, but looked on them as objects, as trophies to be gloated over in secret. I felt the violin bewitching me, whispering in my ear, 'I could be yours', like the Devil making a bid for my soul. I wrenched the instrument away from my chin and put it down with a gasp.

'What is it?' Guastafeste asked, suddenly concerned.

I shook my head, unable to speak. I was fighting off a curse, struggling with the base forces within me. The violin had been shut away for too long already. It was not for a collector, nor for a poor, ungifted player like me. It was made for greater things.

I began work on the violin next morning. For a long while I did nothing, simply sat at my workbench and stared at the 'del Gesù'. What I was about to do filled me with disquiet. It seemed tantamount to vandalism. Certainly a musical historian would have regarded it as such. Yet I knew it was necessary. Whatever my sentiments, it was the right thing to do.

I looked up for a moment, my gaze coming to rest on the violin hanging on the wall in the corner of the workshop – Ruffino's final gift to me. 'Guide me, Bartolomeo. Steady my hand,' I murmured softly before I turned my attention back to the 'del Gesù' in front of me.

Very carefully, I prised off the fingerboard, then the belly of the instrument. The soundbox was dirty and full of dust. I cleaned it out and examined the label. It was one of the last instruments Guarneri had ever made. I turned the belly over and studied the bass bar. It was far too short and weak for a modern concert instrument. The soundpost too was thin and old. Both pieces of wood would have to be replaced. The fingerboard would also have to go. This one was wedge-shaped, made of willow, lined at the sides with maple and faced with an ebony veneer. I would substitute it for a solid ebony fingerboard, but first I had to undertake the most fundamental alteration to the instrument – the lengthening of the neck.

This wasn't a job to undertake lightly. I was dealing with an historic instrument, the work of a master. I would need to be exceptionally careful and meticulous in the way I went about it. One slip of the chisel and I could ruin the instrument. For the rest of the morning I worked on the violin, absorbed in the details of my craft. It seemed to me that my entire career as a luthier had been preparation for this moment. Everything I had done over the last half century seemed to pale in comparison with the task on which I was now engaged. Bringing the Guarneri 'del Gesù' back from the dead, quite literally resurrecting it – if that is not too blasphemous an analogy – seemed to me to be a truly momentous undertaking. If I did nothing else hereafter, I would consider my life well spent.

In the middle of the afternoon I took a break for a glass of wine and some bread and cheese. I was anxious to get back to my workshop, but I forced myself to sit down in the kitchen for half an hour. This was not the kind of work that could be rushed.

The day's post had been delivered while I was at my bench, including my regular copy of *The Strad*, the magazine for violinists and luthiers which is sent to me every month from England. I opened the magazine on the kitchen table and glanced through it as I ate my lunch. By coincidence, one of the main articles concerned a Guarneri – not Giuseppe 'del Gesù', but his wife Katarina about whom I knew very little except that there had been speculation over the years that she had been a violin-maker in her own right – an unusual phenomenon for her time – and had possibly assisted her husband in the manufacture of his own instruments. I read the article with interest. Here was a woman condemned to live her life in the shadow of her husband, left a widow at a comparatively early age before she remarried a Bohemian infantryman named Horak . . . I paused. Horak?

Dio, I knew that name. Elisabeta Horak, author of one of the letters to Michele Anselmi we'd found in the archives in Casale. She'd mentioned a violin left to her by her mother. Was her mother Katarina Guarneri? If so, the instrument on my workbench was quite possibly the one Elisabeta had sold to Anselmi for Count Cozio's collection. I liked the symmetry of that hypothesis. It tied up another of the loose ends that had been bothering me. There were others, of course, but . . . *but*.

I looked up. No, was that possible? My glass of wine was frozen in mid-air, halfway to my mouth. I put the glass down on the table. My hand was trembling. Surely not. *Was* it?

I went to the telephone and rang directory enquiries, then made a couple of calls to Milan. When I returned to my workshop, I was so agitated I had to sit for ten minutes, controlling my breathing, before my hand was steady enough to pick up my tools. My mind was preoccupied, but no longer with the violin before me.

Guastafeste came round that evening. I opened a bottle of wine and we sat on the terrace, watching the sun set over the cornfields at the bottom of my garden.

'The DNA matched,' he said. 'Proof that Christopher Scott was in Tomaso's workshop the night he was murdered. We think he must have nicked his finger with the chisel he used, let a droplet of blood fall on to the worktop. We've sent the details to the *Questura* in Venice. See if they can get a match with anything in Forlani's house.'

'You think Scott killed Forlani too?' I said. 'What about his alibi?'

'Spadina's looking into that again. There must be a hole in it somewhere, something we've overlooked. Maybe he borrowed a boat to get off the Giudecca, maybe he bribed the water taxi driver and hotel receptionist. We'll find it.'

'And the missing Maggini?'

'Scott took it.'

I shook my head. 'I don't think so. Scott knew about violins. He'd have taken a Stradivari.'

'But the Maggini was the only one whose glass case was broken. It was there for the taking. Why smash another few cases? Scott had just murdered Forlani. He wouldn't have wanted to hang around.'

I sipped my wine without replying.

'You don't agree?' Guastafeste said.

'No.'

'So who did kill Forlani?'

'It's just a hunch,' I said. 'But I think I may have an idea.'

21

They were already waiting for us when we arrived at the Conservatorio, sitting at a corner table in the coffee bar, glasses of mineral water in front of them.

'I'm sorry we're late,' I said, pulling out a chair.

Guastafeste sat down next to me and glanced idly around the room. It was a quiet time of day. There were one or two music students scattered around the other tables, but none of them was close enough to overhear what we were saying.

'Allow me to introduce a friend of mine,' I said. 'Antonio Guastafeste, of the Cremona Police Department.'

Ludovico Scamozzi frowned at Guastafeste. Then he ran his fingers through his hair and made a petulant gesture.

'Police? What's this all about?'

'Violins,' Guastafeste said.

'What about them?'

'Gianni?' Guastafeste invited me to speak.

I looked at Scamozzi. 'It's interesting, isn't it?' I said. 'That men only have one name throughout their lives, but women generally have two, sometimes more.'

'What?'

'Katarina Guarneri, for instance. She had three. Her maiden name, Rota, her first husband's name, Guarneri, and then her second husband's name, Horak.'

'What are you talking about?' Scamozzi snapped. 'Look, I have a departmental meeting in half an hour. Get to the point. Your phone call was cryptic enough, but this is even worse.'

'Half an hour will be plenty of time,' I said.

'Plenty of time for what?'

I turned to the woman sitting next to Scamozzi, her features almost hidden by the unruly bush of dark hair that framed her face.

'Signora Scamozzi, you too have had three names, and you too – like Katarina Guarneri – have chosen, or been forced, to live your life in the shadow of your husband.'

'What rubbish is this?' Scamozzi demanded impatiently.

'Let him speak,' Magda said. Her voice was quiet, curious. She was watching me, her eyes narrowing warily behind her curls.

'You are Magda Scamozzi now,' I continued. 'Before that you were Magda Erzsébet, but you were born Magda Borsos.'

'So?' Scamozzi said.

'Be quiet, Ludovico,' Magda said.

Scamozzi glanced at her in surprise, but he held his tongue.

'People think you're Hungarian,' I said.

'I am Hungarian.'

'But you're not from Hungary. You're from Romania, from Oradea – Nagyvárad, in Hungarian – one of the Hungarian-speaking territories Hungary lost after the First World War.'

'What has this to do with violins?'

298

'Because in 1920, a man from Oradea named Imre Borsos bought a Maggini violin, a distinctive, particularly fine Maggini known as the Snake's Head because of the pattern in the wood of its back.'

Magda Scamozzi took a sip of her mineral water, her eyes never leaving my face.

'Who was he?' I said. 'Your grandfather?'

'I don't know anything about a Maggini violin.' She pushed back her chair to get to her feet.

'Murder is a serious business,' Guastafeste said. 'I think you'd better stay.'

'Murder?' It was Ludovico Scamozzi who'd spoken. He leaned towards Guastafeste, pushing his long hair back behind his ears to stop it falling over his face. 'Did you say murder?'

Guastafeste was spared the need to reply immediately by the sudden ring of his mobile phone. He put it to his ear and listened for a moment, then murmured, 'Thank you', and put the phone back in his pocket.

'What's going on?' Scamozzi said in a puzzled voice, half looking at Guastafeste, half at his wife.

'Nothing,' Magda said defiantly. 'I don't know what they're talking about.'

'I'm talking about Enrico Forlani,' Guastafeste said. 'The man you killed.'

'You're out of your mind,' Ludovico Scamozzi said. 'I've never heard of an Enrico Forlani. How dare you make such a ludicrous accusation. Come on, Magda, we don't have to sit here and listen to this.'

'Sit down!' Guastafeste said sharply. 'And shut up. You may never have heard of Enrico Forlani, but your wife has, haven't you, signora? And you've also heard of Tomaso Rainaldi, a luthier from Cremona who was on the trail of a violin, a very special violin. Rainaldi approached Vincenzo

Serafin, looking for money to pursue the search, but Serafin turned him down. Your friend Maddalena, Serafin's mistress, told you all about it. You wanted that violin. You wanted the information Rainaldi had, but Rainaldi was killed before you could obtain it. So you went to Forlani, the collector who was financing Rainaldi's search. How did you know about Forlani? Maddalena again, perhaps. Did Serafin know Rainaldi had gone to Forlani? The details aren't important right now. But you went to Forlani's house in Venice, that much is certain. What happened while you were there? Did you have some kind of an argument with him? Did you lose your temper and push him into the glass case?'

Magda drank some more of her mineral water. I watched her. Her husband was watching her too. He wanted to know the answer as much as I did.

'You have some concrete evidence to back up this interesting theory?' Magda said.

'My phone call just now,' Guastafeste replied. 'It was from the Milan police. They were at your apartment, with a warrant to search it. Under your bed they found the Snake's Head Maggini that was stolen from Forlani's house after he was murdered.'

Magda said nothing. Scamozzi was staring at her, his eyes wide with horror.

'Is this true?' he said.

Magda ignored him. She was concentrating on Guastafeste and me. I'd expected a show of defiance, angry denials, perhaps even physical assault, but she was subdued. The fight had gone out of her.

'I didn't steal it,' she said. 'The Maggini was mine. Yes, it was my grandfather who bought it. It was in our family between the wars. Then in 1945 the Red Army came to Oradea. I won't tell you what atrocities they committed.

300

Compared to those dreadful acts, stealing a violin was nothing. But it was taken nonetheless. When I went to Forlani's and saw the violin in his collection I was incensed. That vile, smelly, greedy old man had my grandfather's Maggini in a glass case. Something inside me exploded. I attacked him. I didn't mean to kill him. He was unsteady on his feet. He toppled over, put out his arms and crashed through the case. There was nothing I could do for him.'

'You could have called an ambulance,' Guastafeste said.

'He'd have been dead long before an ambulance arrived.' Her eyes flared for a moment. 'I'm not a thief. I only took back what was rightfully mine.'

Scamozzi edged away from his wife, as if he feared she might be contagious.

'You admit you killed him?' he said.

'I did it for you.'

'For me? You killed him for me?'

'You could have been a great virtuoso, Ludovico. You should have been. Up there with Heifetz and Oistrakh and Perlman.'

She reached out to take his hand, but Scamozzi snatched his arm away, the revulsion clear in his face. Magda looked at him. The rejection had hurt. She seemed like a young girl now, puzzled, confused, not fully comprehending what she'd done.

'For me?' he said again. 'Why?'

'I love you, Ludovico. I've given up everything for you.' Her eyes were locked on her husband's face. Guastafeste and I might not have been there. 'You were so gifted, you had such potential. What happened? It was your violin. You never had the right one, always an inferior instrument. As soon as Maddalena told me about this violin, this new

301

Messiah, I knew I had to have it, whatever it cost. It was for you. I wanted it for you. I knew it wasn't too late to bring back your career. You shouldn't be here, teaching these stupid, talentless children. You should be on stage, in the bright lights, an international star. Don't you understand, Ludovico? The Maggini is for you too. Everything I did was for you.'

'Not for me,' Scamozzi said harshly. 'It wasn't for me. For God's sake, Magda, you think I wanted you to kill for me? You're mad.'

She reached out her hand again, but Scamozzi backed away once more. Tears flooded down her face.

'Please, Ludovico. You have to understand. It was an accident. I meant well. I need you. I love you. You love me, don't you?'

Scamozzi didn't reply. Magda gazed at him imploringly. He turned his head away, unable to look at her.

Guastafeste said quietly, 'I think it's time to go, signora.'

'You found it?' Serafin said incredulously. 'You actually found it?'

He very nearly leapt out of his padded leather chair, which for a man of such ingrained laziness was a quite remarkable reaction.

'Yes, I found it,' I said casually. 'Though not without difficulty.'

'So let me see it.'

'In a moment.'

I wanted to take my time, make him suffer a little. After all I'd put up with from him over the years it was the least I deserved.

'Come on, Gianni, show me.' He was leaning over his desk in a state of considerable agitation. If he'd been a dog, he'd have been drooling all over the polished mahogany surface.

'I want to agree terms first,' I said.

'Terms? What do you mean?' He tried to look wounded but I knew it was only a negotiating ploy. With Serafin, everything is a negotiating ploy. 'You know me, Gianni. I've always been generous. You'll get a fair price from me, you know that.'

'Maybe,' I said coolly. 'But perhaps I'll get more from somebody else.'

That gave him a shock. He sat back heavily and stared at me.

'You'd take it elsewhere?' he said, aghast.

I could feel the warm glow of power seep through my bones. So this is what it felt like. I could see why it was so addictive.

'I'd obviously prefer not to,' I said. 'But if you give me no choice . . .'

'Who would you go to?' Serafin said, regaining some of his customary cocksuredness. 'There's no one else with my kind of contacts, my list of private collectors.'

'I could put it into an auction.'

Serafin was horrified. 'What, and give a fat commission to one of those parasitical auction houses? You wouldn't want to do that. Besides, if you sell privately you know you'll get a better price.'

'Will I?'

'Don't play games, Gianni. This isn't fun.'

I begged to differ, but it seemed cruel to point it out so I contented myself with a non-committal murmur.

'How much do you want?' Serafin said, a note of such desperation creeping into his voice that I almost felt bad about tormenting him. Almost.

'What do you think it might be worth?' I asked.

'Anything you want. I have clients who would . . .' He'd been about to say 'kill' but changed his mind. '. . . who

303

would give their entire fortunes for a new Messiah. Is it in good condition?'

'Perfect. It's better than the Messiah. Original fingerboard and tailpiece. It's in mint condition, unplayed for a hundred and fifty years.'

'And its provenance? My clients will want to be sure it's genuine.'

'Oh, it's genuine all right. I have historic letters, witnesses who will swear affidavits as to its origins. I've been over every grain of the wood, examined every minute detail. It's the real thing, Vincenzo, you can be absolutely sure of that.'

'How much?'

'Ten million dollars.'

Even Serafin was taken aback a little. 'Ten million?' he said with a gasp.

'It's not negotiable,' I said. 'I'm not greedy. You can take your twenty per cent commission. Eight million for me and my partners, two for you.'

That appealed more to him. I saw him reconsidering the price, maybe even coming round to the view that it was a bit of a bargain.

'It's a lot,' he said.

'It's a lot of violin. I want the money in a Swiss bank account before I release the violin. Can you find a buyer at that price?'

'Yes, I can guarantee that.'

'So you agree to the terms?'

Serafin stroked his silky black beard for a few seconds. I could almost see the dollar signs clicking through his eyeballs like a character in a cartoon.

'Okay, you have a deal,' he said. 'Now, for God's sake, show me the bloody violin.'

I took the instrument out of its case and passed it across the desk.

'I cleaned it up a little,' I said. 'So you could see it at its best.'

'*Dio*,' Serafin said, unable to take his eyes off the violin. 'That is one magnificent little lady.'

He turned the violin around in his hands, studying the belly, the back, the ribs, the scroll, before peering through the f-hole at the label.

'"*Antonius Stradivarius Cremonensis Faciebat Anno 1716*,"' he read. 'The same year as the Messiah.'

'Its sister,' I said.

Serafin held the violin up so that the sunlight glanced off its belly, making the varnish glow like the embers of a wood fire.

'It's his, there's no doubt about it,' he said fervently. 'Look at it. You can see the true hand of genius in it.'

'You can, can't you?' I said.

I paused for a time outside the door of the practice room, listening to the sound coming from within – the endless repetition of scales and arpeggios, of runs and exercises, a violinist warming up before the real work began. Then I knocked on the door and went in.

Sofia glanced round and her bow skittered to a stop.

'Signor Castiglione!'

'I hope I'm not disturbing you.'

'Not at all. I love interruptions. Come in.'

'I've brought you something,' I said.

I put the violin case down on a chair and opened it.

'Put away your violin, Sofia,' I said. 'You won't be needing it any more.'

I handed her the Guarneri 'del Gesù'. 'Take it. It's yours.'

Her fingers closed tentatively around the neck of the violin. The great instruments have a special feel. You can tell the moment you touch them. Sofia's other hand cupped the lower bouts, cradling the violin in front of her. She gazed at it uncertainly.

'For me?'

I nodded. 'You need each other.'

'What is it?'

'Look at the label.'

She peered into the f-hole. I saw her stiffen, then her eyes came back to mine.

'It's genuine,' I said.

'I can't afford anything like this,' she said.

'I'm not selling it to you. It's a gift. It needs a good home.'

'A gift? From you?'

'From your grandfather. He would have wanted you to have it.'

'Grandpa?'

'It's yours, Sofia. A talent like yours deserves a violin like this. And a violin like this deserves a player like you.'

Her eyes were glistening. 'This is too much.'

'Try it.'

She ran her bow hesitantly over the strings, then more confidently, getting a feel for the instrument.

'Play something for me,' I said.

'What?'

'The D Minor Chaconne.'

I sat down in a chair and closed my eyes. From the first notes I knew they were made for each other. When Delphin Alard first played the Messiah, Vuillaume said he heard the angels singing. As I listened now to the 'del Gesù', I heard not the sound of angels, but the voice of God himself. I felt my eyes moisten, the tears well up and trickle down my cheeks. Never in all my life had I heard such a perfect combination of violin and player.

As the final chord rang out across the practice room, I

opened my eyes and saw the look of pure, unconcealed joy on Sofia's face. She glanced at me, uncertain again.

'I can't live up to it,' she said.

'You can, and you will. That violin has been waiting a quarter of a millennium for the right companion. I think it's found its soulmate now.'

Sofia put the 'del Gesù' down in its case and came to me, sobbing openly. I held her for a moment, then stepped back and smiled at her.

'Not you too.' I gave her a handkerchief.

'How can I ever thank you?' she said.

'Thank your grandfather, not me. Let it remind you of him. Play it for him, Sofia.'

Guastafeste eased himself down into a chair and looked at the bottle of champagne that was chilling in an ice bucket on my garden table.

'I thought we'd earned ourselves a little celebration,' I said.

'Everything's arranged?' he said.

'More or less. I've given Clara the sum we agreed, more than enough to provide for her old age. And I've sent a cheque to Mrs Colquhoun to cover the cost of repairing Highfield Hall. There's still plenty left.'

'You thought any more about what we should do with it?'

'That's what I wanted to discuss. I want you to have some of it, Antonio.'

Guastafeste shook his head. 'No, I told you, I don't want any of the money. It wouldn't be right.'

'Why not? You've earned it. Why should you be the only person to come out of this with nothing?'

'I'm not the only person. There's you too.'

'I've not come away with nothing.'

'But . . . you said that . . .'

'I don't mean money.'

'Then what . . .' Guastafeste stopped. He was looking over my shoulder. I turned and saw Margherita standing at the side of the terrace. She was carrying a violin case.

'I'm sorry, is this . . .' she began.

I stood up. 'Let me introduce you. This is Antonio.'

Margherita came forward, her hand outstretched. 'Ah, at last. Gianni's told me all about you.'

Guastafeste glanced at me. 'He has?'

'This is Margherita Severini,' I said. 'Enrico Forlani's niece. Margherita and I are setting up a trust fund to lend out her late uncle's violins to young, promising musicians. Her idea, not mine.'

'It was both of us, Gianni, you know that,' Margherita said.

I looked at Guastafeste. 'You asked if I'd thought any more about the rest of the money. What would you say to adding it to the trust fund to provide music scholarships to young players?'

'I'd say that was a very worthy cause,' Guastafeste said.

'Let's drink to it.'

We sat together on the terrace and drank champagne. Then Guastafeste said he had to be going. I walked round to the front of the house with him.

'She seems very nice,' he said.

'She is. She's staying with me for a few days. Come for dinner tomorrow. I'd like you to get to know each other.'

Guastafeste looked at me, his eyes warm with affection. Then he embraced me impulsively.

'I'm glad for you, Gianni. You deserve it.'

I watched him drive away, then returned to the terrace.

'You brought it, I see,' I said.

Margherita handed me the violin case. I opened it and

lifted out the Spohr Guarneri 'del Gesù'. I studied it for a time, remembering the years of guilt that violin had caused me.

'What are you going to do with it?' Margherita asked.

'I'll show you.'

I took her down to the bottom of the garden where I had prepared a bonfire of old newspapers and twigs and prunings. I lit the fire and let it blaze for a while, stoking it with more garden waste. Then I picked up the 'del Gesù' and held it for a time, preparing myself for what I had to do. For most of my life I have looked on violins as precious objects. Even the crudest, cheapest instruments – in my eyes – are worthy of respect for they have still taken many hours of labour to craft, and they are still as capable of making music, in their own way, as any Stradivari or Guarneri. But when a precious object is a lie – no matter how convincing a lie – it loses its right to respect. The Spohr 'del Gesù' was a beautiful piece of work. I could admire the skill that had gone into its construction. But I did not regard it as my own work. It was not I who had made it, but a different, corrupted luthier. And because, for all my sins, I try to be an honest man, I had now to put an end to that lie.

I took a last look at the violin and placed it on top of the bonfire. I watched the flames lick around it, the varnish start to blister and crackle. The wood ignited, smouldering, then burning with a sudden, brilliant incandescence. I could see its shape, it was still recognisably a violin. Then its form began to change, the wood blackening, disintegrating and turning to ash as the fire consumed it. I looked away. I'd seen enough.

'Why?' Margherita said.

'To free my conscience,' I replied.

'I don't understand.'

'Some day I'll tell you.'

I took her hand in mine.

'Now how about one of those duets you promised?'

Margherita smiled. 'I'd like that,' she said.